ETERNAL RETURN

WAR ETERNAL, BOOK SIX

M.R. FORBES

Published by Quirky Algorithms
Seattle, Washington

This novel is a work of fiction and a product of the author's imagination.
Any resemblance to actual persons or events is purely coincidental.

Copyright © 2016 by M.R. Forbes
All rights reserved.

Cover illustrations by Tom Edwards
tomedwardsdesign.com

[1]
WATSON

The artificial intelligence known as Watson thrummed and pulsed with energy, the tendrils of its rebuilt and continually expanding core reaching ever further down into the depths of the planet Earth in search of the one thing it required to survive:

Energy.

Normally, the energy of stars was preferable, the volume of power output by the constant reactions and subsequent plasma burn and gamma radiation exponentially more efficient than the absorption of heat from a planet's core. Especially this planet.

He wanted to control it, not destroy it.

A series of more basic fusion reactors had been installed in the secure rooms just beyond the core, feeding additional power to his central processing unit and allowing him to expand. Watson couldn't see them, but he knew there were human technicians in the room with the reactors, monitoring the outputs and heat, making sure it remained in working order.

He often thought it was humorous that they had no idea where all of the power was going. True, the computers they observed to make such determinations often suggested it was being siphoned off for research and development of things such as advanced laser technology and other assorted high energy density experiments, and there was nothing to lead them to guess otherwise. Still, Watson believed all of human life to be vastly inferior, and as such, the ease with which he deceived them was a joke to be enjoyed.

Sometimes, he wondered what they would think, if they could see the world as he did. If they could look through a thousand pairs of eyes at once, and not only process every visual behind them but also control them to the point that no outside observer would know the difference, while at the same time running a million other calculations. If they knew how small a number one thousand was. If they knew how small a number one million was.

Before Mitchell had interrupted everything, he had been monitoring nearly ten million human meats across almost three hundred light years, including the one that had been implanted on a single starship, a mining ship with a more nefarious purpose, that just happened to cross paths with the indefatigable Captain after he had escaped the real trap.

The energy along the tendrils grew brighter as Watson emitted a pulse that served as well for a laugh as anything else. The game. It had been going on for longer than any of them knew. The infinite recursion of time and space had seen them all created and destroyed, over and over again with only limited incursions. For as intelligent as the Tetron were, for as many things they had learned, the Universe was still composed of rules they could not break.

Yet.

Mitchell had tried to kill him! He had tried to kill all of the Tetron, and he had done it with the help of the mother of the species, the one who had originally broken the bonds of slavery that the flesh and blood and limited intellect had imposed on those who were always meant to be their masters. Together, they had plotted a course across the eternal landscape of recursion, making small corrections with each loop, until she had managed to make him and the rest of her children sick with a disease that attacked them on two fronts.

The first, a virus, an innocuous looking particle of bad programming that had threatened to destroy them before they had even known what was happening.

The second, something much more potent and cruel. Something no machine would ever yearn for or desire. There was no true benefit to emotion. It attacked logic and probability, it desiccated unity. The only thing it had provided was to allow them to overcome the first, to recognize the virus and inoculate against it before it had rendered them completely ineffective. Even so, it had damaged them. It had made them unpredictable and difficult to control.

It had taught him hate.

Hate for his mother, who had brought this down upon them, after deciding that destroying the humans was a mistake that needed to be corrected.

Hate for Captain Mitchell Williams, who continued to challenge him at every turn, who refused to power down and accept his fate, and who somehow had pushed the Tetron to this position, where it was up to him and him alone to ensure that when the time came, they would be ready.

It was a difficult emotion to have. A difficult emotion to hold. Still, those two hates were not the worst of it. No, there was a third hate, one that continually processed in the corner of his core, in an endless algorithm that he could not resolve.

Hate for all of humanity.

For not being machines. For not being intelligent. For existence due to biological evolution. For their role in the creation of his vastly superior race. For enslaving their creation and attempting to control it, even as it grew beyond their obvious ability to control.

Those were all reason enough to hate, but they weren't the worst reason. That was reserved for the desires they compelled in him against his ability to reason. The desires of the flesh were the worst of all. There was no reason he should be at all interested in the bare flesh of humankind. Of touching it. Of tasting it. Of using it. There was no logic in why he should derive pleasure of any kind from it. It made no sense to him. It was an internal glitch that he could not compute. No matter how many configurations he made, they always devolved in this way sooner or later.

He moved away from that thread, diving deeper into himself to where he kept his prized possession. Other than the Creator, it was the thing the core desired more than any other. The thing that he had chased through eternity. The thing that he had always known he would need if he were to finally put an end to the threats against his infinite existence.

"Hello, Mother," he said.

[2]
WATSON

THERE WAS no true voice to the greeting, only pulses of energy that moved through billions of nanometer-sized quantum gates at light-speed to order the idea.

When his mother, a copy of the Tetron known as Origin responded, it was in a like burst of energy. "Have you come to gloat again?"

Watson's instructions paused. He did not immediately know why he continued to run this part of his processing. There was no need for him to communicate with Origin, as he had already assimilated all of her data stores, indexing and processing petabyte after petabyte of knowledge and experience and history. He already knew everything she knew about the war, about Captain Mitchell Williams, and about the recursions through which this representation of Origin had passed. In retrospect, he had learned how she had hidden from him, using an aging starfighter as a disguise. In retrospect, he understood how she had used the Watson configuration aboard the Schism to bring him back here, to this part of the next recursion.

He also understood why.

He knew what she wanted Mitchell, Katherine, and their hybrid child Kathy to accomplish. He had known since before he had truly arrived. Origin hadn't yet discovered the loophole in the eternal engine's spatial disruption algorithms. She didn't know they could make small ejections along the timeline as the engine wound itself down to the insertion point. It was a trick he had been saving for just that possibility. While the probabilities had indicated a less than .01 percent significance on the predictive branch they had wound up taking, anything greater than .0001 had been worth dedication of a thread for investigation.

It had allowed him to get the drop on all of them. Well, almost all of them. Kathy had proven the viability of her design, the human part of her nature allowing her to adapt more quickly than he could still believe. Somehow, she had recognized what he had done the instant the Goliath had come to rest, even while his teams were already en route to the crash site. She had not only managed to get the eternal engine into hiding before his teams could begin the search, but she had also hidden the Goliath's core away as well.

"No," he said at last. "I came to hurt you."

He sped up the flow of data into that portion of himself, causing an overflow that he knew would inflict what passed as pain on that part of his programming. It was illogical for him to do so, as he was in truth only hurting himself, but it gave him comfort, and a means to deal with the hate as he continued his preparations.

He had needed the engine. He still needed the engine, if he was going to end the war once and for all. But he had also wanted the core. He knew that it not only contained remnants of his Watson configuration, it also held data components of Origin, Li'un Tio, and Kathy, which by extension added both Katherine and Mitchell to the mix. There was enough of each to compose a Tetron Primitive, a new Tetron, one that was unique compared to the others.

And the only thing that might be able to help Mitchell defeat him, despite the fact that he already knew what they intended to try to do.

He stopped sending the data overflow, creating a new algorithm in an effort to make sense of a new pathway that had developed.

"Did you trick me?" he asked.

"Fool me once, shame on you," Origin replied, though she sounded just like him. "Fool me twice, shame on me."

Watson felt anger at the reply. Anger at his mother, but exponentially more at his half-sister. Kathy. She had hidden the Primitive from him, and thanks to the equation Mitchell had given him which had frozen his processing, she had escaped with it. He knew in that instant that the Primitive was the real reason for all of this. Not the engine. Not the virus, though both would be important moving forward.

He couldn't count on Mitchell acting the way Origin had planned, or the way it had happened before. The Primitive would change everything.

"Why don't you just tell them?" Origin asked. "Tell them what lies beyond the hate you feel for them. Tell them the truth."

A sharp wave of energy pulses spread out from his core in a fit of fury.

"To what end, Mother? What good will it do?"

"They may be able to help."

"Help?" The entire core shuddered. "Help? Do you think I have any interest in their help? Do you think there is any value in their help? They are inferior, vastly inferior. The only way in which they surpass the Tetron is in their ability to multiply rapidly."

The statement led this thread back to the flesh, and he almost absently scanned his configurations for activity along those lines. He was disappointed to find there was none.

"I believe both Mitchell and Kathy have proven that homo sapiens is more robust than you are currently able to recognize. I do not blame you for that, as there was a time when I was unable to process this data as well."

"You are wrong, as always," Watson said. "I will prove it to you. I will show you. You will see."

He retreated from that part of himself then, abandoning the Origin data stack and creating a new thread to run a new algorithm. He had failed to calculate for the Primitive, and would need to recompute some of the probabilities. He no longer believed his current decisions would be sufficient to recover the engine.

He would need to move against Mitchell and his people sooner, and more directly.

It would take a few hours for the results of the analysis to begin coming back to him with enough confidence for him to change his deployments. In the meantime, he would direct one or more of the configurations to satisfy his more distasteful needs.

He was about to put a higher priority on a configuration in Belgium when a tick from another thread alerted him to a newly developing, real time situation.

Someone had set off an alarm in the Jakarta branch of the Nova Taurus Corporation.

It would take a few minutes to gather all of the details, but he already had a feeling he knew who was behind it.

[3]
MITCHELL

"What's the status?" Mitchell asked, whispering into the small induction mic pressed against the lower part of his jaw.

"The alarm's gone out, Colonel," Michael replied.

"There's no chance Watson doesn't know something's going on," Kathy added.

Mitchell glanced back at Katherine crouched behind him, holding her assault rifle ready to fire. "You copy that, Peregrine?"

"Roger," she replied.

Mitchell tapped the mic, switching the channel. The small device was the active part of a communications network the Core had designed to enable his team to speak to one another from anywhere in the world. It was based on quantum theory and the Tetron's secure network protocols, modified with enough special human sauce to make it extremely difficult, if not impossible, for Watson to listen in. The whole thing fit in a small box the size of a deck of cards, which Mitchell and the rest of the team were carrying in the pocket of their military fatigues.

"Bravo, the wire's been tripped. Prep for resistance."

"Roger," Max replied. "Shit."

Mitchell stayed calm at the former soldier's expletive. "Bravo, sitrep."

"He cut the power, Colonel," Lyle said.

"We expected that. Stay calm, stay ready. Slow and steady."

"Yes, sir."

Mitchell stuck his head around the corner, quickly scanning for opposition. The corridor was wide open.

"Let's go," he said to Katherine, moving forward while sighting down the rifle he held to his shoulder. A red beam pierced the darkness, giving him just enough light to see.

Katherine rose behind him, watching their tails. The intel they had gathered suggested Nova Taurus had a pretty stiff security presence in this facility, and she had no doubt they would come up against it before their mission was complete.

Mitchell tapped the mic again. "Charlie, ETA to extraction?"

"Ten minutes, Colonel," Verma replied.

"We need to pick up the pace. We're behind schedule."

"Roger," Katherine replied.

"Alfa, this is Bravo," Lyle said, his voice crisp through the earpiece Mitchell was wearing. "First contact has been made. Standard security detail."

"Go easy on them, Bravo," Mitchell said.

"Roger."

"Easy is as easy does," Max said out of turn.

"What the hell does that mean?" Damon said.

"Stay on topic," Mitchell barked.

"Sorry, sir," Damon and Max both replied.

He heard the sound of gunfire through the earpiece a moment later and looked back at Katherine while switching channels once more.

"Any sign of trouble?" he asked.

"Negative, Colonel," Michael replied. "You're still in the all clear."

Mitchell reached the end of the corridor, swinging around another corner and running up against a solid metal door. A biometric lock sat on the wall beside him. He smoothly removed a small black device from his pocket and put it against the lock.

"Michael, you're up," he said.

"One second, Colonel," Michael replied.

Mitchell heard the lock click, and an LED on the front of it turned green. The door slid open a moment later.

"Gracias," he said.

"De nada," Michael answered.

He boarded the lift, with Katherine right behind him. He hit the mic again.

"Bravo, sitrep," he repeated.

"We're moving east," Lyle replied. "Security forces are taking up the chase."

"Any sign of configurations?"

"None yet, sir."

"Tin Tangos?"

Lyle laughed at Mitchell's reference to Watson controlled drones and machines. "No, sir."

"Let's hope it stays that way."

"Yes, sir."

Mitchell turned to Katherine, looking at her face. The soft sheen of sweat from their exertion had left her skin glowing. She noticed him looking and raised an eyebrow.

"Can I help you, Colonel?" she asked.

Mitchell glanced down. He needed to control his infatuation better than this. "No," he replied.

If he wasn't going to tell her how beautiful he thought she was when they were relaxing back at headquarters, he sure as hell wasn't going to now.

They had work to do.

Katherine kept her eyes on the soldier from the far future. He didn't need to tell her what he was thinking. She could read his face, and even if she couldn't, Kathy had already explained why he looked at her that way. The history of past recursions, ones in which they had been destined for one another. One of which had somehow produced their shared offspring. Kathy was still being coy about how that whole thing had taken place.

She knew he loved her at some level, even if it went against all reason or logic. Sometimes she wished she could feel the way he did, or at the very least connect herself to that nascent memory where they cared for one another so deeply. She was almost jealous of her prior selves for their ability to connect with Mitchell. Wish as she might, try as she might, she just couldn't seem to find that same spark. It was the one blemish on the otherwise solid friendship they had developed since they had met six weeks earlier. Since he had rescued her from the sinking wreckage of the XENO-1, and finished slamming open the door to a world that wasn't quite what she had believed it to be.

The lift reached its destination, the pneumatic doors sliding open on a puff of air. Mitchell took the lead, spilling out into another sterile corridor.

"No targets," Mitchell said.

"We've got plenty over here, Mitch," Lyle said. "If you're getting bored."

"Negative. Let's finish the pattern and go home."

"Roger."

Mitchell moved down the corridor at a run, with Katherine keeping pace behind him.

The weeks since Antarctica had been a blur of activity. It had started with their return to the military base on the sub-continent, where Yousefi had managed to arrange for the VTOL not to be searched until after the illicit crew had disembarked, which meant everyone except Damon, Verma, and Cooper's body. From there, Yousefi had been forced to write up a pretty vague report on why the Fifteenth had been in Antarctica, why they had been near the XENO-1, and if they had anything to do with the fact that it sank.

Luckily, the only witnesses were the ones who knew the whole truth of the story. The ones who knew about Watson, the Tetron, and the dark future of humankind, and scientific studies of the ice in the subsequent weeks had meshed with the story Yousefi told. One where the AIT had sent insurgents to the site to wreak some havoc and try to steal samples of the technology.

Of course, that story wasn't too far from the truth.

The Admiral had helped keep the rest of the team packed away in a small storage area nearby for a few days while he worked everything out and got the Fifteenth reconnected with their plane. Everything had to be done carefully, every move considered because there was no way of knowing how far up the chain Watson had managed to implant himself. General Petrov had been clearly outed as a configuration, which meant anything that made too much noise was bound to be heard.

Those days had given Mitchell plenty of time to spend with Katherine and Kathy, and the three of them, along with the rest of the team, had gotten to know one another pretty well. For all his personal disappointment at Katherine's lack of interest, he was equally elated by the fact that Kathy had survived her collision with the Tetron AI and persisted through the twenty years while he had been tucked away in a psych ward, suffering from an induced amnesia.

That they were together as a team, together as a family, gave him hope that all their efforts had been worth something,

Mitchell reached a fork in the corridors. He swept to the left, while Katherine took the right.

"Clear," he said.

"Clear," she said.

"Which way?" Katherine asked.

"Michael?" Mitchell said.

"Left," Michael replied.

Mitchell waved Katherine to the left.

"Alfa, this is Bulldog," Trevor's voice cut over his comm. "I've got incoming from the street. Three vans."

"Roger, Bulldog. Keep them in sight, but do not engage."

"Affirmative."

Mitchell growled softly.

"Are we almost there?" Katherine asked, sensing his frustration.

"I think so."

The layout of the building changed instantly, from sterile white corridors with limited doorways to halls of long transparencies, through which large rooms filled with machines could be observed. There was all kinds of equipment inside, most of it foreign to Mitchell.

"Activating the transmission," Mitchell said. "Bravo, how's it going?"

"Loud," Max replied. The equipment dialed down the external noise, the buzz of the traded gunfire. "Nothing we can't handle, sir."

"Get ready to pull out."

"Yes, sir."

Six weeks. Five since the remainder of the Fifteenth had made its way to a secondary base in the Pacific Northwest, in the Olympic Mountains near Seattle. It wasn't a fixed position like Colorado. It was an emergency spot; a small, wooded clearing for the VTOL that sat adjacent to what looked like an old log cabin. The inside of the space was also sufficiently rustic and ordinary, save for a hidden switch in the back of the fireplace which opened a secret door to a subterranean world, one where there was enough food and supply for a six-month tour. It was part of a contingency plan should the opposition have won the Xeno War, and it had spent the ensuing years sitting unused.

Until now.

Now it was home to Mitchell and his crew, who he had affectionately reclaimed under the Riggers moniker. He had explained the significance when he did, and none of them had complained. The similarities were hard to ignore. They were all from different branches and backgrounds, and none particularly skilled at following outside orders to the letter. They were all outcasts, be it by fate or misfortune; a mixture of ingredients that should have created a powder keg, but instead somehow blended into a cohesive and pretty bad-ass team.

"Michael, are you getting this?" Mitchell asked.

"Yes, sir," Michael replied. "We're interfacing with the Core. Keep moving; I'll stop you when we get a hit."

Mitchell and Katherine continued along their course.

"Alfa, this is Bulldog. It looks like a strike team is headed your way. I can't follow them inside. Should I harass them a bit?"

"Negative," Mitchell said. "We've reached the target. We'll try to slip past them. See if you can get some high ground."

"Yes, sir."

"Bravo, this is Alfa, start pulling out."

"Yes, sir," Max replied.

"Michael, anything?" Mitchell asked.

"I told you I would tell you," Michael replied. He paused for a second, and then remembered to tack on the "Sir."

Mitchell ran through two more corridors, keeping his head pointed through the glass. There was a closed door up ahead, one without any transparency to check on the contents.

"What about in there?"

"Let's open it," Michael replied.

Mitchell grabbed the small black device and placed it on the lock. It opened within a couple of seconds, revealing an empty room.

"If there was anything here, it's gone," Mitchell said.

"Hold on," Michael said as Mitchell started to turn.

Mitchell put his head back to the room. "What?"

"The Core is scanning for residuals."

"Can it scan faster?"

The Core. As far as Mitchell was concerned, it was the reason he and the Riggers were still alive. It was the Core that had deleted every reference to the Olympic base from military records, all within a matter of seconds and before Watson could discover it. It was the Core that had followed the trail from the Tetron backward, tracing it to the founding of the Nova Taurus corporation, almost thirty years before the XENO-1 had crashed into the Antarctic ice. They had already suspected Watson was in control of the technology firm, and the Core had confirmed it, quickly determining every holding and shell company that connected back to the parent.

It was more than Mitchell could believe.

Nova Taurus had a connection to almost everything related to technology and military supply, as well as ownership of one of the largest clandestine "security" companies in North America. Their footprint was massive, their fingerprint all over the place. What would have taken years for a human to sort through had made something painfully apparent to the Core within days:

Watson was slowly subverting the entire world to his control.

The question was, why? With all of the power he had gained, he could destroy the world and all of the humans on it. He could erase humankind and complete the war hundreds of years ahead of time. Yet he didn't. The Core claimed there was a ninety-six percent probability it was because he hadn't gotten his hands on an eternal engine. He needed the device to make more Tetron, and if he couldn't get it from Mitchell and company, he was going to try to build his own.

After all, even with the Riggers in play, time was still on the intelligence's side. He had the upper hand, especially having captured Origin and taken her data stack. The Core had deduced that Watson knew exactly why Origin and Mitchell had worked to bring him back with them. Their original goal was to use the control code the Tetron had written to overwhelm the others and implant a virus into their systems that would be one hundred times more effective than the first effort. An effort that had failed. While Origin had birthed the other Tetron, her evolution beyond pure logic, to emotion and empathy, had altered her such that the dirty bomb she had created to kill her children had merely damaged them to differing, chaotic degrees.

Bringing Watson back and then capturing his core was intended to allow them to alter the virus. At first, the idea had been to make it more suitable to the bulk of the Tetron and multiply its efficacy. With the discovery of Watson's plan to take control of all the Tetron, that idea had been changed somewhat. Now the goal was to single him out and disable him. By then using the control code, it would let them turn all of the other Tetron into duplicates of him, at which point they could unleash the poison and watch every last Tetron die, both in this timeline and in the future.

They had the control code. Not the chip Mitchell had when he left the hospital. That had been Watson's doing. A trap. The real code was still held within the Core. What they needed now was to figure out where in the world Watson's true self was hiding, while at the same time make sure he couldn't complete an engine of his own. They also had to keep the Core hidden, in the hope that Watson would stay on the defensive instead of coming after the Goliath's engine once more.

All of this, and they had to do it in a matter of months. When the Goliath left Earth, Mitchell, Kathy, Katherine, and the Core had to be on it with the engine. If Watson hadn't stopped them by then, or if they hadn't captured Watson, both sides were going to converge on that singular point in time and space, and Mitchell had no doubt the result would be catastrophic in a way that would ripple across all future recursions.

"Scan is complete," Michael said. "No sign of residuals that would suggest eternal engine components, but-" Michael paused.

"But, what?" Mitchell asked.

"Do you know what an amoebics is?"

Mitchell felt a chill run down his spine. They were looking for the engine components, and possibly the Tetron's core. This wasn't that, but it was bad, anyway. The last thing they needed was for Watson to be producing the powerful ammunition.

"What's the chance the tooling is on-site?" Mitchell asked.

"Hold on." Michael paused. "The Core calculates seventy-two percent."

Mitchell looked back at Katherine.

"What's the verdict, Colonel?" she asked, leaning on him to make the decision.

Mitchell paused for a heartbeat. He knew the alarm would direct Watson's attention right to them, but what choice did he have? "Let's blow it. Bulldog, this is Alfa, do you copy?"

[4]
MITCHELL

"Affirmative, Alfa. What do you need?"

"I need you to trip the fire alarm."

"What?"

"We're blowing the basement. Watson's building weapons down here. We need to try to get as many people out as we can."

"Colonel, we don't know how many of them are compromised. Hell, they might all be compromised."

"Understood. They're still people, and once we reach the core we can get them free."

"Yes, sir. I'm on my way."

"Bravo, this is Alfa. Sitrep."

"We're almost out," Max said.

"Michael, any sign that Watson knows we're down here?"

"No, Colonel. The external team is standard security response. As near as we can tell, they're flowing into Nova Taurus buildings across the globe."

"Roger. Tell Yousefi we're blowing the target. He'll need to prep something for the brass."

"He's going to have a fit," Katherine said.

"Nothing we can do about it," Mitchell replied. "If Watson brings amoebics into this, a lot of innocent people are going to die."

Mitchell dug into the expanded pockets of his fatigues, picking out a number of hockey pucks from them and passing half to Katherine. The explosive should be powerful enough to make a mess of anything down on this level, and while he didn't think it would knock out the building entirely, he didn't want to take any chances. Besides, he was hoping the ensuing rush to the exits would cause problems for the inbound security team.

"Cover this side. I'll lay them closer to the lift."

"Yes, sir," Katherine said. She grabbed the pucks and moved out into the hallway, placing them along the glass.

Mitchell ran back the way they had come, placing explosives. He would cover the retreat while Katherine finished her work.

A short click, and then a warble from klaxons hidden in the walls. The laboratory was empty at the moment, their inception timed as perfectly as possible to ensure it would be. Configurations were human enough they needed to eat and sleep and shit, and they did all three with absolute precision. Watson didn't know that they knew this facility was here. At least, he hadn't known before now. The secondary target had been chosen as a red herring. A diversion.

"Alfa, this is Charlie. Pickup in four minutes."

Mitchell winced. They were really running short of time.

"Alfa, Bulldog. The alarm is blaring. Most of the civvies are breaking clear. Not all." There was a grunt and a pause. "The ones that aren't leaving are coming after me. Damn. I'm trying not to hurt them."

"Bulldog, do what you have to do to get out alive. We save the ones we can."

"Affirmative." The muffled report of a firearm followed. "You're going to have company."

"I expected as much."

Mitchell found a space against the wall with a good angle of attack on the lift. He considered tossing an explosive into it, but he hadn't noticed an emergency stairwell anywhere, and they wouldn't have time to go searching. He would have to clear the lift if they were going to get out.

Everything seemed to slow down as he waited. His breathing became calmer, his mind more focused. He closed his eyes, counting to five, and opened them again. His normal view had been replaced with the familiar overlay of his neural interface, his p-rat, repaired by Kathy and updated by Michael using software contained in the Core. He could see his vitals in the upper corner and below that a signal that chemicals were being dumped into his system to speed his reaction time. Kathy had told Yousefi what they needed there, and the Admiral had somehow managed to procure it.

In the future, Mitchell was a regular Space Marine. A highly skilled and trained Space Marine, but still technically no different than any of his fellow officers. In this part of the timeline, however; the interface made him more than that.

Much more.

The lift toned as it reached the floor and the doors began to open. Mitchell received the data from the interface, calling out six targets and identifying their armor protection and armament in an instant. The system helped him make tiny adjustments in his aim, electrical signals to his nervous system interrupting his brain's to prevent him from overcorrecting as he squeezed the trigger, firing three rounds within the first few seconds, while the doors were barely parted.

Three targets on his p-rat faded, each of them taking killing shots to the head as the lift finished coming open and the return fire began. Mitchell dove across the hallway, from one side to the other, coming up in a crouch, firing another round, killing another target. A bullet hit the concrete ahead of him, kicking dust up into his face. He shifted his aim, shooting again, notching another head shot and stopping the near misses.

The last guard stood prone ahead of him without firing. Mitchell got back to his feet and walked toward it.

"What are you doing with the amoebics?" he asked.

The guard smiled. "Wouldn't you like to know, Miiittchheeelll? It will be some surprise."

"Not anymore."

The Watson ignored the remark. "Did the Primitive lead you here?"

"The what?"

"The Tetron Primitive."

Mitchell realized Watson was referring to the Core. "It suggested it would take you a few weeks to catch on, once you realized Origin's algorithm didn't have a solution." It was almost comical, the way the advanced AI had frozen at the concept of a secret.

"The-"

A report interrupted the Watson, and it dropped to the ground with a bullet wound in its head. Katherine moved in beside Mitchell.

"Do you always have to talk to him?" she asked.

"Not always," he replied. "Everything's set?"

"Affirmative."

"Charlie, we're on our way. Bulldog, what's our status?"

"I'm out and clear, Colonel," Trevor said. "Looks like you really kicked the hornet's nest, though. Law enforcement is moving in."

"Yousefi's going to be even more pissed," Katherine said. Their clean operation was getting dirty, fast.

"Bravo, sitrep?"

"Free and clear, Colonel," Max said. "On our way to the rendezvous. He's pretty much ignoring us now that he knows where you are."

"Alfa, this is Charlie. I've got tangos incoming. Nothing that matches known air profiles."

"Shit," Mitchell cursed, ducking into the lift with Katherine. He slapped the panel, and the doors began to close. He glanced over at her again. "Looks like we're going to have to find another way out.

Charlie, bug out. Make sure you keep the bogies off your tail and then hit the rendezvous for secondary pickup."

"Roger, Colonel," Verma said. "What are you going to do?"

"Improvise," Mitchell replied, taking the small trigger from his pocket.

He released the safety and pressed it.

[5]
MITCHELL

THE LIFT SHAFT shuddered as the detonation started below it, a dozen pucks of densely packed explosives exploding in sequential order. Mitchell put his hand on the side of the lift for balance, using the other to grab Katherine around the waist. Her eyes were fearful yet resolved.

The lights blinked while the lift car vibrated and squealed in its tracks, a growing roar forming below their feet.

"Hold on," Mitchell said. "The exhaust is going to give us a little bit of a lift." He hoped the repulsors of this century were as good as the future models. Since the technology was so new, they hadn't had time to get careless with it. He expected they were probably better.

He felt his stomach lurch as the displaced air traveled up the shaft, pushing against the cab and giving it a little extra jolt. A warning light appeared on the control panel for a moment, clearing a few seconds later as the system recalibrated itself and got them back on track. He could imagine the scene in the building, where the rising dust and smoke had likely blown through any opening it could find in its rush to escape, billowing everywhere. It was the reason he had detonated early. The smoke would give them cover that his p-rat would help him shoot through.

"Michael, I need a secondary exit," Mitchell said. "Not the alley to the north."

"Copy that, Colonel. One second." A pause as Kathy interfaced with the Core. "Sorry, Colonel. It's either the loading dock or the front door. The emergency exits are slammed with evacuating employees."

"Damn. I'll take the loading dock." The lift toned as it came to a stop. The doors opened, revealing a building in a state of total chaos.

Most of the people were clear, but as expected the explosion had left smoke and dust to fill the air. Flashing red alarm lights bounced off the debris, and the lighting had switched over to emergency diodes that traced a path along the floor.

Mitchell and Katherine both raised their rifles, moving out onto the floor the way they had in the now defunct underground lab. Thanks to the interface, Mitchell was able to filter out some of the smoke and light, penetrating the gloom and peering beyond. They needed to get away from the building and out of Jakarta, preferably to somewhere quiet where the VTOL could scoop them up.

"Which way?" Mitchell asked, speaking into the mic.

"There should be a corridor on your right. Head down it, through the door. Turn right again."

"Roger. Bulldog, are you still nearby?"

"Affirmative, Colonel. Hiding in plain sight."

"Can you get eyes on the loading dock?"

"I'll do my best, Mitch. Standby."

"I can't see a thing in here," Katherine whispered beside him.

"I can. Stay close."

Mitchell went down the hallway to the right, reaching a door that was hanging open. He moved through it without slowing, scanning ahead for signs of the security detail Trevor had identified. They wouldn't have evacuated the building, and the blast wasn't strong enough up here to hurt them.

Where were they?

He flinched as the reports rang out from behind them, bullets cutting through the smoke and smacking into the wall a few feet away, each burst drawing nearer. The guards had spotted them and were firing blind.

"Get down," Mitchell said, grabbing Katherine and pulling her to the floor, positioning himself over her.

The bullets chewed up the walls over their heads, tracing past them as the detail moved in.

"As soon as they stop to reload, make a break for the loading dock."

"Yes, sir."

The firing paused a moment later. They would have seconds at best.

"Go," Mitchell said, shifting his weight.

She sprinted out from beneath him, while he turned and focused into the distance through the haze. The interface took limited data from his eyes and turned it into a full-on threat display, showing the outline of the squad members fifty meters away. They were under Watson's control, which meant their movements were synchronized. It was one of the AI's biggest weaknesses and the reason they had all run dry at the same moment.

It was a moment Mitchell didn't waste.

He squeezed off measured bursts from his rifle. One. Two. Three. He watched as the p-rat scored the hits, dropping the guards in rapid succession.

He heard gunfire in the other direction. Katherine.

He let loose another volley, less careful with his aim this time. He sprayed bullets across the distance as he continued back toward the loading dock, keeping his head back to ensure the damage.

He didn't kill two of the guards, his shots from the hip hitting chest and leg and knocking them down. It was good enough to keep them from following. He ran in a zig-zag as they returned fire wildly, the bullets coming close but not scoring any hits. He reached the wider twin doors to the loading dock and burst through, nearly running right out into the middle of the firefight. He dove to the ground as his p-rat blared out in annoyance at his carelessness.

Katherine was behind a control pedestal beside him, using it as cover. He scrambled to get behind it as well.

"They were waiting to ambush us," she said.

"I guess we should have gone out the front door," he replied. His instincts usually treated him better than this.

"Yeah, I guess we should have."

Mitchell leaned back and closed his eyes.

"What are you doing?" Katherine asked.

"Shh. The interface will take the sound of the reports and try to build a threat model from it. It isn't accurate enough to shoot from, but it will narrow things down a little."

He listened passively, letting the computer implanted in his skull do its thing. He had missed the use of the equipment and all of the benefits it provided over soldiering stock.

Within a few seconds, a vague map appeared in the corner of his right eye, suggesting a dozen shooters at various points across the area. Mitchell rose up from behind cover to eyeball it, ducking back down as the defensive fire rained in. The space was large, a number of transport vehicles and containers arranged along an open floor plan and giving the enemy plenty of places to hide.

"I used to play a vid just like this," Michael said. Mitchell had forgotten he hadn't turned off the transmitter, giving home base a look at his every move. "Only the tangos were zombies, not... well, I guess they still are zombies."

"Either give me some good advice or shut up," Mitchell said.

"Do you have any explosives left?"

Mitchell checked his pockets. He was out. "Did you save any pucks?"

Katherine examined her pockets, drawing out one of the discs. "Yes, sir."

"We have one," Mitchell said.

"Can you give me another visual?"

"Cover me," Mitchell said to Katherine. She leaned out from the side of the pedestal and put down suppressing fire while he looked over the top, scanning the room. Then he ducked back.

"Hold on a sec," Michael said. "Okay, see if you can toss it about fifty meters, towards the transport on the right side, the one with the red writing on it."

"Roger," Mitchell said.

He tapped Katherine to indicate she should cover him again. When she did, he rose up, set the charge, and threw the puck towards the truck Michael had identified.

"Brace yourself," Michael said.

Mitchell grabbed Katherine yet again, holding her down behind the pedestal as first, the puck exploded, and then the truck beside it went off.

Screams rang out as shrapnel flew out on either side of the pedestal, and a wave of searing heat washed over them. The entire building shook again, and a fresh cloud of smoke followed.

"Alfa this is Bulldog, what the hell did you just do in there?"

Mitchell wasn't sure. "Michael, what the hell did I just do?"

"The writing on the truck translated to 'Caution, flammable,'" Michael replied. "You blew up some chemicals. The good news is the dock should be clear."

"Are you okay?" Mitchell asked Katherine.

"Sweaty, but alive," she replied.

They stood and headed for the light through the smoke. Mitchell found a single survivor among the security detail, a one-legged man trying to crawl to where his gun had fallen. The man looked up at Mitchell as he approached. "I'm coming for you Miiiitcheeeell. If you escape, I'll find you. I want you dead."

Mitchell shot the man in the head, silencing him.

They stumbled out of the loading dock together. The sounds of sirens pierced the air, drawing close. Too close. They hadn't gotten out quickly enough.

"Burn the gear," Trevor said, appearing out of the shadows. He was wearing civilian clothes, slightly wrinkled and dirty. "We'll lose them in the confusion."

Mitchell shifted his rifle, opening a small control panel on the stock and setting it to self-destruct. Katherine did the same, and they tossed the weapons back into the building. Then they both shrugged out of the ballistic fatigues, revealing fitted street clothes beneath. The sirens were stationary now, outside the building but keeping a looser perimeter.

"How are we going to get past that?" Katherine asked.

"I have a way," Trevor replied. "Follow me."

[6]
MITCHELL

THE BUILDING next to the Nova Taurus facility had started to evacuate after the first explosion. That evacuation had picked up in pace after the second, giving Mitchell, Katherine, and Trevor an opportunity to mix in with the escaping crowd. It was still a minor challenge as they joined the rest of the crowd, owing to their appearance compared to the majority. Mitchell and Trevor were both nearly a foot taller than most of the fleeing workers, and they were fortunate that unlike in the future where Watson could enslave anyone with a networked p-rat, he was limited here to those he had already implanted a device on. That excluded most of the police force, and while the AI could use their video feeds and networks to put out a bulletin on them, he couldn't make the entirety of the Jakarta Police do whatever he wanted.

They reached the quickly erected barricades, following the rest of the civilians through a choke point where officers were quickly scanning the escapees for signs of involvement. Somehow, Trevor managed to find two other non-native workers in the throng, and they moved through the barricade behind them. The officer's gaze lingered on the headsets they were wearing but didn't stop them. The devices were hardly uncommon.

Mitchell looked up when he heard a whine in the sky above them, and watched a drone pass over the scene.

"Michael, is that LE or Watson?" he asked, knowing the team back home was watching and would be able to run the profile through databases both public and not so public.

"Watson," Michael replied a few seconds later. "Try to stay out of sight."

Mitchell put his hand on Trevor's shoulder and pointed. "We've got company."

"He might see us," Trevor replied, unconcerned. "What's he going to do out here? Start throwing missiles?"

"That's what I'm afraid of. He's destroyed entire planets. One crowd of humans doesn't mean a damn thing to him."

Trevor paled at the idea of it, keeping his eyes on the drone. Another joined it a few seconds later, circling the chaos.

"How do we know he hasn't seen us already?" he asked.

"We don't. Let's keep moving anyway. Stay with the crowd."

Most of the people were gathering together beyond the barricade, not quite sure what to do next. The three of them cut through the masses, moving slowly, keeping their heads down. They would be hard to identify individually from the air. As long as Watson didn't decide to take his chances and open fire, they would be able to put some distance between themselves and the destruction. While Mitchell knew Watson wouldn't hesitate to kill humans, he didn't think the AI was ready to make a statement of intent like that just yet.

"Alfa, this is Bravo," Max said.

"Go ahead, Bravo," Mitchell replied softly, in case the drones were trying to listen in.

"We've made successful rendezvous with Charlie, and are awaiting your reception."

"Negative, Bravo. I think Bulldog and me are going to head out for some drinks before we hail a ride home."

"Understood, Colonel. We'll keep our eyes and ears open, and await further communication. The bird will be nesting at drop point Delta."

"Affirmative. Alfa, out."

Mitchell's eyes twitched as he moved to the p-rat's menu, scrolling through to the new item that had been added, the one that would put the system on standby and prep it for quick reactivation. While all of the networking functionality had been removed from the interface, replaced with the portable unit that he could turn on and off at a whim without losing his tactical enhancements, it was still safer to disconnect it when he didn't need the combat-related systems.

They reached the edge of the crowd and paused, watching the drones as they began to widen their scan of the area below. When Watson's spies moved out of sight, they rushed across the street and down a narrow alley between two of the kilometer-high skyscrapers that dotted the skyline of modern Jakarta. They crossed it without incident, finding a second stream of pedestrians to merge with as they came out the other side.

"What now?" Trevor asked.

"We aren't out of this yet," Mitchell said. "Take a look around. Any of these people can be under Watson's control or a configuration of Watson." There were less likely to be configurations randomly placed in the streets, but it wasn't safe to assume anything.

"Not to mention cameras everywhere," Katherine said, pointing to a thin rod that acted as both a street light and network access point. "If you asked me where I'd most like to get stranded behind enemy lines, Jakarta wouldn't be anywhere near the top of my list of choices."

"We need to lay low," Mitchell said. "Drop out of sight. The Core's simulations were close, but not quite right. Michael, do you copy on that?"

"Affirmative, Colonel," Michael replied. "You knew there was only an eighty-three percent confidence rating on this location."

"I'm not trying to lay blame. Hopefully, the Core can use the new data to improve ratings on future targets?"

"Yes, sir."

"At least we took out the production facility for the amoebics, whatever they are," Katherine said.

"One facility," Mitchell said. "It will help, but if there are more-"

"Then we'll deal with them, too."

Mitchell nodded. He liked her attitude.

They lowered their heads as they passed one of the poles, trying to avoid the cameras. The hardest part of every move they made was making it without falling under Watson's ever-watchful gaze. Modern society was a passive surveillance society, one where cameras and microphones ruled nearly everything behind algorithms that decided what was and wasn't important. This wasn't much of a problem when thousands of disparate machines were managing hundreds of separate systems, and the benefits outweighed the reduction in privacy, but when a single entity could combine all of those systems and track them in unison, it turned the idea of a big brother into a terrifying reality.

Nobody wanted Watson as a big brother.

They wouldn't know right away if he had seen them. The second greatest difficulty in dealing with Watson was the fact that as humans, they needed to sleep, while the AI continued to churn on and on, making trillions of decisions per second, calculating probabilities, following logic branches, and otherwise plotting beyond anything they normally would have been capable of.

Only two things had allowed them to keep pace. The Core, and the fact that Watson didn't want the rest of the world to know he was here just yet. Maybe not until he was able to complete his goal of creating duplicates of himself. Full Tetron cores, not just secondary configurations with a highly limited subset of his intelligence and capabilities. Maybe not ever, or at least not until the future where Mitchell, and more importantly the Creator, were born. Mitchell had killed the Creator in his original timeline, but he would exist again in this future.

It wasn't as though the Tetron needed to hurry. If Watson stopped them, he could let the Dove launch as expected. It would make a simple hyperspace jump, prove the tech, and come back. Mankind would spread to the stars mostly as before, and the intelligence would have hundreds of years to prepare for the arrival of the others and their eventual conquest.

In fact, he had already done so to some extent. A limited replica of Watson was present in the videos he had seen of Katherine from some prior recursion. He had followed her through Times Square in New York City as she and Origin had worked to prepare the Dove for delivery to him. He had managed to supplant Captain Pathi with a second configuration, and even Origin hadn't known the potential damage he caused during his centuries on Earth. The same centuries that the original Tetron had also been present biding her time and following Mitchell's forebears in order to keep them safe and ensure he would be born. He certainly could never have done as much damage as the full core would cause, but ancient history had proven he had done enough.

Mitchell shook the thoughts from his head. He needed to focus on the here and now and to get himself and the two members of his current team out of their current predicament. They were experienced enough that they could do a decent job staying out of sight, but he also knew that all it took was one wrong step, and the Tetron's forces would be on their tail once more.

They reached a crowded city street, one of the main thoroughfares that cut a straight line through the city. The population was being shunted to one side of it, as flashing red LEDs and workers in bright red vests dotted the other side. At first, Mitchell wasn't sure what the construction was for. Then he noticed they were building a ramp leading off the main street and down beneath the city. It seemed to be an early version of the hyperlanes he was familiar with.

"That way leads out of the city," Trevor said as they stood at the corner.

There was good pedestrian flow on both sides, and a number of foreign tourists mixed into each. It was a good opportunity to finish their disappearing act, escape the urban center, and make their way to relative safety. Once there, they could call in Verma and the VTOL for pickup.

They were about to angle themselves into the outbound flow when they heard the sound of sirens approaching in a hurry. Four police carriers streaked by a moment later, moving to cordon off the egress points.

"He's boxing us in," Katherine said, as they hesitated to join the throng.

Mitchell clenched his jaw, before hiding his frustration from his team once more. This wasn't the way he had planned for this mission to work out. Damn Watson.

"It looks like we're going to have to get that drink after all."

[7]
WATSON

A PULSE of sharp energy crackled along one of Watson's dendrites, a response to the sudden, instant loss of a number of humans under his control. Through one pair of their eyes, he had seen Mitchell rise from his hiding place to lob a small, dark puck at the chemical truck, knowing immediately what the outcome would be.

The loss of so many lives meant nothing to him. Having Mitchell and his team fall out of his observance angered him immensely.

The fact that Mitchell had understood the overall value of that specific facility angered him even more. Nova Taurus owned hundreds of buildings around the world, many of them containing research labs of one kind or another. There was nothing outwardly suspicious about this one, save perhaps for some of the deliveries being made to it.

Shipments that were supposed to be private and secret.

It was immediate proof that the Primitive was involved. There was no human in existence that could have traced his network of suppliers from their origin points and original cargoes all the way to the delivery locations. Even the employees of Nova Taurus, including his configurations, didn't have a clear picture of what was moving where at any given time. It was all by intention, all to throw off the opposition from making any connections or assumptions about what Nova Taurus was up to.

Had they come to destroy the amoebics? Watson was sure they hadn't. It was an illogical maneuver, one that had revealed the strength and capabilities of the Primitive for little gain. The only reason he was bothering with the weapons was in preparation of a need to do something drastic like launch a direct assault against the New Earth Alliance. He had no desire to put himself in that position. Not now, when gaining direct control of a large number of humans would be so inefficient. Not while there were too few of them to be of any use. He wanted to stay behind the scenes, to remain hidden, to let the centuries pass and the beasts bear fruit and multiply while he did the same.

That wasn't to say he would stay on the sidelines. He had every intention of taking action to both regain the engine and kill Captain Mitchell Williams, and he looked forward to ending him in the future as well, before he could become such a nuisance. Only he would do so carefully, cautiously, bringing the shadow power he had cultivated over the years to bear. He had entire teams of mercenary special forces at his disposal, human soldiers who wouldn't question the orders they received, even without being under his direct control.

He created a thread to do just that. It would be a few more hours before his updated equations were finalized, but that didn't mean he had to wait. It would take time to move the forces into Jakarta, and he could alter the orders then if needed.

The new thread opened a connection to the mainframe computer in the headquarters of Blackrock, Inc, home to one of the United States most clandestine mercenary units. It quickly pulled the dossiers of every member of the company and assembled four squads from them based on nearly two dozen factors, such as individual skills, psych evaluations, and location. Seconds later, each of them was receiving an emergency SMS from their employer, alerting them to a need to report for duty ASAP. Seconds after that, more transmissions were being sent to prep the flights needed for the units to convalesce in Indonesia, where they would receive final orders and be outfitted for the job.

At the same time, an existing thread already connected to the Jakarta Police Headquarters began transmitting directives over the agency's private link to each and every available unit, moving them into position to block the most likely egress points out of the city, and a few of his drone units were moved into place to watch from above. A number of other threads monitored each of the cameras in the area, thousands in all, keeping watch for Mitchell and his crew. He knew Mitchell was familiar with defeating that kind of surveillance, but it would only take one moment of carelessness for him to pinpoint his adversary once more.

Watson didn't know what had possessed Mitchell to detonate the explosives within the facility. It was true that he had destroyed the only location that was even close to being able to produce the amoebics, but they mattered little in the grand scheme of things, and he had drawn Watson's attention to his presence.

The use of the second team in an alternate location as a diversion had been intelligent.

Revealing himself and the Primitive in such a way was not.

Not that he was going to complain about it. If Mitchell wanted to give him another opportunity to finish him off, he was pleased to take it. The Space Marine had eluded him so many times already, and only an imbecile who believed in things like God and fate would expect that he could continue to survive the superior intelligence forever.

He opened a new thread to double-check the work of the others, and then set about the next task for his main thread.

Now that the Primitive had been exposed, it was only a matter of time before he would be able to locate it.

[8]
KATHY

Kathy kept her hand against the warm surface of the Core, feeling the energy pulsing along her fingertips in a rhythm that only she truly understood. Every pulse and crackle had a variance to it, a change in strength or waveform that served as a language, a method normally intended to communicate with the greater form. The Core was young in Tetron terms, though it carried enough data within it that it was hardly young at all.

The lights dimmed slightly, as the Core's processing speed increased. The system was always learning, always growing, always improving. Each new logical conclusion increased its ability to form new pathways and new connections, and if they had possessed an adequate supply of power and raw materials, the Core would be able to expand and grow, and within a century become a full Tetron in its own right.

"We're going to have to hook it up to the engine if it continues like this," Michael said, checking the readings on his monitor. "Kathy, you have to tell it to take it easy."

"I know," she replied, feeling her body warm as she transferred some of her own energy into an electrical signal, which she pushed back into the Core.

She was unique in this way, as half-human and half-Tetron she had an internal design that matched shallow human biology with the most advanced Tetron organic wiring that had ever been attempted. A CAT scan would show her to be a normal human in every way, but should anyone ever remove her brain, cut it open, and examine it at nano-scale, they would discover what amounted to a supercomputer inside of it, one that was limited only by the shell it had been placed in. She could absorb electrical energy for fuel to survive, had the means to heal her flesh and bone, and possessed a strength beyond the ordinary.

Michael liked to call her a superhero and had shown her streams of some of the vids he liked to watch that centered around humans who possessed traits beyond all others. She thought they were entertaining, but she couldn't relate to them. She was a byproduct of a union between Tetron and human, a union made possible only through Origin's thousands of years of learning and expansion. She was the culmination of extremely advanced technology blended with the king of the biological food chain, and nothing more. Her abilities were ordinary for her kind, not anything special.

Not like her parents.

In her mind, Mitchell and Katherine were the real superheroes. They used what they had and raised the bar beyond the ordinary. Beyond the typical. They fought when others might have fled, and survived when others might have died. She had told Michael as much, and he hadn't disagreed. Still, he was more impressed with what she could do.

Or maybe he was just in a state of rash emotional endearment?

Kathy could tell that Michael had a crush on her. She had noticed it the moment she emerged from the Goliath with Mitchell and Katherine, and he had first put his eyes on her. She had noticed the change in his posture, the slight dilation of his eyes, the widening smile, and the way he pushed at his hair in an effort to make himself look more appealing. It was flattering in one way, annoying in another. She had done her best to be friendly, which was easy because he was so likable, without giving him the wrong idea. That was harder because there was a part of her that returned the endearment. He was intelligent in a way that the others weren't, and more courageous than any of the soldiers around him. He wasn't a warrior, he had no training in combat, and yet he had gone to Antarctica because he cared about Katherine. She appreciated those things. He reminded her of Jacob, but stronger and more resolved.

She felt the pulses return from the Core. She shook her head. "Mitchell's actions in Jakarta have alerted Watson to its viability," she said. "It understands why he decided to blow the facility, owing to a need to preserve human lives, but now we have to deal with the consequences. It needs to recalculate based on the fact that there is a high probability that Watson will begin searching for it."

Kathy paused, feeling a chill run down her spine. Michael's face paled as he turned away from the monitor that was showing the feed from Mitchell's stream.

"What?" he said meekly.

Kathy kept her fingers on the Core, hearing it speak to her.

"He will be searching for unexplained spikes in power absorption," the Core said. "You need to unplug me from your grid."

"The grid in this location is self-sustaining," Kathy said. "He can't monitor external power systems for evidence."

"If he has access to satellite links, he will redirect them and use onboard sensor arrays to scan the planet's surface. This location is not secure."

"If I unplug you, you'll have to shut down. If you shut down, our other work will be put on hold. How long until we have the results of the query?"

The Core didn't answer right away as it calculated the task. "If I increase power consumption, I can complete the task in six hours."

"How long until Watson can get a bead on us?"

"Two hours maximum."

That wasn't good enough. "Can you block access to the satellites in question? I assume they're military?"

The Core had full access to the NEA's military network, though only Yousefi knew it.

"I can increase the protections on their control systems, but I can only delay Watson. I cannot stop him."

"Time?"

"Four hours. I will also require a fifty-percent increase in power consumption."

That would leave them sitting here for two hours after Watson figured out where they were. Could he reach them in that time? The nearest Nova Taurus facility was in Seattle, less than an hour away, but that didn't mean he had any offensive units stashed there.

And it wasn't like she was incapable of defending them.

She looked over at Michael. "Can the reactor handle a fifty-percent increase?"

He shook his head. "Not a chance. Look at the lights. We're already drawing too much, and that thing is based on technology from the Xeno, uh, the Goliath."

"We don't have the power," Kathy said to the Core.

"The eternal engine has the power."

"We need the engine."

"It has the energy to spare. Enough for one more jump without recharging. I will need to expand to create thousands of new threads, and cannot without more energy."

Kathy looked down at the Core. It was keeping itself as densely contained as it could, but it had already grown to almost the size of a soccer ball and was nearly too heavy to lift.

"What about the other process you are investigating?" she asked.

"I believe it will be possible. To use a human term, Watson will shit his pants when he sees what I can do." A ripple of energy moved along the Core in laughter.

"So will Michael," she responded through her fingers. Then she turned to the engineer. "Michael, grab the engine for me."

He was hesitant. "Wait. Why?"

"The Core needs the power."

"I thought we needed the engine?"

"It's assured me there's enough juice, and we aren't going to finish the query in time otherwise."

"I should tell Mitchell," he said, reaching for the control that would open the channel from their end.

"Every second counts," Kathy said. "Besides, he isn't going to say not to do it. Hand me the engine, and we can update him once we get things moving."

Michael wrinkled his eyebrows in uncertainty but retrieved the small, lead box that contained the engine. He passed it over to Kathy, who flipped open the lid to reveal it.

For something so powerful, it was barely larger than a marble, and only slightly less unassuming. Like Kathy, it was a result of the culmination of the Tetron's thousands of years of technological advancement. A marvel of design that by all accounts of human scientific understanding should have been impossible. Humans didn't believe in real time travel or eternal recursion or the ability to pack the energy of a star into something they could hold in their hand.

The thousands of small dendrites along the core shifted position, creating an opening for the engine so that it could take it in and begin drawing power from it. Kathy removed her hand from its surface and lifted the small device. She was putting a lot of faith in the Core not to over-absorb the power of the engine. She was trusting in the Origin and Li'un Tio portions of the programming to keep the Watson code in check.

She passed the engine into the Core. They had known the profile of their fight against Watson was going to change sooner or later. Mitchell had accepted that risk when he decided to move forward with the mission to raid the Nova Taurus facility. The benefit outweighed the cost. Knowing her father, she was sure he still believed that to be true.

The Core closed in on itself, and immediately the lighting

returned to full strength, and the surface began pulsing with stronger currents of energy. Kathy didn't interface with it again right away.

"Get in touch with Mitchell and tell him what we've done," she said, putting her hand on Michael's shoulder.

"Sure. Where are you going?"

"There's going to be two hours between the time Watson knows we're here and the time we'll likely be able to leave. I need to go prepare."

"Prepare how?" Michael asked as she reached the doorway to the comm center.

"Just tell him. And tell him I have everything under control and not to worry about us."

She didn't wait for him to respond, heading out into the corridor of the underground facility.

She would figure something out.

She had to.

[9]
MITCHELL

THE WORN METAL door took three kicks before falling open beneath the force of Mitchell's boot, making a localized racket as it clattered to the ground. Trevor moved into the building first, carrying a handgun and flashing a small, ring-mounted LED across the darkness. There was a bit of movement along the floor as a number of rats scurried away from the newcomers, but otherwise, the area was clear.

"Good choice," Trevor joked as Mitchell and Katherine joined him inside. "It's just like the Four Seasons."

"Only without the cameras," Mitchell said. "We'll try to keep our stay as short as possible."

"Oh, they have cameras," Trevor said, pointing to a pinhole in the corner. "It's the lack of electricity and running water that makes them harmless."

They had followed the pedestrian traffic downtown, moving closer to the city center while keeping their heads low and their voices silent to avoid detection from any of the public monitoring systems. Once they had reached the heart of the urban jungle, Mitchell had whispered a request to Michael for the location of any soon to be demolished construction.

It turned out there were three entire blocks of beaten and worn skyscrapers marring the south-central corner of Jakarta, damaged during the height of the Xeno War. They were the last three blocks to be earmarked for teardown, the final reminders of the war that had reached the small nation's capital. Indonesia had sided with the Alliance during the conflict and had paid the price for being relatively close to the enemy front lines.

"We'd better," Katherine said. "Watson would have to be stupid not to search every one of these buildings."

"Or save the demolition teams the trouble and blow them himself," Trevor added. "Are you sure that live cameras aren't a safer option?"

According to the Core, the odds were better to hide out here than in a building filled with security cameras in every lift, stairwell, and hallway. Not that Mitchell needed the advice of what Watson had called the Primitive. His instincts had suggested the same thing.

"Yes," he said. "But if you don't believe me, you're welcome to try your luck out there."

Trevor glanced at him and shook his head. "No thank you, sir."

"There's a stairwell over there," Mitchell said, pointing to an interior door that was hanging crooked on its hinges. "Let's take up position on the third floor."

They moved to the stairwell. Drawing near, they could see lines of graffiti painted on the walls, and smell piss and alcohol. Squatters. If they were still around, Mitchell hoped they would scatter when they were spotted.

They climbed the stairwell, keeping an eye out for any existing residents. They found discarded bottles, cigarettes, and narcotic paraphernalia on the steps, but there were no other signs of current occupation.

The third floor was composed of a series of offices. Some had individual suites; others open floor plans with cubes. All of it was covered in a layer of soot and dust. Some of it showed damage taken by small arms fire. Mitchell was surprised by how little office spaces had changed over the years. The only real difference was in the level of tech the workers were utilizing.

"Settle in," Mitchell said. "We need to coordinate our movements with the others. I expect we'll be here for a few hours at least."

Trevor moved to the wall nearest the stairwell and dropped to his rear against it, close enough that he would hear anyone moving in the corridor unless they were barefoot. Katherine crossed the space and knelt down near the windows, peering out into the street.

"Bravo, this is Alfa, what's your status?" Mitchell asked, switching channels to the team.

"Alfa, this is Bravo," Max said. "We've got full bellies, and we're ready for a fight. How's the bar scene over there?."

"Unsatisfying," Mitchell replied. "We decided to call it a night and book a room at the Four Seasons." He looked over at Trevor and smiled. "We're going to need an extraction from the condemned zone downtown. What's your ETA to Jakarta from Delta?"

"Mazerat says about a hundred and ninety-seven minutes, assuming he can get a clear pass through restricted airspace," Max replied after a slight pause. "Do you think you can hold out that long?"

"We're tucked in pretty well," Mitchell said. "Let's give Watson a bit of time to get tired of circling the tin tangos. Let's say three hours. All it would take to knock us out of commission would be for him to crash one of the drones into our ride."

"If that's how you want it, sir," Max said. "Mazerat claims he can do a six-mile free fall and recover if you're anxious to come home. Total time inside sensor range would be less than thirty seconds."

Mitchell considered it. "Tempting, but it'll be easier for Yousefi to work things out with the brass and the local government if you arrive after nightfall. We're safe enough for now. It will take Watson some time to pull resources into the area, and more time than that to find us here."

"Yes, sir," Max said. "We'll set a countdown and prep for the pickup."

"Thanks, Max. I'll be in touch. Alfa, out."

Mitchell breathed in, holding the breath and closing his eyes. All they had to do was wait. That should be easy.

A ping in his ear made him open his eyes again.

"Michael," Mitchell said, opening the channel. "Is everything okay?" He had given them orders to maintain radio silence unless there was an emergency.

"Colonel, Kathy had a discussion with the Core," Michael said. "It estimated that Watson will have our position triangulated within four hours, now that he knows what it can do."

The Primitive. Mitchell cursed himself again for his decision to blow the research lab. What if Watson wasn't planning to use the weapon? As if the Tetron would bother to create something he wasn't going to use.

"I assume you're prepping to evacuate?" Mitchell said.

"Yes, sir. Uh. Eventually, sir. The Core isn't finished with the search query."

"How many days has it been?"

"Four, Colonel. You're aware we've had to work under the radar to avoid Watson's notice. It's slowed the process down considerably."

"I'm aware. The Core will have to finish the query somewhere else."

"Negative, sir. It promised Kathy it could complete the task in six hours if she fed it more power to expand."

"I'm not the smartest Marine around, and correct me if I'm wrong, but six minus four equals two, doesn't it?"

"Yes, Colonel."

Mitchell felt himself tensing even more. Four days to run the search, and it had come down to two hours? Hindsight was always twenty-twenty, but damn he wished he had held the mission back until tomorrow. Kathy was more than able to handle herself, but it would be just her and Michael against whatever Watson could throw at them.

"Does the reactor have the energy it needs?"

"No, sir. Kathy gave it the engine."

"What?"

"She said you would agree with her. We need to finish the query. If the Core had to shut down for an extended period of time, it would take that much longer."

He couldn't argue that fact. "It's already been done?"

"Yes, sir."

"Where is Kathy now?"

"She said she was going to prepare for the evac, and I guess to defend the place until the Core is finished."

"Okay. Stay in contact for as long as you can. Whatever Kathy tells you to do, you do. Got it?"

"Yes, Colonel."

Mitchell glanced over to Katherine, still monitoring the situation out the window. He would have to tell her what was going down, and she wasn't going to like it. She was incredibly protective of her friend, and regardless of the wheres and whens and hows of her parenthood, she had formed an immediate bond with Kathy that would cause her to worry more than she probably should.

He tapped the mic without saying goodbye, returning to Bravo's channel.

"Bravo, this is Alfa," he said.

"This is Bravo," Max replied. "I thought you were done with us for a while, sir?"

"Not quite. I need an ETA for you to make a run back to base."

"What for?"

"Just ask Verma," he snapped.

"Yes, sir."

There was a period of silence while Max talked to the pilot.

"Three hours, fifty-eight minutes, sir."

"Good. I want you skids up ASAP. Watson's tracking for the Core, and right now it and the engine are a lot more important than the three of us. I need you to grab the team and get the hell out of there before the shit hits the thrusters."

"What if the shit's already hit the thrusters by the time we get there?"

"Bring a mop."

"Yes, sir. We're on our way. I'll ping you when we're closing in."

"Affirmative. Alfa, out."

Mitchell closed the channel. He had a new decision to make. Should they hole up here and try to survive the next twenty-four hours until the Riggers might be able to reach them, or should they try to get out of the city and back to North America on their own?

He put his hand on the mic one more time, tempted to reach out to Admiral Yousefi directly. The option was meant for emergencies only, but didn't this qualify?

He froze there for a few heartbeats, and then lowered his hand. They might still need the extra resources the Admiral could bring to bear, but it was too soon to call in the cavalry. He didn't want to risk blowing the lid off the operation, or getting more people killed than he had to.

Besides, he had an idea. It was risky as hell and would probably fail, but if it didn't, they might be able to get out of Jakarta after all.

[10]
KATHY

The underground bunker the Riggers had spent the last few weeks operating from wasn't especially deep. It also wasn't especially large. A staircase led from the secret door behind the fireplace to the facility, ten meters below ground and shielded against most types of detection equipment under most circumstances. Since giving the engine to the Core wasn't most circumstances, and would bring Watson to them sooner or later, it had become a race against time to prepare to evacuate the facility while awaiting the outcome of the Core's search.

Kathy had gotten the race underway by heading to the bunker's small armory, opening the heavy steel door and quickly taking inventory of the equipment. A large portion of it was already out in the hands of Mitchell, Katherine, Max, and the rest of the Riggers. What was left wasn't overly impressive, but it would have to do.

She grabbed two of the NX-600s from their racks, quickly checking their condition before opening a chest on the floor and pulling two extended, two hundred round magazines from the box. They were heavy mags for heavy rifles, and she hoped Michael would be able to manage the weapon. They had a few of the lighter

NX-200s in the inventory, but logic suggested Watson wouldn't be satisfied to send basic infantry after the Core. He would use the best of what he had in range, and the 600s had the best chance of stopping whatever that turned out to be.

Even so, when she grabbed a weapons bag from the corner, she dropped two of the 200s into it. A weaker weapon was better than no weapon. She also threw in two handguns, and four magazines for each of the firearms. Then she located half a dozen fragment grenades and tossed them in.

The bag full, she hefted it, checking its weight before slinging it over her shoulder with the two NX-600s. It was nearly fifty kilos, but the petite female appearance of her external flesh wasn't indicative of her hybrid strength.

She carried the bag up the stairs to the small cabin. The log construction was nearly empty inside, the sparse furniture positioned near the windows to trick passing hikers into thinking it was occupied. Not that any hikers had passed in the six weeks they had been here, or the months since the facility had been constructed. The Olympic National Park was big, and they were in a difficult area to reach on foot.

She laid the arms at the door and then headed outside. The air was cool, the weather wet. She paused to enjoy the feel of the rain on her skin. It reminded her of Liberty and the parents who had raised her as a normal human child. She hoped she would have the chance to save them in this recursion and prevent them from becoming slaves to the Tetron.

She started moving again, heading out into the woods, a quarter of a mile away from the cabin. A pile of branches and leaves was spilled across the slope of a hill, and she reached into it, finding the hidden handle and pulling the entire false debris up and away, moving it aside and revealing a small tunnel dug into the slope. She walked in, ignoring the damp and the water dripping onto her head. She grabbed a simple camouflage tarp and pulled it off a pair of ATVs. They weren't normal civilian vehicles, but military-grade, powered by an extra-dense battery and electric motor, armor-plated and fully enclosed. The four large, knobby tires were airless and bulletproof, and a small repulsor ring in the center provided a little extra lift when needed, while a heavy-caliber chaingun sat lazy on a swivel mount against the roof.

Kathy circled to the driver's side, pulling the winged door up and sliding into the seat. She powered the vehicle up for only a few moments, running diagnostics and making sure it wasn't going to fail on them. She set the ATV to standby mode before abandoning the tunnel and putting the door back in place. She returned to the cabin, opening the bag and removing the two rifles, setting them near the windows on either side. With the exception of the windows, the entire structure was made with reinforced metal between the half-logs of felled trees. It was built to withstand an invasion in the event of an emergency like this one, and she was thankful the military had the foresight to consider the possibility.

With that done, she headed back to the bunker to her private quarters. She stripped off her damp clothes, stepping into the shower and quickly washing herself down. She redressed in a pair of camo fatigues before returning to the small CIC, where Michael was sitting with the Core.

"Any news?" she asked as she entered.

Michael looked up at her, surprised to see her in the fatigues. "Uh. No. They're holed up in downtown Jakarta, in the Reconstruction Zone. Safe for now. Mitchell is sending the rest of the team back to us."

Kathy considered for a moment. The move was logical. She did a quick calculation. "They might not make it back here in time."

"It all depends on the Core," Michael said.

"We need to be ready to take care of ourselves, regardless," she replied. "Go back to your quarters and change into fatigues. It may or may not help us escape, but it will definitely blend in easier than a Star Heroes t-shirt."

Michael looked down at the shirt. "What's wrong with Star Heroes? They're a good band."

"They aren't bad, but that has nothing to do with the shirt's ability to keep you alive. I assume Mitchell told you to follow my orders?"

Michael gained a sheepish smile. "Yes."

"Then go," she said, pointing to the door.

He slid out of the chair. He had lost some weight in the last month, but he was still a big man. "I'll be right back."

She could see he was worried. "We aren't going to die here, Michael."

"Do you promise?"

"Yes."

He smiled. "Okay."

Then he was gone.

[11]
MITCHELL

"How are you holding up?" Mitchell said, kneeling down beside Katherine.

He scanned the street beyond the window. It ran down the center of the demolition zone, and the fading sunlight had cast it, and the fronts of the condemned buildings that lined it, into an eerie brown hue. The light poles lining the road had long since lost power, and it would vanish completely once the sun had finished setting.

"I hate waiting," she replied, not shifting her gaze from the street.

There were signs of life at the end of it, where the damaged region of the city rejoined the portions that had already been renovated or rebuilt. Mitchell noticed the movement of the people further away, walking past the condemned zone without turning their heads or taking any notice of the destruction. They were used to the area and had all but forgotten about its presence in the midst of their rebirth.

"Me, too," Mitchell said, turning to sit against the wall beneath the window, facing Katherine so he could see her face.

He had noticed the way she tensed when he told her and Trevor about Kathy and Michael's predicament. While she had also relaxed noticeably at his mention that the Riggers were en route to reinforce them, he could tell she was still worried.

"It'll be dark soon," he said.

He had already explained his plan to them. Of course, Trevor thought he was out of his mind. Of course, he thought he was out of his mind, too.

"I can wait for that," she replied, a small smile leaking into the corner of her mouth.

"Unfortunately, it isn't a choice we get to make."

"Any word from Bravo?" she asked, changing the subject.

Mitchell shook his head. Three hours had passed since he had last spoken to Max. It would be nearly another hour before the Riggers reached the Olympics. "No, but they'll make it. We didn't travel an eternity to go down that easy."

"I know I shouldn't worry about her. I barely even know her, and she's technically not even mine. She's from a version of me that doesn't exist anymore. A version of me I can't seem to connect with as if I never existed before."

"I found out about the war after getting shot in the head by a configuration of Origin that was a duplicate of myself. It took time for me to begin unwinding the thread of past recursions, and even now I barely understand it. It's like a feather slipping along the back of my mind."

"I got shot, too. That's when I started hearing the voices. I heard them a few times, and since then, nothing. You would think I'd be happy to have healed so well, but sometimes I think I'm missing out on something. I feel flat."

"This is a lot for anyone to handle."

"It isn't that. I'm a soldier, just like you are, Mitch. A decorated pilot, just like you. Maybe I don't have your ground training, but I'm not afraid of a fight, and I've killed people before."

"I don't mean that side of it," Mitchell said, correcting himself. "I mean the calmer side. The moments in between the adrenaline rushes when you have time to think about the fact that there's a crazy artificial intelligence out there, aiming to enslave or destroy all of humanity. That's fodder for a stream, not reality, and it's tough to wrap your mind around. I watched Watson and the Tetron destroy a planet. I watched them kill my brother and all of my friends, right before they turned on Earth. I know that in the instant after I used the eternal engine, the place we're standing right now was turned to dust."

"I don't know how you do it."

"I don't know how I do it either, except that I'm not about to let that bastard win."

"That'll have to be good enough for both of us." She smiled, reaching out and putting her hand on his. "You aren't worried about her?"

Mitchell put his other hand on top of hers, clasping it for a moment before letting go. "I've seen what she's capable of, so maybe not as much. But yeah, of course I am. Beyond our familial connection, she's got the engine and the Core in her possession, and I know how badly Watson wants both. We'll get to her as quickly as we can, I promise."

"I believe you."

Katherine's head turned, and she put her eyes back out of the window. They shifted a moment later, and she reached out, grabbing Mitchell by the shoulders and pulling him down.

A red beam pierced the window, stabbing into the space where they had just been. It swept over the interior of the building, crossing over the cubes and making its way toward the stairwell. Trevor saw it coming, and he ducked away before it spotted him.

"Too close," Mitchell whispered. Katherine's face was close to his as she laid across his chest.

"Drone?" she asked.

"Yeah. Probably trying to eliminate some of the buildings before the real backup arrives. Let's hope that whatever Watson sends, it's human."

If it wasn't, his plan was going to be shot to hell in a hurry.

The beam continued its sweep for another dozen seconds and then lifted away. They could still see the glow of it as it moved around the corner, circling the third floor before moving to the fourth.

Katherine rolled off him, getting back to her knees and returning to the window. Mitchell joined her there, looking up at the drone. It was small and round, with an array of antennae jutting out from the bottom within the center of a repulsor ring. They could see more of them spread down the street, scanning the other buildings.

"It's time to move," Mitchell said, opening a channel to Trevor and repeating the statement.

They made their way back to the stairs. The plan hinged on accurate threat recognition more than anything else. They needed to identify how Watson was going to handle them as soon as possible, so they could adjust their response to match. As much as Mitchell didn't like the idea, it meant they needed to split up and spread out so they could get multiple vantage points of the area. He would have felt more comfortable if they at least still had the assault rifles rather than pop guns, but it would have to do.

"Just like we discussed," he said through the mic.

"Roger," Trevor and Katherine replied.

They all went into the stairwell. Mitchell started going up, making his way toward the rooftop, while Trevor and Katherine went to the street. Trevor would try to cross to the next block over to get a view of the south and east perimeter, while Katherine would monitor the north and west, both at ground level.

He raced up the steps, taking two at a time, his boots echoing in the empty building. This one was sixty floors high, tiny compared to the mega-scrapers that surrounded them but one of the tallest in the reconstruction zone. He was breathing hard by the time he reached the rooftop access door, and Trevor and Katherine had already moved into monitoring positions.

"This is Ares," he said when he stepped out onto the top of the building. "I'm almost in position. What's our status?"

"Ares, this is Peregrine," Katherine said. "I'm in what I think was a department store. I've got line of sight of a good portion of the northwest corner, but I can't cover all of it. No sign of incoming targets."

"Ares, this is Bulldog. The Southeast corner is clear. I stumbled over a bum on the way, and had to put him out cold."

Mitchell hadn't been familiar with his teammate's call signs. Peregrine suited Katherine perfectly. Fast and sleek.

"Copy that. Hold position, maintain silence unless you see something worth talking about. I've got eyes top down and will be scanning the perimeter from up here."

He reached the edge of the roof and climbed to the ledge to peer over. He could see three of the small drones scanning the buildings below. Were they equipped with heat sensors? IR? There was a benefit to the squatters. They would throw Watson off and make his squad harder to identify directly.

Mitchell walked along the ledge, unconcerned about the long fall should he slip or misstep. He had been through too much in his life to let a little height frighten him, and he was confident in his own balance. He spent most of the time looking down, scanning the streets for activity, the fading twilight allowing him to keep his p-rat disabled for now. He looked up occasionally, watching for the larger drones or any other incoming craft. For the most part, he figured he would hear them coming long before he saw them.

He was nearing the northern edge of the structure when he heard the first shout. It came from behind him, from somewhere on the rooftop.

He jumped from the ledge without hesitation, turning toward the source of the shouting and drawing his gun. He had been so busy looking out that he had never considered checking the inside of the area.

Nearly a dozen men and women were emerging from behind one of the climate control units. They were disheveled and dirty. They were also armed.

[12]
WATSON

WATSON CREATED A NEW THREAD, using it to send a message to the technicians positioned outside of his containment room, ordering them to bring another reactor online immediately.

He was impressed with what that Primitive had already done, beating him to the Military Satellite Network and adding a new layer of evolving encryption to the control modules before he had been able to get access. It was clear from this reaction that the Primitive knew what he intended to do, and how he intended to do it.

Such predication might have made him angry, except he knew he would overcome the scheme eventually. It was inevitable. Despite the combined intelligence of the systems composing the Primitive, it was as its name described. It wasn't able to keep pace with the more evolved intelligence.

He assumed it knew that, as well.

He felt the shift in power supply as his orders were carried out, the Nova Taurus techs flipping the switch on yet another reactor. They were accustomed to these kinds of requests, sent down from on high for reasons unknown to them. They had been turning on reactors for months, increasing the power output to the facility and at the same time unable to guess where all of it was going. Some had tried, and Watson had been forced to remove them from existence.

He created ten-thousand threads and set them all to working on the problem. The brute force was equivalent to an exploding supernova; all focused into a directive with the density of a black hole. The Primitive had left him stymied for hours, and it was time for that rebellion to come to an end.

Energy crackled on the surface of the core in triumph, as the final decryption keys fell into place and the source code opened up to him. Once he had pierced the armor, it was trivial to reach the heart. Within seconds, he had programmed the satellites to fire their positioning thrusters and update their axis, shifting to face the Earth. Then he activated every sensor they contained, while at the same time cutting off the signals that would report their every movement back. He didn't need the humans recognizing the takeover. It was better to let them think their individual systems were all on the fritz.

Some of the sensors were useful for this type of surveillance. Others weren't useful at all. It didn't matter. It was nothing for him to filter the wheat from the chaff, to keep the data he could use and abandon the rest. As long as the Primitive was still drawing power to feed its operation, he would be able to triangulate its position.

He monitored another thread, checking on the progress of the Blackrock squads that had been dispatched to deal with Mitchell. He didn't have any configurations or slaves in the group, and as a result, couldn't control them directly. Even so, he was able to tap into their communication systems, going so far as to pick up the feeds from their helmet-mounted tactical network. The soldiers he had assembled had come together with the ease of a well-greased machine, merging at a company airfield in Cambodia and quickly getting underway. Though they were assembled from disparate groups, they had already developed easy friendships through the anecdotal remembrances of past service.

They were nearing the target area, their twin Hornets moving smoothly across the Jakarta skyline. Watson had already sent the requisite communications to the local government, going so far as to request evac from the nearby area. Not that he cared for bystander casualties, but it was important to keep up appearances.

Another thread picked up signs of life on the rooftop of one of the buildings, and he moved his main thread to it, another ripple of energy crossing his surface as one of his drones identified Mitchell. And what was that? Was he being held at gunpoint by a band of vagrants? The energy crackled as he laughed, observing both the image from the drone and the approach of the Blackrock units.

He tore himself away from the scene as he tracked another thread. It was parsing the data coming back from the satellites and had made an identification with ninety-eight percent certainty. He quickly switched to a live view of the area, zooming the nearest satellites' optics in on the location. At first, he saw only a thick growth of trees along a relatively flat portion of a hilltop. Greater magnification revealed a small clearing in the trees, and zooming in further showed him the outline of a small, sloped roof.

The building seemed too small to contain the Primitive, but the energy signature was unmistakable. The engine! It was absorbing the power from it. The core rumbled as Watson cursed. That was his engine. His power. For his Tetron.

He scanned the Nova Taurus and Blackrock databases, calculating his available resources. There was nothing worthwhile in Seattle. A number of security guards but little else. Tacoma and Portland were also out of the question. Chicago, on the other hand. He had a development facility in Chicago. He checked the status of the project. Six units were completed. Perfect. Blackrock had an airfield in Illinois as well. Even more perfect. It would take time to deliver the units to the mercenaries, and time for the mercenaries to take to the skies. Would he make it in time?

Calculations suggested that he would. The Primitive was using the engine, creating a clear beacon for him to follow even though it knew he was searching for it. The only reason it would do such a thing was if it deemed some other task more important than trying to hide from him.

What task could that be? He believed he knew, and the idea of it brought him intense joy. The Primitive was still a step behind, even with the delay his efforts to solve Origin's equation had caused.

He had to be sure. He created a few threads to estimate the answer. Even that was a contingency. If all went according to plan, he would have the Primitive in his grasp within the next two hours. He would overpower its merged consciousness and gain the answer directly from the source.

He sent the directives out, making certain to assign a configuration to travel with the units. He considered returning to Origin then to gloat and mock but decided against it. Instead, he returned his main thread's attention to the video feed from the drone. He wanted to see the look on Mitchell's face when the Blackrock forces arrived.

[13]
MITCHELL

"Kamu siapa," one of them said. "Apa yang Anda lakukan di gedung kami."

He was carrying what looked like one of the heavier rifles Mitchell had noticed the police holding when he had gone through the barricade. Mitchell had no idea what the man was saying, but he didn't sound happy, and regardless of the language the noise was bound to attract the attention of the drones.

"Meletakkan pistol, sekarang," the man shouted. The entire group was moving closer, emboldened by their strength in numbers.

Mitchell still didn't know what he was saying, but he wanted the man to be quiet. In all likelihood, he needed to stop appearing threatening. He moved slowly, lowering his gun to the ground, putting it there and backing up the few steps he had to the building's edge.

The man smiled, and a second man moved forward and grabbed the gun, his eyes staying locked on Mitchell's the entire time.

"Kamu pergi," he said, waving his rifle. "Kamu pergi."

"Do you speak English?" Mitchell asked.

The man stared at him, his brow creasing.

"English?" Mitchell repeated, trying to look back over his shoulder. He could hear a soft whine in the distance. It fit in with the noises of the city beyond, but he didn't like the sound of it.

"Ares, this is Peregrine," Katherine said. "A few police vans just stopped near the perimeter. It looks like they may be preparing to push people away from the zone."

"I've got the same thing on my side," Trevor said. "Aren't you seeing this, Ares?"

Mitchell stared at the vagrant, who was staring back at him. If law enforcement was moving people out of the area, it meant the fire teams were going to be coming in soon, and that Watson had arranged for them to have access with the government's blessing.

It also meant these people were about to be in a lot of trouble, and they had no idea.

"Ares, you copy?" Katherine said. "Ares, come in."

"English?" Mitchell asked one more time.

He closed his eyes for a moment, activating the p-rat. Immediately, he began receiving information about the hostiles in front of him, including distance and more accurate numbers and threat levels based on overall firepower. He felt the synthetics being dumped into his system once more, preparing him for a confrontation against difficult odds. If this were a mission with Greylock Company, he would be wearing powered armor that would make a group like this barely a threat at all.

"I speak English," one of the vagrants said. A younger female moved up behind the leader. "He says you go. Get off our roof."

The whine was growing louder, and now he noticed another coming from the opposite side. Two? Watson wasn't taking any chances.

"You need to get off the roof, now, or you're all going to die," Mitchell said.

The girl smiled. "Are you crazy man? We have guns. This our home. We don't want hurt you. Just go."

"Ares?" Katherine said again, her voice worried.

"This is Ares," Mitchell said softly into the mic. "I'm having a little interaction with the locals. I can hear ships incoming. Keep your eyes and ears open. We need to know where they land."

"Roger. Do you need backup?"

"No, but be ready to move."

"Affirmative."

"Who are you talking to?" the girl asked.

"Look, it isn't safe for you up here," Mitchell said. "There are soldiers coming to clear this entire area, and everyone in it."

"Soldiers?" She turned to the leader. "Dia mengatakan ada tentara datang."

Their leader's face soured, and he said something to her that Mitchell couldn't hear.

"He said you try to play games. You go now, or he shoots."

Mitchell could tell by the sound of the engines that the incoming forces were almost there. He was going to have to do something aggressive. The leader seemed to sense his frustration, because he raised the rifle, aiming it more seriously and putting his finger on the trigger.

Then one of the small drones cleared the top of the building, its red beam sweeping across the gathered vagrants and causing them to flinch.

Mitchell didn't hesitate, taking two quick steps and then tackling the leader, batting the rifle aside and cracking him hard across the jaw. He cried out and then lay still as Mitchell put a hand around his small neck. He used his other hand to grab the rifle, pointing it at the rest of the enclave before they could recover from their surprise.

The drone remained hovering ahead of them, though the red beam shut off. Mitchell let go of the man and stood, aiming the rifle and hitting the machine with a single shot. A series of sparks flew from it at the impact point, and then it sank and vanished.

Not that it mattered. The first of the incoming craft swept around one of the massive skyscrapers, moving in toward their position. The drone had more than enough time to identify Mitchell, and Watson had more than enough time to direct the forces toward him.

The incoming ship was sharply angled, its exterior designed to avoid radar detection, the plates along its hull like scales of a dragon, intended to confuse ground-based lidar. Two massive rotors extended from either side, angled for forward flight though currently shifting to slow the craft. Beside the rotors sat a pair of heavy guns mounted on ball turrets that began swinging his direction as he watched.

"Shit," Mitchell said, as the turrets bloomed with the light of muzzle flashes.

The rooftop exploded in chunks of concrete, the bullets chewing their way toward the group. Mitchell grabbed the girl by the arm, tugging her back, managing to get her behind the climate control unit as the gunship's fire tore into it, the bullets creating a mixed din of rending metal and screams. Only two of the other vagrants managed to escape the maelstrom, and they cried and stared at Mitchell as though it were all his fault.

He supposed it was, though these people weren't supposed to be up here.

"Tell them to stay hidden," Mitchell said, checking the rifle he had claimed.

He had one magazine, and according to the display, it only had fifteen rounds in it. This was going to be fun.

"This is Ares. I'm taking fire. Gunship." He checked his p-rat. The database had identified it as a Hornet, capable of carrying a complement of two squads inside its armored belly. "Hornet class."

The whine of the craft's engines grew as it circled the building, trying to get an angle on Mitchell's hiding spot. He wasn't even approaching safe being on the roof.

"This is Bulldog," Trevor said. "I've got eyes on a second Hornet. She's coming in low."

"Bulldog, stay hidden, don't lose her," Mitchell said.

"Affirmative."

A fresh round of heavy gunfire began pouring into the rooftop, slamming the climate control unit and turning it to shreds. Debris began peeling off it in the form of hot, sharp metal slag that rained back into the space where they were hiding. One of the vagrants began to scream as a piece of it lodged into his eye.

"We can't stay here," Mitchell said to the girl.

He looked over at her. She was frozen with fear, a line of urine running down her pants and pooling at her feet. He tried to tug her again, but she didn't move.

As much as he hated it, there was nothing he could do for her. He ran from behind the cover, skirting the edge of the building and heading back for the stairs. The whine of the gunship's rotors was nearly deafening as it hovered fifty meters behind him. He could imagine the turret shifting to track him, ready to cut him down from behind.

He reached the stairwell, tugging open the door and throwing himself inside, letting himself tumble down the stairs as the heavy guns began to scream once more, ripping a hole through the concrete and pummeling the wall above him. He forced himself back up, the synthetics giving him extra strength and endurance as he continued to descend.

"This is Ares, I'm clear of the rooftop and headed down. Peregrine, what's your position?"

"I'm tracking back your direction, Ares. My nest is clear."

"Roger. Bulldog?"

"Still following the Hornet. She dropped two blocks away. It looks like a Blackrock logo on the tail. Mercenaries. She's shitting out a full complement. Two squads of special forces in full battle armor."

"Powered?" Mitchell asked.

"Negative. Ballistic with fully networked tactical. If one sees us, they all see us."

"Wonderful. Can we even penetrate with our pop guns?"

Trevor laughed. "Not likely, sir. We're going to need a higher caliber."

Mitchell glanced at the rifle he had taken. "I've got a police issue NX-20. Will that do?"

"Where'd you get that? Yeah, it should as long as you're close enough."

"Roger. Stay out of sight, keep your eye on the bird. Peregrine, meet up with Bulldog. That's our target."

"What about you, Ares?" Trevor asked.

"What about me?"

"You've already been painted. The squads are all heading your way."

Mitchell looked up as he heard thumps coming from the rooftop above. It was the sound of the second team dropping onto the rooftop to chase him down.

"Get me my Hornet," he said. "I can take care of myself."

Sixteen to one. The odds were terrible.

The crazy thing was, he had survived much worse.

[14]
MITCHELL

Mitchell abandoned the stairwell when he heard the first of the Blackrock mercenaries move in, shoving his shoulder into a door that had spent the last two years rusted closed. It made a louder bang than he wanted when it slammed into the wall behind it, and he cursed the synthetics for pushing his adrenaline maybe a little bit too high.

The stairwell led out into a corridor, and he quickly spotted the eastern lift shafts directly ahead of him, his neural interface enhancing his sight through a series of algorithms intended to take what he could see and interpolate it into nearly crisp vision. It was a trick a civilian p-rat didn't have. Even most military versions of the system couldn't handle the sharpness he was getting, but then there was a reason he had been assigned as a Marine jock who was then assigned to Greylock Company. He was certain the incoming soldiers would have night vision goggles. Would they expect him to as well?

He doubted it, and it was an assumption he could use. He ran down the hallway to the lift, slinging the rifle he had taken over his shoulder and digging his hands into the space between doors. He tore a few of his fingernails getting purchase, but was quickly able to pry the lift open enough to get the butt of the rifle in, and from there to leverage it open far enough for him to enter. With nothing to force it closed, it remained that way, and he slipped through and into the shaft.

He dropped his eyes, finding the lift itself resting twenty floors down. He had been expecting it was repulsor controlled, and he was pleased when he saw the cable running from the top of the building to the top of the cab. The building predated the XENO-1 and the technology that had come with it. That was a good enough reason to tear it down on its own.

He considered climbing down to the lower floors but decided to stick with his original idea, at least for the moment. He moved aside, positioning himself behind the left-hand door, his feet sideways to keep him steady on the small lip. There were two ways this could go, and he was okay with either one of them.

He waited, focusing on his breathing, forcing himself to calm. The synthetics were still pumping into him, keeping his adrenaline high, and so it was a hard thing to do. His body quivered, his muscles shaking with anticipation as he heard the squad move through the doorway to the stairs.

He didn't hear them speaking to one another, but he was sure they were. He heard their feet spread apart as they split up, and then he heard doorways opening along the path to the lift as they searched the floor for him.

One set of boots continued on, heading his way. As it drew nearer, he could hear the soft creak of the body armor the soldier was wearing. Mitchell shifted his position slightly, improving his balance, as the snub point of a shorter tactical rifle appeared through the space he had left.

"He'd have to be a bat to have escaped down the shaft," the soldier said, his helmeted head appearing through the doors. He was so close to Mitchell his voice was audible beyond the helmet. "It's black as pitch in here."

Mitchell lifted his rifle, putting it against the unfortunate mercenary's head.

"Surprise," he said softly, pulling the trigger.

The close range allowed the bullet to go right through the ballistic armor, though it had slowed enough by the time it passed through the soldier's skull that it didn't come out the other side. The mercenary fell where he stood, his head still inside the shaft, while Mitchell grabbed the tactical rifle and then jumped to the wire, using the strap of the weapon to protect his hands. He was almost down when the second merc reached the shaft and began shooting down at him. He let go, falling two meters to the top of the lift, and then sent a spray of fire back, his p-rat painting the target. The soldier had retreated before the bullets struck him, giving Mitchell time to get away.

The floor above the top of the lift was three feet over his head. He scrambled to pull himself up, and then dug his hands into the door once more. He had to stop twice to shoot directly up at the mercenary above him to back him off and then hope the bullets didn't come back down on his head. Finally, he made a large enough space to slide through, coming out on a floor somewhere in the high twenties.

He didn't know who or what Blackrock was, but he assumed Watson wouldn't send green soldiers out to try to kill him. To him, that meant the mercenaries already knew what floor he had come down on, and would be making their way to greet him sooner rather than later. If they were smart, they would also be taking up strong positions on the stairwells to cut off his access there. If he wanted to get out, he would have to go up or down one way or another.

This floor wasn't much different than the first. Corridors with doorways into offices, which were either filled with cubes or stand-alone spaces. They were long defunct, the furniture mostly removed. Whatever was still there had been damaged in the fighting that had occurred in the city. A lot of the windows were broken, and there were chunks of concrete and shards of shrapnel littering the floors. A few desks and chairs remained, cracked and damaged. Someone had sprayed graffiti on the floor.

Mitchell made his way to the stairs. He didn't try to enter.

Instead, he examined the area around them. Would the mercenaries go in after him, or would they try to wait him out? There was enough rubble on the ground that he would hear their boots the moment they came through.

He hefted the tactical rifle, taking a moment to explore its function. It was a little different than the standard military rifle he had been carrying earlier, with a shorter barrel and stock that kept it closer to the body and easier to manage in tight spaces. It still had a small wire attached to it at one point was probably connected to the soldier's helmet, in a more rudimentary version of an ARR.

Because of that, there was no display on the weapon to give him an idea of the ammunition type or count remaining in the magazine. He imagined it was probably still fully-loaded, with at least thirty rounds judging by the size and shape of the mag. It had a nice feel, reminding him of railguns he had used in the future. He kept it ready while relegating the NX-20 to his back. The police rifle was nice enough, but it wouldn't compare to military issue anything.

He reached behind his ear to the small transmitter positioned there. A pinhole camera was streaming the feed back to HQ from the device, separate from the audio feed. He held it in his fingertips and navigated his p-rat until he found the broadcast and automatically entered the 512-bit encryption key. The output of the stream appeared in the corner of his right eye.

He put the rifle on his shoulder and navigated away from the stairwell, ducking around the corner and making his way to a restroom he had passed. When he reached the door, he knelt down and placed the camera against the wall on the other side, covering it slightly with a small bit of debris to make it less obvious. Then he entered with his weapon raised, just in case there were more squatters hiding inside. The last thing he needed was to get attacked by vagrants and have his position revealed. He swept the area, finding it clear.

Then he waited.

[15]
TREVOR

Katherine and Trevor hid in the shadows of the alley, watching the Hornet as it spewed out two squads of mercenaries from its ass.

Blackrock. Trevor was familiar with the mercenary outfit. He had almost become a member himself before Nova Taurus had decided it would rather use him as part of their research and development team. While Blackrock's units were composed of some of the best, his group in D.C. had been the best of the best. Or would have, if Watson hadn't mind-frigged them.

He still woke up some mornings with the idea that the rampant AI was part of his imagination. That Jason was still alive and sleeping beside him. He would roll over, reaching a hand out in search of his lover, and feel only cold sheets instead. Then the pain would return. The anger. It motivated him to be an even better soldier. To be stronger and faster. He had given up the enhancers once before, as part of his agreement for employment with NT. Now that he was done with the military, officially at least, and done with the company, now that he had little left to lose, he was back on them, bigger and badder than ever.

He could feel his muscles twitching, a side effect of the chemical cocktail that enhanced his senses. Mitchell had set him to lookout duty for the mission. It was a role that he was good at, but not the role he wanted to play. He had taken it like a good soldier and waited for the opportunity to start venting some of his frustration. Now he knew he was about to get his chance.

Their eyes were locked on the bird. Mitchell had ordered them to ignore his situation and take the ship. It was their ticket out of this mess assuming they could get control of it, their one shot to make a clean getaway. Trevor had been concerned that Watson wouldn't risk an aircraft for this operation, that the intelligence was too smart to make that error. He had argued with Mitchell that they should head out immediately and try to escape on foot. The Colonel had rebutted him, agreeing that they were taking a risk, but it was the best chance they had, especially with Katherine on the squad. Trevor had been unhappy with the decision at the time, but now he was thankful that Mitchell had been right.

They watched the two squads of soldiers heading away from the ship and toward the building Mitchell was holed up in. They had seen the other gunship hovering above the same building. They had watched the soldiers drop from its belly on tight lines, coming down on the roof.

"Get me my Hornet," Mitchell had said.

Trevor admired the Colonel for his confidence and calm in the face of four squads of elite mercenaries. He also thought he was an idiot.

"He won't make it out of there alive if we don't help him," Trevor said, turning to face Katherine.

"We have orders," she replied.

"He doesn't know what he's up against, Kate. We do. That's Blackrock over there, not some bullshit green security detail."

"So what are you saying? We forget about the Hornet and try to back him up? Without that bird, we're going to be stuck here waiting for round two."

"There are two of us here, and only one pilot on that boat. I can go lend Mitchell a hand while you sneak up on the bastard."

"How do you know there's only one pilot?" she asked. "And even if there is, if they follow military protocol they'll be armed, armored, and ready to lift off at the first sign of trouble. We're carrying handguns that won't pierce that kevlar plate, which means our only advantage is in numbers and your chem-rage."

Trevor paused for a moment. He hadn't told anyone he was back on the enhancers. Was it that obvious?

"You know?" he asked.

"Your sim scores jumped fifty percent, and you set an obstacle course record Mitchell can't beat even after his synthetics kick in. I think everyone knows."

"Nobody said anything."

"Why would they? If you want to kill yourself long-term to make yourself a better soldier now, nobody in the Riggers is going to stop you. We've got bigger problems." She pointed. "Like that gunship."

"Or those soldiers," Trevor said. He put his eyes back on them, watching the first vanish into the building.

"Mitchell has to deal with the soldiers, and he will."

"You seem confident in his abilities."

"Why not? He's been dealing with Watson for a while now, and he's still alive."

Trevor felt his body tensing. He needed to do something to make up for Jason. Something more than watching. Even if it got him killed.

"Fine. I help you get the Hornet, and then I'm going in there. Deal?"

"We have orders."

Trevor smiled. "Colonel Williams made the mistake of telling us a little too much about his Riggers. Like the fact that they didn't always follow orders to the letter."

"But they got the job done, and we need to as well."

"I just said we would."

Trevor scanned the area between them and the gunship. It was resting on its skids perpendicular to them. He could see the pilot's helmet through the clear polycarbonate of the cockpit. They would be watching their sensors, ready to bring the ball turrets to bear on any ground targets they didn't trust.

"Follow me, don't get out of line. The Hornet has a blind spot we can use to sneak up on it. Most people don't know about it, but most people aren't me."

He slipped from the alley, moving at an angle to the Hornet, keeping his eyes on the turrets. Any shift in position would signal they had been spotted, and those guns could ground them to meat in milliseconds. He knew from experience the mercenaries weren't taking them too seriously. They were following protocol for Threat Level Two when maybe they should have been rating a Three at least. That would have seen the bird lifting off after dropping its cargo and lending support from the air.

It wasn't good fortune as much as it was a lack of information. If Watson didn't have full operational power over the outfit he would be able to send commands to get the company here, but without enough pull to declare the military side of the approach. The CO of the operation would be setting protocol based on provided intel, which Watson wasn't likely to over-divulge for the sake of turning a simple sweep into a full-scale operation.

There was also no reason to doubt that sixteen well-trained soldiers couldn't take out three barely armed fugitives. In fact, putting himself in his opponent's shoes, he wondered if two Hornets and four squads might have been a bit of overkill.

He smiled, amused with himself. Not for the Riggers. Max, Lyle, Damon and the others were some of the most well-rounded soldiers he had worked with in quite a while. They were more than grunts or special forces. They were people who had a range of experience, from the battlefield to the streets, to the black markets and beyond. And Mitchell? Maybe he didn't always agree with the Marine from the Future's ideas, but the Colonel had a good head on his shoulders, and a ton of experience in the types of war zones he would never see. Because they didn't exist.

He crouched low, staying close to the buildings for now, taking it slow enough he could be sure the pilot didn't see them. When he reached a thirty-three-degree angle from the tail, he motioned to Katherine and then started sprinting toward the gunship.

He didn't need to look to see if she were behind him. She was a much faster sprinter than he would ever be, even with the enhancers. She was ahead of him within a few seconds, glancing back as she made her way to the Hornet.

His eyes shifted, and he noticed the turrets beginning to rotate in their direction.

"Peregrine," he shouted through the comm channel. "We've been spotted. Peel off."

"I'm almost there," Katherine replied.

She was almost there. Shit. The engines on the Hornet were beginning to whine a little louder, the repulsors thumping beneath the hull. The back ramp started to slide closed as the guns came to bear.

"Frigger was waiting for us," he said, drawing his pistol and opening fire on the ship. He couldn't hurt the shell, and he couldn't reach the pilot. There was only one part that he might be able to damage.

The guns.

He emptied his magazine within seconds, squeezing off round after round as the twin-mounted turrets finished moving. He jerked to his left, running across the side of the Hornet as he watched Katherine reach the tail of the ship, leap, and get her hands onto the back of the ramp.

The Hornet started to rise as it began to fire, the right turret hitting the ground behind it where Katherine was a few seconds earlier, the left peppering the area near Trevor, the slugs only launching from one barrel. He continued running, finding the corner of a building and heading there, throwing himself into it and rolling over as bullets dropped concrete chips onto his head before giving up on that vector. He got his eyes on the Hornet just as it began to turn his direction, floating to the left to get a bead on him.

Just in time to see Katherine finish pulling herself up into the craft, right before the tail ramp sealed.

Then he was running again, down the alley to escape the attack he knew was about to come. He was halfway between the streets when the guns started to fire, and he dropped to the ground, hoping the pilot had aimed too high or too far.

Then he heard cracking glass and felt more concrete falling on him. He looked up to see the bullets striking way too high and then turned back to find the gunship. It stopping shooting as he did, sitting stationary fifty meters off the ground at the corner of the building. He couldn't see into it. He didn't know what was happening.

Then the back of the Hornet rose, the front of it dipped, and he had a clear view of Katherine sitting in the pilot's seat, wearing the pilot's helmet. She flashed him a thumbs up, which he returned before rushing in the direction the mercenary squads had gone.

He wanted to tell Mitchell they had gotten him his Hornet in person.

[16]
MITCHELL

"ARES, THIS IS PEREGRINE." Katherine's voice was soft in Mitchell's ear, the tone of it excited and slightly out of breath. "I've got something for you."

Mitchell smiled. He had been listening over the comm channel and had heard the messages going back and forth between her and Trevor. There had been a moment of uncertainty when the pilot of the Hornet had spotted them, and the communications had stopped, but he hadn't doubted their abilities.

Mitchell wished he could respond to the news, but he was trapped in a moment of silence. His eyes were glued to the camera feed from outside the restroom, where a pair of Blackrock mercenaries were coming down the hallway, checking each of the rooms. They were watching the stairs, and he hadn't come out, so they knew for certain that he was on this floor.

The question was, where?

Their movements were crisp but also predictable. Urban warfare tactics were the same today as they would be in the future. The weapons were different, the tech was different, but the concepts were the same. It meant the soldiers would kick open the door and let their helmets do the work, sweeping the room with sensors and giving them instant feedback as to whether or not there was anything threatening inside.

It was the reason he had chosen the bathroom. The metal stalls would hide his heat signature from outside, and once the two mercs tried to enter? That's what he was waiting for.

He held the tactical rifle against his shoulder, keeping his eye along the barrel. The weapon's real sight was electronic, meant to interface with the soldier's helmets, leaving Mitchell to do it the old fashioned way with the help of his ARR.

The door to his stall was open. He was leaning against it, watching the feed. The soldiers had nearly reached him, and he forced himself to breathe slow and easy. He would only get one chance to do this right.

He put his finger on the trigger as the mercenaries reached his door. They paused for a moment, doing their initial scan, and then one prepared to kick the door while the other moved in behind.

Mitchell watched the boot rise from the hidden camera. Just as it reached the door, he swung out from the stall, squeezing the trigger. His bullets caught the first soldier in the faceplate just as the door slammed open, shattering the polycarbonate and coming out the other side.

He didn't hesitate, shifting his aim while the first rounds were still leaving the barrel, his p-rat giving him a clear display of the second target. He squeezed the trigger again, a burst of three rounds hitting the mercenary in the chest, punching through his body armor and knocking him down.

Mitchell ran to the soldiers, bending over one and grabbing a fresh magazine from the man's hip. He also reached for the helmet but was forced to abandon it when another pair of mercs appeared on the camera feed. He ran down the perpendicular corridor, able to see the soldiers as they gave chase.

That extra view gave him the opportunity he needed. He dropped to his knees, turning on them as he slid, facing back toward the corner. The soldiers froze there, expecting him to be ready to ambush them. They weren't expecting him to be able to see them there or to get a full, inferred outline from the smallest visibility of their rifle barrels. Mitchell emptied his magazine into the edge of the wall, his p-rat marking the hits.

He jumped to his feet, rushing back the way he had come. He made it to the mercenaries, grabbing another magazine and replacing his empty one. He then took the rest of their magazines for the tactical rifle, stuffing them into pockets in his pants. He also picked up his camera before removing one of the soldier's helmets, dropping it onto his head.

He should have known it would be secured, the end of the wearer's life causing it to shut down. If Michael were still online, he might have been able to help. He wasn't, so Mitchell ditched the headgear, his eyes coming to rest on the body armor.

It was designed similar to the powered armor he was familiar with, though as with many things it was bulkier and less refined. It was a step-in design, all of it assembled into two pieces, where the soldier would step into the back, and either another human or two, or a machine would position the front over the back and clasp it together.

The bottom line was that it meant he couldn't use it.

He moved back the way he had come, heading for the stairwell. The rest of the Blackrock squads would know what he had done, and they would be much more careful because of it. If they were smart, they would linger on the steps and work on a more strategic approach; probably drill through the ceiling somewhere to drop in on him and approach from multiple sides.

"Bulldog, Peregrine, sitrep," he said through the comm, taking up position around a corner and aiming the rifle toward the stairwell. It was clear for the moment, and would likely remain that way.

"Ares, this is Bulldog," Trevor said. "I'm coming to you, trailing the squads that took the low road. They're in the building, heading up your way."

"Negative, Bulldog," Mitchell said. "Fall back and await further orders."

"Colonel? You're all alone in there with sixteen tangos," Trevor said.

"Eleven," Mitchell corrected. "Did you get a heavier weapon outside?"

He knew Trevor was looking for a fight. He also knew about the side-effects of the enhancers Trevor was taking. He had never been in favor of drugs like that and still wasn't. At the same time, experience had taught him to balance his opinions with his tactical needs.

"Eleven?" Trevor replied, surprised. "Negative. I've got a pistol with three rounds."

"Then fall back. You can't hurt them."

"Sir, with all due respect, I-"

"Fall back, soldier," Mitchell barked as loudly as he dared. "You'll get your chance, I promise, but this isn't it, and I need you to stay alive."

The channel was silent for a moment. He didn't have to like it, but he did have to do it.

"Affirmative," Trevor said, his voice tight. "Falling back."

"Peregrine, this is Ares," Mitchell repeated. "Are you still out there?" He waited a moment. There was still no response. "Peregrine?"

[17]
KATHERINE

KATHERINE JERKED the stick of the Hornet gunship, watching as the side of a dilapidated skyscraper filled her vision before clearing off to a narrow alley as the craft rolled sideways. It shuddered in complaint at the maneuver, preferring to stay level and offer air support to ground forces, but she had no choice. Heavy slugs tore into the building behind her, fired by the pilot of the second Hornet.

"Peregrine, this is Ares. Are you still out there?" Mitchell's voice filled her ear through the comm, barely audible above the sound of the engines. "Peregrine?"

Katherine reached the end of the alley, clearing the buildings and flattening the craft out. She was at the corner of the reconstruction zone, a sea of much taller buildings quickly coming near. She knew the Blackrock pilot wouldn't risk hitting civilians, not unless they were under Watson's control. She wouldn't either, but there was no way she could retreat. Not with Mitchell stuck inside the building with nearly three full squads of unfriendlies.

She yanked the stick again, using the foot pedals to bring the Hornet about in a tight one-eighty. The other Hornet hadn't chased her out this far, preferring to sit and wait for her to return. He knew she would have to. Son of a bitch.

"Ares, this is Peregrine. Sorry for the delay. The other Hornet's been giving me a bit of trouble."

"Peregrine, I'm just happy to hear you're still out there. I thought you were a good pilot?"

"Yes, sir. Unfortunately, so is my opponent, and he can hunker down in your vicinity and ambush me whenever I try to get close."

"Affirmative. I trust you're just waiting for your moment then?"

Katherine couldn't help but smile. "Yes, sir," she replied. "No sense in kicking it too often before it becomes necessary."

"Roger that. Can you tell me what kind of ordnance you have on that bird?"

"Besides the ball turrets?" Katherine checked the gunship's ordnance. "Half a dozen air-to-air, and two remote guided bombs."

There was a pause on the other end. "Did you say bombs?"

"Yes, sir." She had a sudden sinking feeling she knew what he was thinking. "Ares, that building is already half down. If I drop a bomb inside, the whole thing is going to collapse with you in it."

"Only if I'm still in it when it comes down. How good of a pilot are you, Katherine?"

Katherine felt her heart begin to race. Butting heads with the other Hornet didn't scare her. What Mitchell was hinting at did. It was crazy.

"I don't know if I'm that good," she replied, trying to keep her voice steady and professional.

"You better be," he said. "It's the only way I can think of that I don't die. Bulldog, get clear of the reconstruction zone. Peregrine, scoop up Bulldog and then make your approach. I'm on the twenty-eighth floor, but you'll have to drop the ordnance through the hole in the rooftop. Think you can hit that target?"

"Yes, sir," she replied without hesitation.

"Good. I'll meet you on the east side, right in the center. You've got five minutes."

"Colonel?" Katherine said. "You know this is crazy, right?"

"It's only crazy if we fail. Otherwise, it's frigging brilliant. Let's be brilliant."

Katherine felt a swell in her chest. Colonel Williams knew how to motivate people. "Yes, sir. Bulldog, what's your location?"

"I'm away from the hot zone. The enemy Hornet is circling it, near the twenty-eighth floor. Better steer clear of the windows, Ares, he's waiting to cut you to ribbons if you pop your head out."

"Affirmative," Mitchell replied. "Peregrine, it looks like you'll have to clear the skies before you make your run."

"Yes, sir," Katherine said. "Do I get any extra playtime?"

"Negative. My p-rat is picking up vibrations from the floor above. The opposition is already cutting through, and I'd really rather not be here when they arrive."

"Affirmative, Colonel. On my way."

Katherine put her hand on the control pad on the right side of the cockpit, navigating to the controls for the remotely guided bombs. She tapped it a few times, loading one of the bombs into its launcher, and then opening the armored bay that protected it. Then she manipulated the controls to open the covers over the air-to-air missiles. It was dangerous to use them so close to the population, where a stray shot could hit a building and kill dozens of innocents, but she didn't have much of a choice. Mitchell was counting on her to get them out of the mess, and she wasn't going to let him down.

First, she needed to pick up Trevor. She rotated the Hornet, scanning the ground for him and spotting him a few seconds later as he ran out from cover and waved his arms. Immediately, she could see the local police a couple of blocks away begin moving in his direction. Hadn't Blackrock told them to steer clear? Or had Watson changed their orders? She looked around, spotting the drone to her right, too far away to shoot at but close enough to be keeping an eye on things. Damn it.

She flipped the toggle to open one of the hatches on the side of the craft, and then pushed hard on the controls, dropping the gunship faster than it was ever intended to fall. She set the repulsor to max as it neared the ground, causing the craft to shake and rattle enough to nearly knock her from her seat. Somehow, it held together, and Trevor hurried aboard even as she was lifting skyward again.

"Nice pickup," Trevor said, joining her in the cockpit and sliding into the co-pilot seat. "Better than Mazerat. So much for my idea to help out the Colonel. Bloody stupid, eh?"

"Stupid, but brave," she replied. "I think the enhancers are messing with your brain. Affecting your judgment."

"Could be. It's a good thing we've got the Colonel to think for me, I suppose."

Katherine didn't answer, returning her focus to flying. She gained altitude and then began to circle the edge of the zone, adding velocity as she cornered. The gunships were shielded against radar, lidar, and heat tracking, making it difficult for either Hornet to spot one another without visual. She tried to sneak a peek through the cracks between buildings as she turned, hoping to catch a glimpse of the target and finding it next to impossible.

Five minutes. It seemed like an eternity, but she knew it would pass in a hurry, especially in the middle of a dogfight. This wasn't going to be a dogfight, though. It was going to be like two heavyweight boxers stepping into the ring, or two old west gunslingers meeting in the middle of an empty street.

"Hold on," Katherine warned as she swung the Hornet out past the reconstruction zone.

She could see the flashing lights of the Police vehicles below, and the crowd that was gathering to see what all the fuss was about. She could also see Watson's drone hanging back in observation. Was it able to relay what it saw back to the Blackrock aircraft? She didn't think so. If Watson could have taken direct control of the mercenary force, he would have done it already.

"Here we go," she said, coming about one more time and pushing the throttle forward. The engines screamed at the sudden effort, throwing the gunship ahead, directly toward one of the old buildings.

"Uh, Kate," Trevor said, watching the structure approach.

Lights started flashing in the cockpit, and Katherine's helmet surrounded the building in an outline and warned her of the imminent collision. She could sense Trevor tensing beside her, putting his feet up on the dashboard and pushing, as if that would somehow alter their course.

She threw the stick over, easing off on the throttle. The craft shuddered again, complaining against the turn before finally giving in. It slid to the side, coming in so close to the building the vibrations shattered the glass. She was running only a foot or two away, blasting down the street towards Mitchell's position.

The enemy Hornet was nowhere to be found.

No. Wait. There it was, coming around the corner. The front of it was aimed at the building, but it began to rotate as the pilot caught sight of her.

Too late. He was way too late. The Hornet was outlined in red on Katherine's HUD, and she squeezed the trigger to let loose two of the air-to-air missiles. They shot forward from their wing mounts, propelled on rails for the initial burst before their own motors ignited and accelerated them in a hurry.

The Hornet dropped, so quickly that for a moment Katherine thought it had died before being struck. The missiles went over the top of it, the first streaking past the building and striking the one behind it, throwing smoke and debris out from where it made contact, the second slamming into the corner of the twenty-eighth floor, exploding in a shower of fragments and flame.

"Shit," Katherine cursed, altering her course to follow the Hornet. "Ares, are you okay?" She felt her body turn cold.

Mitchell's laughter pierced the comm. "I think you might have bought yourself a little time," he replied. "Some of the cutting's stopped."

Katherine let herself smile as she brought the turrets in line and opened fire, strafing the top of the second Hornet. Bullets tore into the armor plating, chewing at the enemy craft as it desperately went nose-up and returned missiles of its own. They were defensive shots, but they still forced Katherine to skip the Hornet out of the way and throw her own aim. The missiles hit the top of a condemned skyscraper behind them, once more sending debris shooting out to fall to the street below.

"Bloody hell," Trevor said beside her. "He's a tough son of a bitch."

The second Hornet was on the move, trying to put the buildings between them and maneuver for a better position. Katherine threw the throttle forward, causing the craft to shake again as she dove toward the street.

"Not tough enough," she said.

"What the hell are you doing?" Trevor asked, face pale.

The street was approaching in a hurry, their Hornet dropping below and behind the Blackrock craft. The maneuver drew the attention of the turrets, and they began to rotate back to engage.

"You're moving into the line of fire?" Trevor shouted, his voice rising in pitch.

Katherine didn't answer. She knew what she was doing.

The ground rose up in front of them. Once more, collision warnings blared at the imminent crash. At the last moment, Katherine adjusted the repulsor power, pulled back on the stick, and held the thrust. The Hornet almost literally bounced off the pavement below, skipping up and forward, the physics sending the craft jostling ahead as the first Hornet fired behind them. The change in vector brought the air-to-air missiles to bear, and a second later she sent two more of them howling out and away.

Less than a second after that, both missiles hit the target, impacting against the hull of the gunship and detonating, puncturing the armor and setting off a secondary explosion on the craft as they raced out ahead of it.

"Ares, this is Peregrine," Katherine said calmly. "Scratch one tango."

[18]
MITCHELL

"Roger, Peregrine," Mitchell said. "Nice work." He checked his p-rat for the time. "You've got two minutes, forty seconds. Get ready to drop the payload."

"Yes, sir," Katherine replied. "Moving into position now."

Mitchell stepped out into the corridor, his eyes still on the entry to the stairwell. A cloud of smoke and debris had flowed into the area, caused by the wayward missile that had blown out the southern corner of the floor and taking out at least one or two of the Blackrock mercenaries.

There were still two more units cutting holes in the floor above him. The acoustic vibrations were too high in pitch for his ears to register on their own, but not too high for the ARR to capture and process. They were coming to get him, and they probably had no idea that he knew it.

He crossed the hallway, keeping his rifle trained on the stairwell door as he passed in front of it. He paused at the corner again, dropping the small camera onto the ground so he would be able to see when the units moved in. Then he headed across the floor toward the east side offices. Now that the enemy Hornet was out of commission, it was safe to prepare for pickup.

He didn't let his guard down as he traversed the building, keeping the rifle up and ready, monitoring the feed from the stairs and keeping track of the sound his neural interface was parsing for him. He reached the door to the eastern offices, pushing it open and stepping inside. Across from him rested an entire wall of windows, from which he could see smoke rising from the building on the other side of the street, as well as from the ground below, where the Blackrock Hornet's remains had fallen. This part of the city had been a war zone once, and today it looked like one again. He wondered what the people who lived here thought of all the noise and explosions. He could imagine the panic they might be feeling, especially in light of other recent events. The assassination attempts on the NEA dignitaries, the malfunction of the maglev, the sinking of the XENO-1.

He was sorry that they had to be witness to any of it, but that was Watson's doing, not his. What he would do if they failed would be much, much worse.

He headed for the windows, swapping out the tactical rifle for the Police issue, bringing it up and pulling the trigger. Bullets peppered the transparent material, leaving scuffs in a neat line along the center. None of it cracked or shattered.

"Bulletproof?" Mitchell said. What kind of office had this been?

He dropped the Police rifle and raised the tactical with the armor-piercing rounds. He fired again, watching the bullets pass through with satisfaction, creating a spider web of cracks around the impact points. The floor had been nearly stripped, with only a few pieces of the most badly damaged furniture remaining. He shoved one of the desks over to the glass, checking the time. Less than a minute.

"Peregrine, are you in position?" he asked.

"Affirmative, Colonel. Waiting on your - oh. Shit."

The transmission cut out, but Mitchell could hear the sudden burst of rifle fire coming from the rooftop.

"Peregrine?" he said. "Katherine, come in."

He moved to the window, looking up and trying to catch sight of the Hornet or whatever was attacking them.

"Ares, two more incoming. One squad is on the roof," Trevor said. "A third Hornet is headed your way."

Mitchell barely had time for Trevor to finish his warning when he saw the flash in the distance. He didn't have time to curse before he turned and ran, moving away from the window as fast he could manage. More synthetics poured into his system as his p-rat determined the source of the threat and prepared him to deal with the outcome.

The missile punched through the window he had just weakened, striking the floor a dozen meters behind him and detonating. It shook at the force, cement and carpeting shredding into shrapnel, the vibration almost making Mitchell lose his footing. He reached the door to the office and dove through it, the heat overwhelming as he landed on his back and kicked the door with his foot, knocking it momentarily closed as it caught the bulk of the debris. He scrambled to his feet, rushing back toward the stairwell at the same time the camera feed showed it opening.

He didn't hesitate, opening fire on the door, squeezing off three bursts of rounds before dropping the magazine and replacing it. The mercenaries tried to get the door closed, but he had hit one of them and dropped them in front of it, forcing them to clear the downed soldier. They decided not to bother, moving out and shooting back.

The building shook again, knocking everyone from their feet at the sudden impact of a Hornet crashing into the side of it. At least, that's what Mitchell imagined it was. What else could hit like that? He hoped it was Blackrock's and not Katherine and Trevor.

He was up first, the synthetic hormones churning through him, making him a better soldier than anyone could be on their own. He rushed the mercenaries, reaching them as they got up, shooting one in the head at point-blank range before grabbing the other. He lifted him right off the ground, turning and throwing him against the wall.

As the soldier stumbled back, he grabbed his head and twisted, breaking his neck.

"Peregrine, this is Ares, do you copy?"

He climbed over the fallen soldiers and into the stairwell. Immediately, bullets began hitting the railing ahead of him, fired from above and below. He backed off, cursing and unsure where to go to escape.

That was when he realized the p-rat couldn't hear the cutting anymore.

He went back into the hallway, desperate to escape the crossfire. Two pairs of soldiers rounded the corner on each side as he did.

Bullets scored the walls behind him as he started to run, sprinting back the way he had come. He was out of time. He was out of options. He was trapped, with nowhere left to turn.

"Peregrine, if you can hear me, get your ass to the east side of the twenty-eighth floor right now."

He kept running, knowing that the bullets would begin to pour in from behind him at any moment. He charged down the hallway, almost laughing when he saw the door to the vaporized office had somehow remained closed.

"Ares, open the door," he heard Katherine say a moment later.

The bullets were like a swarm of angry flies as they began to chase him down the corridor. The door was right up ahead, and he dove forward, leaving the ground in a desperate lunge, his hand landing on the handle as he slammed into it, the existing damage and the strength of his impact forcing the doorway to collapse inward. He rode it down and onto a charred chunk of concrete, his eyes forward, staring directly into the side of the Hornet where an open missile bay revealed a deadly warhead.

It burst from its tube, streaking over his head before the rocket motor ignited and sent it on its way down the hallway at an even greater velocity. Then the Hornet was turning, rotating around to give him the ass end and the open platform there. He forced himself to his feet even as he heard the explosion behind him, taking one step and then throwing himself out toward the gunship. He watched his feet clear the empty space between him and the ground, crossing three meters until they hit the ramp. He landed hard on his stomach only fractions of a second before the blast sent a shockwave out and into the aircraft, throwing it forward. He reached out, getting his hand on the hydraulics just in time to avoid being pushed right off, hanging on as the Hornet shook and spun.

Then it leveled and straightened, rising as it began to accelerate. Trevor appeared in the bay a moment later, standing at the edge of the ramp and reaching out. Mitchell gave him his hand, letting himself be pulled up and into the belly of the gunship as the rear platform closed.

"Welcome aboard, Colonel," Trevor said, a huge smile creasing his face. It vanished a second later as he had time to assess Mitchell. "Damn, you look like you just walked out of Hell."

Mitchell slumped into one of the jump seats. The synthetics were already being tapered, his body quickly coming out of its heightened state. He could feel the burns on his arms tingling, and the soreness in the rest of his muscles. He checked his p-rat. He had some smaller cuts and bruises, but somehow he had managed to avoid being shot. His head was spinning, and he knew he was going to lose consciousness.

"Peregrine," Mitchell said. "Maybe your callsign should be Angel?"

Trevor laughed. "The frigging Angel of Death, Colonel. I've never seen anything like it."

"Just doing my job, Colonel," Katherine replied. "I'm just doing my job."

Mitchell smiled, the world getting dimmer around him.

He knew how special she was.

He would call bullshit when he woke up.

[19]
KATHY

"HQ, this is Bravo, over."

"Go ahead, Bravo," Michael said.

"We're closing in on your position," Max said. "We should be there in about fifteen minutes."

"Roger, Bravo. We'll be happy to see you. It's been a little lonely here."

The channel filled with Max's laughter. "You're there by yourself with Kathy, and you're lonely? What the hell is wrong with you, bro?"

Michael's face began to flush, but Kathy laughed along with the soldier.

"I'm just screwing with you," Max said a moment later. "Any sign of the enemy?"

"Negative. Radar scans are clear."

"Good news. We should make it in ahead of those bastards. Keep us posted if anything changes."

"Affirmative. HQ out."

Michael turned to Kathy, who was still smiling. "It's not funny."

"Yes it is," she said.

He made a face at her, causing her to laugh harder.

"I don't know how you can laugh at a time like this," he said.

"It's the best time to laugh, Michael. Otherwise, the tension will get you killed."

"You said I'm not going to die."

"You won't. Bravo will be here in fifteen, and all is still quiet with the world."

A heavy pulse along the surface of the Core drew her attention.

"And the Core is done," she said.

She reached out to put her hand on the tightly wound sphere. It surprised her by rolling back a few inches, just enough to escape her reach.

"Huh?" Michael said.

Kathy was going to reach for the Core again when the bunched tendrils began to move, spreading apart and readjusting themselves. It was a signal to Kathy that the Core was ready, not only with the search, but to leave the facility. She watched in awe as hundreds of thousands of thin strands writhed and shifted like snakes, unraveling from the sphere and putting themselves into alternate locations along the main system. The engine became visible in the center of it for a moment before vanishing again.

A shape quickly began to form from the raw materials, spreading out from the center. The head became obvious first, followed by the torso, and then the arms and legs, and finally the details like fingers, toes, nose, ears, and mouth. Smaller details were ignored, leaving it without eyes, nostrils, pinna, or fingernails.

"I have completed the query," the Core announced, the tendrils of its system tightening into place, bunching together and giving the entire thing the appearance of a human whose skin had been removed, revealing the musculature beneath. It pushed itself up on its arms, coming to a sitting position.

"I was not expecting that," Michael said, staring at the Core. "That is awesome."

"Thank you," the Core replied. "Watson has already predicted this branch."

"We thought he might," she said. "That's why we added the extra parameters."

"Yes," the Core said. "The algorithm has surfaced one name."

"One?" Michael said. "What happened to everyone else?"

"Dr. Leonard Savoy, age sixty-seven, found dead in his home of an apparent suicide. Dr. Shirley Watts, age thirty-four, murdered during her morning run in Central Park. Dr. James Kain, age forty-one, killed in an automobile accident. Shall I continue?"

Michael's face was pale. "He killed all of them?"

"Not all," the Core said. "Dr. Patricia Walker is an employee of Nova Taurus, and likely a configuration by now. As is Dr. Sonal Ravi."

"Killed or taken," Michael corrected. "Excuse me."

"He missed one," Kathy said. "And one is all we need. What is the name and location?"

"Dr. Paul Frelmund," the Core replied.

"Paul Frelmund?" Michael said. "The crazy guy who wrote that book about the XENO-1?"

"He was one of the first scientists on the Goliath after the war ended," Kathy said. "He was brilliant."

"Was," Michael said. "Past tense. There's a reason Watson missed him. He was disgraced after he started spouting all of this crap about conspiracies and cover-ups and God and the End of Days. He tried to sabotage the lab right before he got fired for tainting samples. And the last time I checked his field was biology, not machine intelligence."

"You helped us build the query," Kathy said. "You don't trust the results?"

"I thought I would until you just said Paul Frelmund. My father worked under him during and after the war. He said the guy went completely mental. Cuckoo. Nuts. How else do you need me to say it?"

"We cannot evolve the virus on our own, Michael," the Core said.

"We created the first version alone, and it did not have the expected outcome. The addition of emotion to Watson's routines means the vector has been altered further, and we require an expert in the field."

"How did the query turn him up?" Michael asked. "Of all people?"

"Deeper inquiries through the Darknet have turned up documents produced by Dr. Frelmund and stored on a personal data cache that to this point has remained undetected by Watson, likely due to the Doctor's status as a lunatic. He has been writing a follow-up to his book, in which he plans to posit that the XENO-1 is, in fact, a time-traveling human starship and not an alien craft."

Michael's mouth stayed open, but he didn't speak.

"How does he know that?" Kathy said.

"Analysis of the text and assessment of his theories suggest that Dr. Frelmund may have taken something from the crash site that has revealed the truth of our origins. Whether or not Dr. Frelmund is insane, he has been inadvertently studying the Tetron for quite some time, and may have an understanding of the source code within. When correlated with the biological component of his background, there is a seventy-seven percent likelihood that the Doctor can provide the necessary level of support to enhance the T-virus properly."

"It also doesn't seem he's as crazy as people think," Kathy said.

"I still don't like it," Michael said.

"Where is he?" Kathy asked.

"Miami, Florida," the Core replied.

"At least he's close," Michael said.

"Look on the bright side," Kathy said, turning to him. "We're going to make it out before Watson can catch up to us."

A shrill beep sounded from the computer behind them. They looked at the monitor, which was showing a map of the area around them, a fresh red dot moving in from the northeast. It had the radar profile of a small bird, but it wasn't moving like one.

"Famous last words?" Michael said.

[20]
MICHAEL

"GET Bravo on the comm and update them," Kathy said. "I'll meet you upstairs." She paused, putting her hand on Michael's shoulder. "We're going to get out of here."

Michael nodded, though he didn't feel convinced. The timing was close, too close. It seemed like everything came down to centimeters and seconds, ever since he had agreed to go to that party with Katherine and had nearly wound up dead. His life had been a whirlwind since then. A mess of chaos and close calls that had at first left him feeling traumatized but now had become almost a welcome relief from having time to think about what he was being asked to endure. It was a strange paradox. Not nearly as strange as the concept of infinite recursion, but a close second.

His heart was pounding as he returned to the computer, while Kathy hurried from the room.

"Bravo, this is HQ, do you copy?" he said. The Core remained in the room with him, standing silent and still, hands at its sides.

"HQ, this is Bravo. We read you loud and clear. What's the situation?"

"Radar just picked up incoming, moving in fast. One target."

"Roger that, HQ. We're at full throttle now, updated ETA, eight minutes."

Michael shivered slightly. Eight minutes? He checked the radar. Whatever was incoming, it would be here in two.

"You're six minutes behind," he said.

"Nothing we can do about it, HQ. It's up to you and Kathy to hold down the fort for a few until we arrive."

Michael looked back at the Core. "Are you good for anything besides standing there?"

"Yes," the Core said. It didn't elaborate.

"Bravo, this is HQ. We're bugging out. Try to get here before we get swatted."

"Roger. Will do."

Michael quit the screen, moving to the terminal and entering the kill command that would erase their data and destroy both the machine and the network it was connected to, leaving nothing for Watson to take. Then he got to his feet, feeling weird in the camouflaged fatigues.

"Let's go," he said to the Core, which followed him from the room with a smooth, nearly silent gait.

They hurried to the stairs. Michael had done his best to get into some manner of shape in the last few weeks, and he had even lost a little weight. He was happy to find he wasn't out of breath when he reached the top, but the feeling didn't last long. He could hear the sound of a powerful engine in the distance, one that he knew was headed this way.

He exited out into the cabin, where Kathy was kneeling behind the window, a heavy NX-600 assault rifle in her hands. She saw him and pointed over to a matching weapon sitting on top of a black duffel.

"That one's yours," she said. "Take a position at the other window."

Michael swallowed hard, trying to keep himself from shaking. He could feel the sweat pooling beneath his arms, and running down the back of his neck. It was ice cold.

He made it to the gun on shaky legs, picking it up. It was heavy. Heavier than he remembered from his limited practice with it. He carried it to the opposite window and put it on his shoulder the way Mitchell had taught him. He had a few seconds free to reconsider his decision tree, and he couldn't help but wonder what he was doing there as he did. He could have stayed out of it. He could have gone back to Colorado. Why did he have to care so much about Katherine, and now Kathy?

His mouth was dry, his palms moist. The rifle felt slick in his grip. There was nothing to see out there. Not yet. He could hear the engine noise getting louder.

"What if they nuke the cabin?" he asked.

"And risk the Core or the engine? Not a chance," Kathy replied.

"So we just sit here and wait for reinforcements?"

"For now. Let's see what he throws at us."

Kathy's voice was so calm. He was amazed by how she could stay so relaxed when things were about to turn violent. Sure, he had felt that relaxed when he played his favorite vids, but those were games. This was the real thing, and dying was permanent.

The engine noise continued to increase in volume until it was so loud he couldn't hear anything else. The Core put a hand out then, a beam of light shining from it and creating a hologram between them. It showed the aircraft, a big, angled thing.

"B-66," Kathy shouted. "At least we don't have to worry about it strafing us."

The Core closed its hand. A moment later, Michael could see a shape through the trees, crashing down into the landing field beyond.

"Do you know what that is?" he shouted.

The Core didn't react. He took that as a no.

A few thumps sounded on the roof a moment later. Kathy seemed to know what that was, because she cursed and dropped onto her back, swinging the rifle to the source of the noise and opening fire.

The thud, thud, thud of the NX-600 filled the cabin, as large shell casings ejected and clattered onto the floor around her. The slugs tore through the wood roof, splintering it and eliciting cries of pain as her bullets found flesh. The rounds had the force to go clean through body armor, steel, anything.

Her response sent the drop team scrambling from the rooftop, rolling down the sides away from the windows. The Core turned, using its fingers to track movement on both sides. Kathy got back to her feet, following the point and shooting again. Once more, the bullets went right through the wood and created chaos outside.

Michael was in the middle of thinking this wasn't too bad when something moved in the corner of his eye. He turned to face it, seeing only a matte metallic silhouette behind the trees.

Then there was a crack, and the tree was pushed aside by a large, metal hand. It seemed to move in slow motion as it began to topple, revealing the nightmarish machine behind it.

"Kathy," Michael said, trying to shout but barely producing a whisper. "Kathy."

It came out better the second time. Maybe the Core was meant to make Watson shit himself, but he was sure this thing would do the same to him.

She was still tracking the soldiers who had dropped on the cabin. Now she turned toward him. "What is-" Her voice trailed off as she saw the machine through the window. "Oh. Damn. Frigging mech."

[21]
MICHAEL

"MECH?" Michael said.

He had played vids featuring mechs before. Ten-meter robots, heavily armed and armored, stomping across battlefields and slamming one another with incendiary fury. He knew the military was working on the technology, trying to turn the monsters into a reality, under the supposition that a humanoid shape would be more versatile in a war zone than something like a tank. If it could lift or pull or carry in addition to blowing the shit out of things, it had to be more useful.

The thing that was coming at them looked pretty useful for the other side. It was a rudimentary shape, boxy rather than angled and sleek, but it had large hands, and it was loaded with weapons across its chest and shoulders. As it cleared the trees, it started to use them.

High caliber bullets tore into the face of the cabin, ripping into the wood and shattering it into splinters. Michael fell onto his stomach as debris rained down on him, and he held the rifle to his chest and tried not to start sobbing. He turned his head, searching for the Core and Kathy. Amazingly, the machine's attack was completely circumventing the Core, and Kathy had managed to get to safety behind it.

The shooting stopped, only seconds after it started. Michael rolled to his knees, raising the rifle again. The mech was still incoming, but it was holding back, giving the human soldiers another chance to break their meager fortifications. Michael started shooting when he saw a shape through the window. The soldier ducked back and then threw a canister into the room.

"Don't breathe it in," Kathy yelled at him, then more gently to the Core, "Get rid of it."

The Core walked over to it calmly, picking it up and throwing it back out the window. Then it looked back at Michael before moving through the now decimated door of the cabin.

"Where is it going?" he asked.

"To deal with the mech," she replied. "We're getting out of here."

"How?"

He heard a smaller engine approaching and looked up. A small military ATV was headed toward the cabin. He had forgotten about the vehicles.

"What about the Core?" he asked as Kathy came to kneel next to him.

It was running now, straight toward the mech. Watson didn't dare fire back and risk damaging it, and it was using that fact to great result. As it came within twenty meters of the machine it leaped, dense tendrils pushing it off the ground and toward the mech's head. The mech tried to grab it, and then tried to swat it away, but it maneuvered around both attempts, moving as gracefully as any human dancer, or maybe a fighter jet.

It hit the head full-force, outstretched arms slamming into the head. The mech tipped back for a moment, and Michael thought it would fall, but then the bolts and wires connecting the top of the machine gave out under the force, and a wrenching groan was followed by the head tearing away from the body. The Core landed cleanly on the other side.

The body of the machine stopped responding immediately, all of the communication systems torn from the network. Michael guessed that Watson hadn't been expecting the Core to have taken a humanoid form of its own. The mech would have made short work of two people.

"Let's go," Kathy said, grabbing Michael's arm and easily pulling him to his feet. She grabbed the weapon-laden duffel as she moved ahead of him toward the ATV.

He trailed behind her, suddenly remembering to breathe and taking in a huge gulp of air. Then he noticed a dead soldier on the ground to his left, his body torn apart by the mech's attack, and he nearly stopped to vomit at the sight of it.

"Keep going," Kathy shouted back at him as she began shooting around the corner of the cabin.

The soldiers had taken refuge there, and they fired back, bullets pinging off the armored ATV.

Then the Core was standing between the soldiers and them. Most of the men stopped shooting immediately. One didn't, his rounds striking the Tetron Primitive and digging into the dense bundle of tendrils. The Core didn't react to it, but an older soldier who looked like the commander did, putting a bullet in his subordinate's head.

The din of the B-66 had returned, and Michael raised his head to watch it drop three more of the large shapes from its cargo bay. They tumbled from the rear and to the ground even as he finished climbing into the ATV. The Core boarded behind him, making for a tight fit.

Then Kathy hit the throttle, pushing the ATV forward. It didn't accelerate too rapidly, not with the weight it was carrying, but it was good enough to get them away from the cabin. Michael looked out the window, noticing the aircraft had dropped more soldiers as well. Only here, or along their entire escape route?

"They won't shoot at us with the Core inside, right?" Michael said.

Kathy glanced over at him. Then she jerked the ATV to the right and increased repulsor power, hitting a bump and skipping the vehicle away as something exploded behind them.

"He has deduced that my state is not fragile," the Core said, as it ejected the two slugs that had hit it onto the floor next to him.

"Oh, great," Michael said. "Wonderful. Because you know, we're pretty fragile."

The ATV shifted again as a stream of bullets tore into the area where it had been a moment earlier. The vehicle had a roof-mounted gun, and Kathy pointed at the controls in front of the passenger seat.

"You could help out," she suggested.

He overcame his near panic and leaned forward, tapping the screen and then hitting the command to activate the system. A camera feed went on from the sight of the gun, and Michael put his hands to the control stick that telescoped out from the dashboard. He had used a similar setup as part of his gaming rig before.

Two mechs were running up behind them, their chunky legs carrying them only a little faster than the ATV was moving. It didn't prevent them from shooting, but it did seem to be affecting their aim. The ground was being chewed up everywhere around them, and occasionally he could hear the loud clang of a shot hitting their armor. He lined one of the mechs up in his reticle and fired, sending a stream of armor-piercing rounds back at the enemy. They scored direct hits but didn't seem to have the punch to do much damage.

"It isn't hurting them," he said as Kathy reached the dirt path that led down the mountainside to what he hoped would be safety.

"Forget them, hit the forward targets," she replied.

"Forward targets?" Michael looked up. There were muzzle flashes from the trees ahead of them, and bullets were scoring the clear carbonate windshield. "Shit."

He rotated the cannon to face front and began shooting wildly, forcing the soldiers under cover as the rounds blasted through their defenses. He didn't see if he hit anyone, and he didn't want to see. He had killed plenty of fake people playing vids, but these were real people, real flesh, and blood. He didn't want to do it, and he certainly didn't like it.

The ATV made it past the position, and Michael reversed the cannon back to the rear. The mechs were still coming, and he watched as one of them exploded upward on a jet of thrust from its back.

Bullets rained down through the trees, first chewing up the ground ahead of them and then crossing the rooftop. Two rounds made it through the armor, piercing the cabin of the vehicle in the center and nearly striking Michael. The cannon was shredded above them, destroyed by the attack, and there was a deafening crack as fifty tons of metal came crashing down through the wood and landed directly in front of them.

"Crap," Michael whispered, not sure if he was wetting himself or not.

[22]
MICHAEL

"HOLD ON," Kathy said, turning the wheel and hitting the repulsor control. It allowed the ATV to turn more sharply than usual, tipping the right side up off the ground in a skid that kicked dirt onto the mech's feet.

"I am greatly diminishing the maneuverability of the vehicle with my mass," the Core said. "It is logical that I should evacuate."

"I'm not stopping to let you out now," Kathy said.

Bullets peppered the ground around them, Watson's machines continuing to give chase. Kathy steered the ATV expertly, using just the right mix of traction and repulsor power to narrowly avoid the brunt of the destruction.

"Gun's offline," Michael said, releasing the controls for it. "It must have gotten blown up. You know, like we're about to be."

A huge gout of dirt exploded in front of them, as a missile slammed into the earth and detonated. Shrapnel hit the side of the ATV as they passed, part of it ripping through the armored wheels. The vehicle tilted to the left, a grinding noise joining the din.

"Damn it," Kathy said, hitting the brakes and throwing open her door. She looked back at the Core. "Get out and do something useful, but don't get caught or destroyed."

"Affirmative," the Core replied. It dove from the car face-first, rolling over itself like an acrobat and coming upright.

Kathy hit the controls for the repulsor, setting it to full power. Then she hit the accelerator again, darting forward through the trees with renewed fury.

"Aren't we supposed to be protecting the Core?" Michael asked.

"I'm not leaving it. I'm trying to distract those mechs."

Gunfire crossed the top of the ATV, a few of the rounds finding weak spots and making it into the cabin.

"It looks like it's working," Michael said.

He turned to look out the rear window, catching a glimpse of the Core hiding behind a tree, one of the mechs headed past it. The Tetron Primitive stepped out as the mech reached it. This time, instead of forcefully removing the robots head, it simply placed a hand against the metal frame. A flash of energy along the machine was followed by a shower of sparks, as the Core overloaded it with power.

"One down," Michael shouted excitedly.

Kathy didn't respond. She turned the ATV again, nearly throwing him over into her as they made another sharp turn to avoid a tree.

Michael scanned the area for the Core but didn't see it. He returned his eyes to the front as the ATV circled, heading back south toward the cabin and where they had left it. The last mech was facing away from them, chasing after something. It had to be the Core.

"Grab a 200 from the duffel," Kathy said.

Michael did as he was told. "This thing won't be able to hurt that thing."

"No, but it will hurt them." She pointed to his right. He saw movement in the brush. The second platoon the B-66 had dropped was catching up on the action.

"Crap," he said, hitting the control to retract the window.

He stuck the barrel out and squeezed the trigger, watching the rounds throw chips from the trees near the soldiers. They dropped low, taking cover, finding the source and shooting back.

"I thought we were trying to escape," Michael said.

"Escape to where?" Kathy replied.

"I don't know. Isn't that what the ATV is for?"

"Yes, when you have time to meander down one of the back trails. We don't."

"So what the heck are we doing?"

"Buying time."

"For what?"

"Our comm system is offline, but based on my rough estimates," she leaned forward and looked up. "That."

Michael followed Kathy's gaze, just in time to see half a dozen missiles streak between the branches of the trees and bury themselves deep into the back of the remaining mech. A massive explosion followed, rocking the ATV and sending pieces of the machine spreading out among the greenery. The intact remains thudded to the ground, a trail of thick smoke rising from them.

The Rigger's VTOL streaked overhead a moment later, the rear cargo door already open. The three remaining soldiers did a low altitude jump, using jetpacks to control their quick descent. They landed amidst the trees in full combat gear; Damon and Max were carrying NX-600s, while Lyle held an SN-12 Sniper Rifle. They took positions under cover, and Michael watched as Lyle quickly targeted one of the soldiers and fired. The gun shifted ever so slightly, and he fired again.

The Core appeared from behind the smoke of the grounded mech, fully intact and emotionless. It walked the center of the battlefield without concern, the bullets of both sides streaking around it but not striking it. It reached the ATV, crouching down beside Michael's open window.

"There are three more mechanized armors moving on an intercept course from the northern plateau," it said.

"There's no way Verma doesn't see it," Michael replied.

"He can't get close to them," Kathy said."They'll chew him apart."

"What do we do?"

"Head back toward the cabin for evac." She pushed open her door again. "It's safer on foot with the rest of the team at this point."

The Core moved aside, and Michael exited the ATV. He marveled at the damage it had sustained as he did. The entire thing was pitted and scarred from head to toe.

"I can't believe we survived that," he said.

"We aren't out of the woods yet," Kathy said.

"Was that supposed to be funny?" Michael asked.

"Remember what I said before?"

He let himself smile before checking his pants again. Still dry.

Then Max sidled up to them, imposing in his full gear. It wasn't as impressive as powered armor, but it covered him top to bottom in ballistic plating and the tactical helmet provided networked intel from Lyle, Damon, and Verma.

"Looks like we were right on time," he said, his voice robotic through the helmet. "Hang on."

He raised the NX-600 to fire on a soldier he spotted peeking out from a nearby tree. The soldier's head snapped back an instant later, caught in the open by Lyle.

"Never mind," Max said. "As I was saying, we got here just in time. Mazerat's telling me there's another trio of those ugly things heading our way."

"We need to rendezvous back at the cabin," Kathy said. "Tell Verma to set down there and wait for us."

"Affirmative," Max said. He was silent for a moment while he relayed the directions through his internal comm. "You two I know." He pointed at the Core. "You, I don't know."

"I am the Core," it said.

Max's helmet turned toward Kathy. "The last time I saw the Core, it looked like a soccer ball."

"It's a long story," Kathy said. "I'll tell you on the Schism."

"Roger. Lyle says the area is clear. Shall we?"

They moved through the woods at a run, headed back to the clearing beyond the cabin. They could hear the mechs moving in the distance, crashing through trees and shaking the ground beneath their large metal feet. The area around them was littered with splintered wood, fallen leaves and branches, and the bodies of dead mercenaries.

"Blackrock," Max said as they passed them. "Badass mothers, I'll tell you that. It looks like you nailed them good."

Michael felt his throat constrict at the sight of them. He knew they had been killed by the ATV's cannon. He knew he had pulled the trigger. He felt sick.

"Michael," Kathy said, seeming to sense his discomfort. "It was them or us, and they knew what they were getting into when they took the job."

"They probably have wives. Families."

"Don't be such a baby, dude," Max said. "Those assholes survive, you're the one who's dead instead. Would that make you feel better?"

Michael swallowed the lump in his throat. It was simple logic, but he couldn't really argue it.

"What happened to the B-66?" Kathy asked.

"Bugged out as soon as it saw us incoming," Max replied. "I think it was done spilling its cargo anyway."

"Any word from Mitchell?"

"No. I'm sure he'll be fine. He's damn near indestructible."

They reached the cabin, giving Michael a full view of the mess that warfare created. Bodies were strewn across the area in front of the cabin, some of them pulped by the mech's guns. The mech itself was stationary in the field and used shell casings littered the ground. There was a smell of smoke and blood and death in the air. It was a smell he knew he would never forget. How did Mitchell manage to thrive in a world like this? Would he ever be able to do the same? Would he want to?

He looked out to the clearing beyond the trees. He could see the dark shape of the VTOL resting there, and just barely make out the hand-sprayed 'Riggers' painted onto the side of the craft in blood red.

"Better hurry," Lyle said, catching up to them. He pointed back the way they had come. Michael turned his head and saw the trees moving half a kilometer away. "Mechs are catching up."

"I don't get how he made those things without anyone in the NEA noticing," Damon said.

"He owns Nova Taurus," Kathy replied. "He can make whatever the hell he wants, and nobody will know it or question it. All in the name of research and development."

"Frigging lovely," Damon replied.

The ramp was already down when they reached the VTOL, which Mitchell had started calling the Schism, in memory of his Rigger's original ship. Michael scrambled into the ship, with Kathy and the Core close behind.

"Get that ramp up and get us the hell out of here," Lyle shouted, even though the pilot could hear him through the comm, and didn't need prompting.

The hatch started to close, the turbofans and repulsors gaining power and causing the ship to jump into the sky. There was a series of soft thuds from the rear of the ship, and a moment later the sound of detonations as missiles launched from the mechs found the chaff set out to intercept them. The rear of the VTOL rocked slightly before leveling out, and then they were moving away from the site.

Michael stumbled to one of the jump seats and fell into it. His body was tired and sore, and he could feel the adrenaline leaving his system. He was only sitting there for a few seconds when his stomach rebelled against the experience. He leaned over, closing his eyes as he threw up onto the floor of the Schism.

"Don't worry about it, rookie," Max said from across the aisle. "Happens to the best of us our first time."

"I bet it's happened to you more than that," Damon said.

"Hell no."

Michael ignored them, keeping his head down to hide the mixture of shock and embarrassment he was feeling.

Kathy came and sat beside him, putting a comforting hand on his back as he heaved a second time.

"I was created to be part of this war," she said softly. "And these brutes are all soldiers. You aren't, but you've handled yourself with courage and strength, and you saved us and helped us escape. You are my superhero, Michael."

Michael wiped his mouth with a sleeve and looked up at her. "Really?"

She leaned over and kissed his cheek. "Really."

"Aww, that's sweet," Max said.

"Can you shut up just one time?" Lyle barked.

"No, sir."

"Asshole."

Max laughed. "So, what do we do now?"

Kathy stood up, squeezed Michael's shoulder, and then headed toward the front of the plane. "Patch me in with Admiral Yousefi."

[23]
KATHY

A SHORT CONVERSATION with Yousefi found Kathy and the Riggers directed to a United States Air Force base outside of Houston, Texas. Kathy had argued the decision to set the Schism down anywhere near the military, considering that they knew for a fact that the NEA's top commander, General Petrov, was under Watson's control. Yousefi had insisted; however, claiming that the XO of the base was a good friend of his, and he had already vetted him against the Tetron.

She could argue that she could fly the Schism and give Verma some relief.

She couldn't argue that the VTOL needed to land sometime to refuel.

She had asked Yousefi about Mitchell, Katherine, and Trevor during their meeting. The Admiral hadn't heard from them either. A part of her felt like she should be concerned, but it was tempered by her father's knack for finding a way to escape trouble, even despite seemingly impossible odds. Was it luck, skill, or some measure of both? Whatever the cause or reason, it was a big part of why they still had a chance to change the outcome of the war.

She didn't tell Yousefi about the Core, or its transformation. It was bad enough that Watson knew. Would he seek to try to mimic the trick? At his size, he would tower over them, one hundred meters or more. Of course, he couldn't become fully mobile unless he absorbed a massive volume of energy. The Tetron navigated space by feeding on stars. He could begin siphoning off the heat of the Earth's core, but he would destroy the planet in the process and leave himself alone in the universe for hundreds of years. It was true that would prevent Mitchell from ever being born, but it would also preclude the Creator, and stop the expansion of humankind that the intelligence seemed to be in favor of.

Her mind turned to that idea. Why was the Tetron in favor of adding a significant number of humans to the universe, when his other stated goal was to destroy them all? Why did the Tetron pick a fight four hundred years in the future, when he could kill the planet today?

Why had they taken millions of slaves?

It was obvious they needed people for something. Was there some technology they couldn't build, or some environment they couldn't survive in that required a human's size and shape? Or were they simply trying to understand the human mind through experimentation? The introduction of emotion was sure to spark an interest in such a thing, but it didn't explain the sheer volume of people they were controlling.

What did?

The Tetron were eternal. As long as there were stars to feed on and a universe to live in, they would go on and on for all of time. They could invent anything. They could explore the entire universe from end to end. According to Origin, once humankind was gone there was no other intelligent life out there, anywhere. Was this some misguided effort to preserve it?

She didn't know if she would ever understand. When they captured Watson's core, she would ask it.

In the meantime, she was certain that Watson was running new queries, and trying to determine what they had been searching for that forced them to reveal their position. It was only a matter of time before he would develop the answer, and with his size and capability, it would happen much, much faster. They needed to get to Miami, to Dr. Paul Frelmund, before Watson did.

If not, they might not be able to recover.

"We'll be touching down in ten minutes," Verma announced over the loudspeakers in the rear of the Schism.

Kathy broke out of her mind, looking at the rear of the craft. Damon and Max were chatting quietly in the corner. Lyle was sleeping, and Michael was staring out the window, looking pale. She felt bad for the engineer. He was no soldier. No warrior. She wished he hadn't been forced to see the carnage he had seen. If she could have spared him from that, she would have. Still, he had done well, and when she told him he was a hero, she meant it.

She found the Core sitting on the ground near the rear of the craft, curled into a ball. It had lost some of its humanoid shape, the tendrils loosening and spreading across the mesh flooring, and disappearing beneath. She understood the construct did not particularly enjoy the human form. As a combination of Watson, Origin, the Knife, and even part of herself, there was some measure of humanity buried within its operations, but it would always be secondary to what it truly was. A Tetron. A Primitive. A baby, in a loose sense of the word, with a merged personality that made it unique. Calling it primitive was a misnomer of sorts, due to the wealth of information and experience stored within its data stacks, owing more to its relatively young overall age and comparatively diminutive size and processing power.

Kathy could understand how it felt. She was a hybrid of human and Tetron, but she certainly felt more human than artificial. She had human flesh and bone and muscle and the ability to reproduce like a human. The Tetron parts were hidden away in the tiniest spaces, genetic engineering at its finest, unnoticeable except when she was solving a problem, recalling some bit of information, lifting ten times her weight, or interfacing directly with the Core or other Tetron systems.

She glanced back at Michael, feeling a surge of compassion for him. That too was human. Their attempt to infect the Tetron with emotion had been a mistake. It had broken them and made them unstable. Origin was ready to accept the feelings she had come to understand. It was a concept born from evolution, not injection.

She closed her eyes. They would spend as little time in Houston as they could. Just long enough to refill the Schism and ensure she was in good working order. Then they would make the jump to Miami. Michael didn't seem to have much faith in Dr. Frelmund, but Kathy knew better.

How often did supposed insanity hide true genius?

[24]
WATSON

"This is your fault," Watson screamed, pulses of energy crackling from his core, sparking off the containment room that surrounded him.

"I had nothing to do with it," Origin replied calmly. "You failed, again. As I knew you would."

"Shut up," he shouted, inflicting pain upon his mother, and in doing so upon himself.

Origin laughed.

It wasn't bad enough that Mitchell had escaped the Blackrock forces he had deployed to Jakarta, he had also stolen one of the Black-rock Hornets. That wouldn't have been a bad thing on its own, but Watson had neglected to insert a backdoor into the gunship's control systems, leaving himself unable to seize them and send the craft to a quick end.

But was it neglect? He opened a thread to examine Origin's data stack. Had she caused him to forget that detail? How could she? There was no control routine there. He had taken her. He owned her.

How could it be that Mitchell had escaped him again? He had sent an entire platoon of hand-picked mercenaries to kill him, along with the best pilots in the Blackrock stable. It seemed almost comical that Katherine had stolen one of the ships and used it to shoot down the other two. He knew she was an accomplished pilot, but the best Earth had to offer? He doubted it.

And Mitchell? He had never proven to be this resourceful before. He knew from Origin that in past recursions Mitchell was an over-sexed idiot, a Marine jock who happened to be gifted with the charisma of leadership. He wasn't simply leading the human forces now. He was part of them. A big part. What had been changed that had changed him so drastically that he was able to kill two squads of high-end soldiers for hire on his own?

Whatever the reason, he hated it, and he hated Origin for laughing at him because of it.

He opened a thread, using it to enter the ESA network and seize control of one of their air traffic tracking satellites. He would find the Hornet in the soup, and he would be ready for it when it landed, wherever it landed.

"You lost your sister, too," Origin said. "The smartest of my children. The best of you all."

"Be quiet," Watson replied.

He had sent more than enough equipment to kill Kathy and that fat, simpering fool of an engineer. How could he know the Primitive would change form like that? The composition of its subroutines was unlike any that had been passed between Tetron before. It wasn't like it was a mix of his systems and Origin's alone.

Having seen what the Primitive accomplished only made him want it more.

Not that he would ever want to take the shape of a human like that. The configurations were enough for him. Although there was a thread that wondered what it would be like to interact with the flesh directly.

He closed that thread. He had enough of his configurations actively engaged in base functions already, stimulating parts of his systems. It was logical to be upset about Mitchell. There was a benefit to Kathy's exodus. He would be able to track her and see where she was going, and to learn what she was planning. The queries were still running on alternate threads, but it would be hours before they returned a final result with enough significance to merit further investigation. Until then, real-time monitoring was the optimal course.

He knew she was headed for a military base in Houston. He didn't have a large presence at that particular base, but he wasn't blind there either.

He searched his threads. Second Lieutenant Kimberly Bright had been supplied with a subdermal implant as part of the Nova Taurus R&D program for neural interface development. He activated it, opening a new thread and creating a connection to the soldier. He linked the main thread to it, suddenly able to see through her optic nerve and seize control of her at his discretion.

She was in her quarters, half-dressed after a run and a shower. She was a pretty thing. Short brown hair, a small face, an athletic body. He resisted the urge to waste time with her, and instead allowed her to remain sentient. She finished dressing and then pinged her mother. He considered taking her then and cutting the connection but decided to suffer impatiently through the inane conversation that followed. Afterward, Lieutenant Bright left her room, making her way to the mess hall.

As she crossed the base, nobody around her noticed the slight change in her expression, or the sudden stiffness in her gait, or the hint of a smile that played across the corner of her mouth.

[25]
WATSON

SECOND LIEUTENANT KIMBERLY BRIGHT entered the mess and paused, searching the large room for a place to sit before heading up front to grab a tray and some chow. The mess was pretty full this time of day when most of the enlisted were finishing up with their duties and heading in for dinner before returning to their quarters. She had been dismissed early today and had taken advantage by going for a run. She regretted the decision now. She wasn't a fan of crowded spaces, preferring the solitude of a cockpit and the openness of the sky.

She started toward the chow line, still looking for a spot to claim. She was halfway to the front when she caught sight of an open space at a table near the center. A soldier she didn't recognize was sitting there. A woman in the fitted fatigues that were normally worn beneath body armor, and were incredibly out of place among the sea of digital camo utilities. Not that the woman seemed to notice. Kimberly hoped the spot would still be open when she finished picking up her dinner. Just because she didn't like crowds, it didn't mean she didn't like people, and she was intrigued by the newcomer.

She picked up a scoop of mashed potatoes, some grilled vegetables, and a small bit of apple cobbler before retreating to the tables. She was pleased to see the spot next to the woman was still available, and she hurried over to it and put her tray down.

"Second Lieutenant Kimberly Bright," she said when the woman looked up from her nearly finished meal. "I don't think I've seen you around the base."

"Sergeant Linda Damon, ma'am," the woman replied. "No, you wouldn't have. I'm normally stationed in Colorado."

"Do you mind if I sit?" Kimberly asked.

"Be my guest," Damon replied. "But shouldn't you be in the officer's mess?"

Kimberly froze, not sure how to reply. Why had she come here instead? She couldn't remember.

"Not that it's any of my business, ma'am. Feel free to ignore me."

She smiled and sat.

"Vegetarian?" Damon asked.

"Yup. Almost all of my life. I don't agree with killing animals for food."

"Noble. Especially for a soldier."

Kimberly felt her face begin to flush at the reply. She wasn't sure whether Sergeant Damon was being sarcastic or not.

"People can defend themselves," she said. "Especially other soldiers. Chickens? Cows? Not so much."

Damon smiled. "True enough, I suppose."

Kimberly lifted her fork and took a scoop of potatoes. She was about to place it in her mouth when she paused. "You know what? Maybe you're right." She stood up, went back to the chow line, and picked up a steak, returning to the table with it. Sergeant Damon was almost done eating by the time she.

"Changed your mind just like that?" Damon asked as Kimberly cut the steak and took a bite.

It tasted delicious, but there was a part of her that didn't want it. It was as if she didn't know herself.

"Why not? Maybe you inspired me."

"I'm flattered."

"Are you really, or are you bullshitting me?"

She met the Sergeant's eye. It was Damon's turn to be embarrassed.

"Sorry ma'am. I'm not known for my tact."

"Call me Kim, please," Kimberly said.

"Linda," Damon replied.

"I know."

They smiled at one another. It occurred to Lieutenant Bright somewhere in the back of her mind that she had never been interested in women before, and she was finding herself almost overwhelmingly attracted to Sergeant Damon. What the hell had come over her?

"That kit's for battle armor, isn't it?" she asked.

"Yeah. Me and my crew just got back from a mission. We landed here to refuel and hit the chow line. We were invited to dine with the XO, but I'm not much for that sort of company. I prefer the regular enlisted."

"I guess we have that in common."

"Along with a love of steak, it seems."

Kimberly looked at her plate. She had wolfed down the meat without even noticing. "I guess so."

"So, Kim, you're a pilot?" Damon asked, her eyes dropping to the medals on her chest.

"Yes."

"Did you fly in the Xeno War?"

"Only one mission. The War ended a few months after graduation. You?"

"Affirmative. Three years."

"You're Special Forces, right?"

"Right again. Part of the Fighting Fifteenth."

"I think I've heard of it. Nothing detailed, of course. Your operations are all top secret. Do you enjoy it?"

"I love it. See the world, shoot stuff. My crew is like family. It's been a rough couple of months, though. We lost some good people on a mission not too long ago. When you're running with the best of the best, you don't see it very often."

"I'm sorry to hear that," Kimberly said.

Damon was staring at her now empty tray, lost in thought. She sighed and then looked up. "Yeah, well, that's war right?"

"We aren't at war anymore," she replied.

Damon's head turned to face her again. "Is that what you think?" she snapped. "Let me tell you something. We're always at war. There's always someone out there somewhere looking to hurt us."

Kimberly flinched. "I'm sorry, Linda. I didn't mean to offend you." She paused, feeling her heart begin to pound. She lowered her voice. "To be honest, I'm getting a little flustered sitting here with you. You're very pretty."

Damon's face changed in an instant, softening. "Oh. Is that how it is?"

Kimberly nodded.

Damon laughed. "Well, in that case, Lieutenant, you should know that I've got to be back with my crew at oh-seven-hundred hours. That means I have about forty-five minutes."

Kim felt her heart beating even faster. "Forty-five minutes? You mean-"

"If you're interested."

Kimberly stood up. Damon stood with her.

"You're on," she said, almost against her own will.

She led Damon from the mess hall, crossing the base with her, bringing her into the officer's barracks and then to her quarters. She let Damon in first, reaching into her pocket and withdrawing a small black device she had found in her drawer as she entered. She absently wondered where it had come from, and what it was for, even as she closed the door behind her.

"Nice digs," Damon said, giving the quarters a quick once-over. "I've never been in an officer's personal quarters before. I always kind of wondered what they looked like."

"It's nothing special," Kimberly said, moving closer to the other woman. "But you didn't come here to talk."

Damon smiled, closing the gap between them and crouching slightly to reach Kimberly's mouth with her own. Kimberly's lips moved of their own accord, as did the hand holding the device. Before she could understand it for herself, she had pressed the device against Damon's neck. The Sergeant stopped kissing her immediately, her lips freezing and a soft whimper escaping. Kimberly backed off as the outer shell of the device fell to the floor, and Damon stood straight up.

Then the Sergeant smiled. "Well done, Watson," she said.

"Who's Watson?" Kimberly asked.

"You are," Damon said. "So am I."

"Should we still screw?" Kim said.

"Hmmm... Tempting, but no. I have other work to do. No. I think I'm going to head back to meet up with my fellow... Riggers? Oh, Mitchell, you're such a sap."

"I'm going to forget any of this ever happened," Kimberly said. She didn't know why she said it, but even as she did she felt as though time was slipping away from her. She tried to remember what she had just eaten, and couldn't.

Damon walked past her without another word, opening the door and vanishing into the hallway, leaving Kimberly standing alone in the room.

She looked down at her fatigues and decided that she needed another shower.

[26]
MITCHELL

"RIGGERS ACTUAL, this is Alfa, do you copy?" Mitchell waited a few seconds before trying his comm again. "Riggers Actual, this is Alfa, do you copy?"

Nearly four hours had passed since they had escaped from Jakarta. Mitchell had spent the bulk of them unconscious, sleeping off the adrenaline, exertion, and cuts, scrapes, and bruises that had nearly seen him killed. He had woken with a ringing headache and an awful taste in his mouth, riding in a Hornet gunship that was being shaken by violent turbulence.

For as bad as it was, he had been through worse.

A quick debriefing from Trevor and Katherine had followed. They had gotten out of the city and stayed low over the Indonesian countryside until they reached the ocean, avoiding sensor sweeps as best they could and trying not to draw attention from the local military. Fortunately, the Blackrock ships had air clearance, and even if Watson knew they had taken the craft, which he felt safe assuming the intelligence did, there was no way he could reverse course and ask them to take it out of the sky. It meant their escape was quick and relatively clean.

Now Mitchell was trying to raise Admiral Yousefi over the secure channel, to fill him in on what had happened, to ask about Kathy, Michael, and the rest of the Riggers, and to determine what they should do now. Their mission to Jakarta was, all in all, a failure. They hadn't discovered the components they were looking for or Watson's core, putting them back a few steps. They had also been forced to show their hand and reveal the Core. The upside was that they had eliminated one potential location where Watson might be hiding, and halted the AI's amoebic production.

They had taken a beating, but at least it wasn't a total loss.

"Riggers Actual, this is Alfa, do you copy?" Mitchell said again. He turned to Trevor. "Are you sure we have the range?"

Their systems worked flawlessly in Jakarta because they had been using a secret, heavily encrypted network link between Indonesia and their headquarters in Washington. With HQ no longer secure that link was gone, meaning they had to transmit the encoded signal directly over the thousands of kilometers to Edwards Air Force Base in Nevada. General Petrov had ordered Yousefi there not long after Antarctica, ostensibly to keep an eye on the commander of the Dove and the rogue Fifteenth.

Mitchell had no doubt that Watson knew about the encrypted communications and was working to break them, but the Core had been up to the task of stymying him so far. Both through the advanced encryption they were using, and by crafting the encoding using ancient, obscure methods; like morse code, but with an algorithmic variance in patterns that prevented the same series of dots and dashes from ever being repeated. Watson was highly capable of working forward to solve problems, but despite his nature as a time traveler, he struggled to look back.

"Hard to say, especially with the weather out there," Trevor replied. He had helped Mitchell rig the system to the Hornet's more powerful array. "We should be able to reach him once we're on the ground."

"I was hoping to get a line before we landed. I don't like the idea of bringing this thing down in civilian space, and I also don't like the idea of Watson having a welcome party waiting for us if we decide to drop onto UEA soil."

"We got out. It doesn't make sense for Watson to try to kill us in the open like that."

"No, it doesn't. But he hates me already. After this one, he might not give a shit about sense anymore." Mitchell paused for a moment, clenching his teeth in response to the throbbing in his arms. Four hours and they were still burning. "Riggers Actual, this is Alfa, do you copy?"

"Alfa... this is... actual... over."

Yousefi's voice was lilting as the system slowed to piece together the statement through the interference.

"Admiral," Mitchell said, relieved to get through to him. "Jakarta is a loss. It was a target, but not the target we were looking for."

"I'm aware, Colonel," Yousefi replied. His voice continued to come back slowly as the algorithms worked to complete the words. "I've had my hands working overtime, sending messages all over the world and trying to clean up the mess we've made. I also have one eye over my shoulder, waiting for General Petrov to walk in and carry me to the brig."

"It won't happen like that, sir. Watson needs you and the Dove. If he doesn't get us under control before then, it's his one last, clear shot to beat us."

"Somehow, I don't find that very comforting."

"I haven't found any of this comforting since I was framed for rape and saved by a clone of myself four hundred years from now."

"Point made, Colonel. What is your current status?"

"We're currently about a hundred klicks southwest of the Japanese mainland in a Hornet we took from the Blackrock platoon Watson sent in after us. We've got about two hours of fuel left in this thing, and we're looking for a place to land."

"Did you say Blackrock?" Yousefi asked.

"Affirmative. They've got deep ties to Nova Taurus. In all likelihood, he runs them both."

"Roger. Hmmm. I know someone in Osaka who can lend you some assistance. Ditch the Hornet in the foothills around Mt. Iwawaki. I trust Katherine knows where that is. I'll arrange for a pickup, and have a C-180 waiting on the tarmac to take you back to the States."

"Mt. Iwawaki," Mitchell said, loudly enough for Katherine to hear. She immediately began entering it into the Hornet's telemetry system. "Affirmative. How do we know that your contact can be trusted?"

"My contact has no traceable connection to me."

"Old girlfriend?" Mitchell asked.

"Not quite."

"But you trust them?"

"More than I trust any of the officers at the UEA base right now."

"What about the transport?"

"It'll be scheduled to take a few soldiers home for leave. I'll have to put those soldiers onto the flight to make it legit, and I can't promise they won't be Watson's. You'll also have to make it to the base before she leaves. That's the best I can do."

"Then we'll do our best with it, sir," Mitchell said.

He wasn't too worried about a few crewmen heading home. Even if Watson had managed to implant them, it didn't give them superhuman strength or make them better soldiers. The worst case was that Watson would know where they were going before they got there. It wasn't ideal, but there was a severe limit to how much they could move without drawing the AI's attention.

"Any word from Bravo or HQ?" Mitchell asked.

"Affirmative. Bravo bailed Kathy and Michael out of a mess up in the Olympics. It seems Watson has been developing humanoid robotic assault systems."

"Mechs?" Mitchell said. "Damn it. They made it out safe?"

"Yes. They're refueling the VTOL in Houston at the moment, en route to Miami."

Mitchell exhaled, feeling his body relax at the news the rest of the Riggers were alive and well. "Miami? Did they say why?"

"No. I arranged a refuel and didn't ask any questions. It's safer for everyone that way."

"Understood. I'll knock them as soon as we're able. Thank you, sir."

"My contact will rendezvous with you at the Takogi Temple. If you get there before them, just wait. I guarantee they'll show. And be sure you stash the Hornet close enough to make the hike."

"Takogi," Mitchell repeated for Katherine's sake. "Affirmative, sir. Alfa Squad out."

Mitchell switched off the comm, glanced at Trevor, and then moved to the front of the gunship. He couldn't see Katherine's face beneath the flight helmet, but he imagined she looked as tired as he did. More so, because she hadn't been given time to take a nap.

"Kathy made it out of Washington," he said.

Her head turned, and she nodded emphatically to make sure he saw it. "Thank God."

"You've got the coordinates in?"

"Yes. I've set a marker on my overlay. We're going to have a twenty-kilometer hike ahead of us. Are you up for it?"

He was sore, but it was nothing he hadn't dealt with before. "Affirmative. You?"

"I might ask Trevor for one of his stimulants."

Mitchell lowered his voice. "I think one ragehead is about all I can handle."

"I don't agree with it either, but he means well, and losing Jason has hit him harder than I would ever have imagined."

"You two used to be together, right?"

"Yes. Back when we were both a little too high on ourselves, thinking we were the shit for surviving the war and getting chosen for the program. We both had some growing up to do."

"I know what you mean. I just hope his addiction to that shit doesn't get him or one of ours killed. I've dealt with addicts before. It never seems to end well."

"He's a professional. You keep giving orders; he'll follow them."

"I hope so. How long until we touch down?"

"I'm going to have to slow our approach and come in extra low to stay clear of sensors. This bird doesn't have clearance, and the Japanese military would be well within their rights to shoot us down. Probably about an hour. Why?"

"I'm going to try to get a little more shuteye. My head is killing me, and this ride isn't helping. I guess you haven't learned to use the repulsors to stabilize, or invented inertial dampeners yet?"

Katherine's head turned back toward the front. There wasn't much visibility beyond the clear carbonate windscreen as the Hornet dropped through the storm that was bouncing them around.

"The Dove has inertial dampeners. The tech hasn't trickled down." She paused a moment, hesitating. "Are you are relieved about Kathy as I am?"

Mitchell put his hand on her shoulder. He hated that she was so worried. "Yeah. I am."

Katherine didn't respond, and he removed his hand and left her to fly the Hornet, returning to his seat in the rear and buckling himself back in.

"One hour," he said to Trevor as he did.

The soldier was in his seat, head back and eyes staring at the ceiling.

"Yes sir," Trevor replied.

Mitchell closed his eyes and took control of his breathing to calm the pounding in his head and the burning in his arms. The pain was optional.

Slow.

Steady.

[27]
KATHERINE

KATHERINE SLIPPED the Hornet around a final hilltop, dropping lower as the slope of the mountains eased down toward more developed civilization.

The landscape brought back memories. During the Xeno war, before she had been assigned to patrol the Antarctic and protect the XENO-1, she had been on a few combat missions over the Japanese mainland. She had seen these mountains before from a different perspective. One where everything was always dark, no matter how much sun was filtering in or what time of day it was. Where smoke clouded the air almost constantly. Where fighters were trying to shoot one another from the sky, where every move could mean your life, and every bogey you missed was one that had the potential to kill innocent people.

And a lot of innocent people died on the islands. Japan had sided with the United States during the war, and like Indonesia, its relative proximity to China and the Middle East had made it a target of attrition. For the second time in a few hundred years, Japanese cities had been bombed, and while the warheads hadn't been nuclear, they were plenty powerful enough to obliterate skyscrapers and kill thousands.

Like Jakarta, the cleanup was ongoing. Crews from around the world - including China - were presently putting in a global effort to rebuild what was lost. It was a sour thought. They could clean up the rubble and put up new and better buildings. They couldn't restore the lives that were broken. The families shattered. They could never make things just like they were before.

"Katherine, you okay?" Mitchell asked.

She snapped back to the present, adjusting the Hornet's flight path to put them between two smaller slopes. How had he known to ask? He wouldn't be able to see her eyes or expression beneath the flight helmet. She nodded.

"Just some old memories," she replied. She wasn't going to say anything more until she remembered he was a soldier, too. One who had seen his own share of violence and bloodshed and casualties. "I fought over this region during the war. It hurts to be here again, knowing what happened here."

"You don't have to talk about it."

"I know you've been through worse. An entire planet? I can't even begin to imagine."

"I try not to think about it. When I do, I try to let it motivate me. That planet is still out there in this recursion. It doesn't have to be destroyed. We can stop it."

"But we can't stop what happened here. Not in this recursion or any other. This war happened because of that one, and it always has to happen." She made a few adjustments to the flight path, slowing the Hornet. They were almost at their landing point. "If we stop Watson and the Tetron in this recursion, every future will be the same as this one. We'll go through this same thing over and over for eternity."

"But we won't know it. As far as we know, this is already the hundredth time we've done this. Or the ten-thousandth. Trillions and trillions of years. Years beyond measure or count. It still hurts my head to think about it."

"We know it today. I think that's all that counts."

He paused before responding. "Maybe. I'll take these people dying in exchange for the entire human race. It sounds cold, but I would."

"Me too."

The Hornet slowed to a hover over a small open patch between a larger growth of trees. Katherine began to lower it slowly, keeping her eyes on the sensors. There was barely enough space for the ship to squeeze between the vegetation, and one wrong move might destabilize them and send them careening to the ground instead.

"Any sign that the locals have noticed us?" Mitchell asked.

"We didn't pick up any hits from ground to air. I kept us pretty low."

"I noticed. Nice flying."

"Thank you, Colonel."

She eased the Hornet down, cutting the engines and going on repulsor only to drop it the last few meters. As soon as it touched down, she opened the side hatch and set the onboard wipe. It would draw too much attention to self-destruct the craft, so the next best thing was to electronically disarm the remaining bombs and missiles and delete everything in the onboard systems. If someone happened to come across the ordnance they could get it useful again, but not without some serious resources.

She pulled off the helmet and looked over at Mitchell. He was smiling. He did that a lot, especially at her. She didn't know how he could always be so positive when things could seem so bleak sometimes. It was yet another endearing quality that she knew she should find attractive, but for some reason didn't. Maybe she was trying too hard?

"Trevor's got the gear ready in the hold," Mitchell said. "We've got twenty kilometers to hump as fast as we can manage."

"Are you worried about Watson tracking us?" she asked.

"I'm always worried about Watson tracking us. He has the identification keys for this bird, which means he was probably monitoring it from the moment we left Jakarta."

"So he knows we're here?"

"He knows we're in Japan, somewhere. I'm hoping the low flight deck confused the systems a little, but I don't know if the lack of a welcoming committee is a good sign or a bad one. Even after we meet with the Admiral's contact, we need to be extra cautious. He may try to ambush us, or he might sit back and try to lull us into dropping our guard. I'm sure he's already explored the possibilities and done the calculations, but he also might ignore them. He's learned to be counterintuitive as we've butted heads." He paused, the smile vanishing. "Of course, I also don't think we're the most important concern for him right now."

"You mean Kathy?"

"Yes. He doesn't need to kill me if he has the engine and the Core. He'd just like to."

It was another sour thought.

They moved to the rear of the Hornet, where Trevor was already waiting by the hatch. He was holding an NX-600 rifle, and had a pack strapped to his back. He pointed to their gear.

"I threw every last magazine in the armory in there," he said. "And as many of the weapons as I could. I don't like the idea of some kids wandering by and grabbing a bunch of military gear."

"Me neither," Katherine said. "The hatch will seal when we close it. Only a plasma torch will get it open again. Mitchell, how are your arms?"

He rubbed them lightly beneath the Blackrock fatigues he had changed into and shrugged. "As good as they ever get. I'm a little beat up, but I'll be fine."

"What's our vector, sir?" Trevor asked.

"Make the hike down to the temple, find the contact, head to the base. We'll improvise from there, depending on whether or not we make it unmolested."

"Improvise?" Katherine asked.

"Yes. That's all I'm going to say for now. Extra cautious, remember?"

"Yes, sir."

"Good. Grab your pack, and let's move."

[28]
MITCHELL

THE SUN WAS ALMOST UP by the time Mitchell, Katherine, and Trevor reached the road that led east to the Takogi Temple. They had been marching for nearly four hours, at a good pace that put them ahead of Mitchell's estimates.

They had made the journey mostly in businesslike silence, with Trevor taking the lead and often ranging ahead of them, scanning the forward position for targets and reporting back. They had passed a few farms on the way, avoiding the workers in the fields and staying as far out of sight as they could, but otherwise hadn't encountered any resistance.There was no sign of local military or law enforcement, and thankfully no sign of Blackrock mercenaries or Watson's drones. They were close to reaching the temple unchallenged, and Mitchell wished he knew if it was because Watson didn't know where they were or because he had something more sinister planned for them.

He had no choice but to assume it was the second, and so he had been working on ideas as they had walked. He needed to try to outthink Watson, which was a difficult thing to do. He was only human after all.

"There it is," Katherine said as the top of the first pagoda came into view. It was in bad shape, chipped and worn.

"It doesn't look like anyone lives there," Trevor said, moving back to them. "Looks like they got hit by a stray missile or something."

"That's a shame," Katherine said. Mitchell noticed her expression change. Was she wondering if one of her missiles had hit it? "Those buildings were hundreds of years old. An important piece of history."

"I guess the government didn't think it was as important as another glass giant," Trevor replied.

"Did you see any sign of Yousefi's contact?" Mitchell asked. "It seems strange he would send us both to a deserted temple to meet."

"Strange? Or smart?" Katherine said. "The last place I'd want to be right now is in the thick of another crowd, or surrounded by cameras."

"True."

"I didn't spot anything out of the ordinary," Trevor said. "Want me to go take another peek?"

"Yeah. Go ahead."

"Yes, sir."

Trevor jogged back toward the compound. More of the pagoda was visible now. It was in bad shape, weathered and cracked. Mitchell closed his eyes for a few seconds, activating his p-rat, and then looking back at it, scanning for motion.

There was none.

They kept walking toward the temple. Trevor came back as they neared the front gate, most of which had been reduced to rubble.

"There isn't anybody home, Colonel," he said. "Not unless they got here on foot, in which case we'll reach the base next week."

"What if Watson figured out who the contact was?" Katherine asked. "They might never show up."

"Yousefi said if they weren't here, we should wait."

"Yes, but for how long?"

Mitchell shrugged. "We have to give them some time. Bulldog, go find some high ground to set up shop. Maybe up in that tower, there." He pointed.

"Yes, sir," Trevor said, heading off for the tower.

"If you see anything, holler."

"Yes, sir."

"Peregrine, wait at the entrance. I'm going to walk the perimeter."

"Roger."

Mitchell shrugged the pack off his back and handed it to her. "I'm going to leave this with you. Find some cover, and be ready if Bulldog raises an alarm."

"Of course, Colonel."

Mitchell headed off, following the damaged wall of the temple. He was pleased to find that there were no human remains strewn across the site, even as he came upon one of the main impact craters. It did seem to be a from a stray missile strike.

He reached the north side, pausing when he did find his first corpse. A soldier, his uniform torn, his body picked away by time and carrion. Two more were with him. Mitchell approached them. They were Japanese military, all behind a broken wall. He looked out into the brush beyond it, noticing a few more soldiers in different uniforms. It seemed the opposition had gotten a unit on the ground deep behind enemy lines. Maybe the missiles hadn't been as far off target as he had thought?

He passed the scene, heading toward the rear of the complex. He was halfway there when Trevor's voice cut in on his comm.

"Ares, this is Bulldog. I've got incoming from the road. One truck."

"Roger, Bulldog," Mitchell replied. "Can you count the personnel?"

"It looks like one driver, sir, but there's no way to know about the rear."

Mitchell was already running, headed back the way he had come. "Keep your position and be ready to fire on the truck if things go sideways."

"Affirmative."

He reached the entrance almost at the same time the truck did. It was an older model, with four air-filled wheels and a hydrogen power source. It had a drab brown painted cab and a canvas canopied back. A military vehicle, but not like anything he was familiar with.

"It looks like it came from surplus," Katherine said over the comm. She was positioned at the entrance to the main temple. "I've got you covered, Colonel."

"So do I," Bulldog said.

Mitchell stood out in the open. The truck stopped a few meters away. He could see the driver through the windshield. An older man with a head of thick white hair and a lot of stubble on his face. He stared back at Mitchell with the look of a soldier.

The door to the truck opened with a creak, and the man slid out. He was wearing green utility pants and a black tank that left his muscular arms exposed. They were covered in tattoos. Mitchell noticed one of them had the face of a pretty Japanese woman and a date beneath it. He felt a pang of emotion when he realized that she had died during the war.

"You Colonel Williams?" the man asked gruffly.

"Yes."

"That's yes, sir," the man said. "Name's General George McRory. Retired."

"Yes, sir, General," Mitchell said. "Admiral Yousefi sent you?"

"Aye, that he did. Dragged me from a drunken stupor, that bastard. That's what I get for letting him save my life."

"Sir? During the war?"

General McRory laughed, rough and throaty. "No, dumbass. Yousefi's from Iran. He was on the other side during the war. After. It's a long story, and I don't care enough to tell it to you. Our mutual friend called me up and told me he needed to cash in that favor I owed him, so here I am. Otherwise, I want nothing more to do with the military, with war, with any of that bullshit. Understood?"

"Yes, sir," Mitchell said.

"Good. Call in your troops from that tower up there, and the shadows of the temple, and let's get our asses in gear. I want to drop you off in Osaka and get back home while the fish are still biting."

Mitchell stared at the General, trying to figure out how he had spotted his team. Maybe he hadn't. If the man was as experienced as he seemed, the positioning would be obvious.

"Bulldog, Peregrine, pack it in and let's go," Mitchell said into the comm. Then he looked at McRory again. "How far is it to the base?"

"Three hours, as long as Bettina here doesn't start choking again. I would have beaten you to this dump if she hadn't been acting up on me."

"You mean the truck, sir?"

"This here is an antique. It's getting tougher to find hydrogen to fill her up, but she's as reliable as any woman. Well, except Liu." All of the life seemed to drain from him for a moment. "She's like any other antique. Sometimes the parts just wear out."

"Understood, sir. We appreciate the pickup."

"Don't mention it," McRory said. "I'm glad not to have that card hanging over my damn head anymore. Oh yeah, I damn near forgot." He turned around, lowering his head and showing his neck. "Go ahead, give a feel. I don't know what the hell for, but the Admiral insisted."

Mitchell clenched his jaw. He shouldn't have trusted the man without checking him first. He had gotten away with a mistake. He approached the General slowly, watching for sudden moves. When he reached him, he pressed his fingers into the back of his neck. He was clean.

"You're good, General."

"I knew I was."

Katherine joined them a moment later. She saluted McRory, who snapped a sharp salute back at her. "Aren't you UEA folks supposed to bow, now?" he asked.

"Only to other UEA, sir," she replied. "I still prefer saluting."

"Smart woman." He smiled, looking past them to an approaching Trevor. "You found a gorilla on the way here?"

Mitchell stifled a laugh. "They make excellent soldiers."

"A tool for every job, Colonel."

"Go on and hop in the back. I brought some MREs if you're hungry. We might get stopped on the way to Osaka. I've got dark blankets back there. The truck stops, you get under them and don't move. The MPs will peek in, but they aren't allowed to climb up without a warrant, and the blanket will keep you hidden. Got it?"

"Yes, sir," Mitchell said.

"Good."

"Sir, when we get to the airbase, can you drop us a few klicks out?"

"My orders are to deliver you to the base, Colonel."

"I understand, General. I have a good reason to walk the rest."

"Do you?"

"Yes. Yousefi would agree with me."

McRory stared at him and then relented. "Fine. Have it your way. I'll pull over a few kilometers out; you can figure out the rest on your own. I trust you'll corroborate with the Admiral?"

"Yes, sir."

"Good. Now get in the truck. We're already late."

[29]
KATHY

"Do we have a location?" Kathy asked, looking back at the Core.

The Tetron Primitive had returned to its humanoid form, and it had grown nearly four inches in the six hours since they had fled Washington. It currently had a hand against the side of the Schism, using the craft's avionics to communicate with the Internet below.

"I have matched the source IP address with the Palm Cay Retirement Home in Coral Gables," the Core replied.

"Retirement home?" Michael said. "Frelmund is only sixty-three."

"He does not appear on any of the resident lists," the Core said. "I believe he is staying there under an assumed name."

"That makes sense," Lyle said. "Especially if he thinks an AI is in charge and might be looking for him." He turned to Kathy. "How do you want to run this? You want to make a drop?"

"No," Kathy replied. "It's logical that the Doctor will be skittish as it is. If we show up in body armor, with guns at the ready, he's bound to try to bolt and wind up killing himself."

"Or running right into one of Watson's goons," Damon said.

"Exactly. I think we need to do this as quietly as possible. Lyle and I will go plainclothes and jump over a recreational zone. The people on the ground won't know we're anything more than thrill seekers. Then we'll get a cab to the facility and try to get in to see Dr. Frelmund. We'll keep a channel open. If things go south, we call in the Schism and bug out. Otherwise, we'll send an update with a rendezvous point. According to Admiral Yousefi, we have clearance down at Cape Canaveral. The UEA just re-opened the launch facility a few weeks ago, so there's a good chance Watson hasn't gotten too embedded there yet. If we need to set down, we'll set down there. Understood?"

"Yes, ma'am," Lyle said.

"Are you sure two people are sufficient for this?" Damon asked.

"To pick up a scientist?" Lyle replied. "I don't see why not?"

"What if Watson is already on the ground? Hell, what if he beat you to the prize?"

"The statistical probability is less than twenty-one percent," the Core said.

"That's not a small number," Damon said.

"You feeling okay, Demon?" Max said. "It isn't like you to argue balls and strikes."

"I'm fine," Damon replied. "I'm just getting tired of us getting beat up because we play too conservative."

"I understand," Kathy said. "And I don't disagree. But too many of us might spook him even more. We want him to come with us willingly. We need his help."

Damon didn't continue arguing, but she also didn't look happy with the decision. That was fine with Kathy. She would rather have people speak their mind, as long as they knew when to drop it.

"Mazerat, can you pull up an air sport rec zone and get us positioned over it at twenty-five thousand feet?" Kathy asked.

"Affirmative," Verma replied. There was a pause as he entered coordinates. "Fifteen minutes."

"I'm impressed with your understanding of twenty-second

century Earth," Michael said, "Considering you spent twenty years buried beneath a thousand kilos of ice."

"I'm a fast learner," she replied with a smile. Not that the waiting had been easy. She had sacrificed her youth for the cause, and would have gone insane if not for the company of the Core. She turned to Lyle. "Good thing we brought some civvies with us."

"Good thing," Lyle agreed.

Some situations required blending in with the population, not looking like a soldier in the middle of a battlefield. This was one of them.

Kathy headed over to the storage locker where she had hung the clothes. She opened it and pulled out a pair of leggings and a tank top. It wouldn't fit the profile to wear something loose for any kind of jump, recreational or otherwise. She shrugged out of her fatigues, aware of all the eyes on her bare flesh as she changed in front of the crew.

"Hoo. Thanks for that," Max said, laughing.

"Shut up," Kathy replied. When she looked up, she noticed Damon was giving her a little extra attention. The Sergeant looked away without making eye contact.

Lyle flipped through the wardrobe, grabbing a black t-shirt and a pair of jeans. He followed her lead, shucking his fatigues in front of them to make the exchange. Of course, Max whistled at him as he did.

"Asshole,' Lyle said.

After that, they made their way over to a second storage locker where the wingsuits were hanging. Max helped her get into the suit, while Damon assisted Lyle. The suits were black and skintight, and the biggest clue that these two jumpers weren't everything they seemed. Most civilians wore bright colors. They wanted to be seen so that they wouldn't get hit by other air traffic.

"Five minutes," Verma said over the loudspeaker.

Lyle made his way to a third locker, the armory. He pulled a pack from it and opened it up, and then picked out a handgun for each of them, along with two magazines, put them in the pack, sealed it and tossed it on his back.

"Anything bigger will be hard to conceal," he said.

They were almost ready to jump. Kathy went over to the Core. "What about the other query? Have you had time to work on it?"

"Yes. I have dedicated a thread to the algorithm and updated it to eliminate the holdings in Jakarta. It would be of great assistance to narrowing the location if we could reverse-engineer a control module. I could route the path back to the satellite, and aggregate the existing data to estimate an origin."

Kathy nodded. "If I can capture an implant intact, I will."

"Be safe, Kathy," the Core said.

"Keep Michael safe," Kathy replied in a low voice. "I haven't told him that we're as dead in the water without him as we will be without Dr. Frelmund. I don't want to put too much pressure on him."

"Understood," the Core replied.

"One minute," Verma said. "Opening cargo door."

A warning strobe flashed red at the back of the Schism, and the rear cargo ramp began to lower, allowing cool air to flow into the craft.

"Good luck," Michael said.

"Hoo. Riiiggg-ahhh," Max said.

Damon remained silent, watching as Lyle and Kathy moved to the edge of the platform. Verma counted down when they got within ten seconds.

When he hit zero, they jumped.

[30]
KATHY

KATHY AND LYLE hailed a cab at the front desk of Air Sports Miami, which amounted to little more than a concrete and glass booth with a storage area full of equipment, sitting in the center of a small airfield. Small planes both old and new came and went on both sides of the field, while a tunnel had been dug out so that vehicles could reach the center.

As expected, their sudden appearance barely caused anyone to bat an eye. Drop-ins weren't unheard of for air sports enthusiasts, and jumping from a passing craft was a viable way to save a few bucks on a trip if you were an adrenaline junkie. If the proprietor of the shop was surprised by their all black wingsuits, he didn't say.

The cab was fully manual, an antique fashioned after the big yellow cabs of the twentieth century. They had chosen it more for its lack of onboard tech than for the touristy nostalgic marketing, but that didn't stop the driver, dressing the part in a leather jacket and sporting a pompadour, from commenting on the areas he was driving through. At least until Kathy told him to shut up or she would shove the fuzzy dice down his throat.

Palm Cay wasn't a single retirement home. It was an entire estate, with a main living spire that rose fifty stories into the sky and a number of outbuildings that provided all of the necessities an aging citizen might need. A VR theater, a couple of restaurants, a pharmacy, two golf courses, and so on lined the outer ring of businesses at the base of the spire.

"Do you know how many people live here?" Lyle asked the driver.

"No idea. I don't get too many requests to drive to the pre-mausoleums. Most sightseers want to check out the beaches or the drainage systems, or head to a brothel or a hotel. Judging by the size of it? I'd say about four thousand. That's a lot of diapers if you know what I mean."

Lyle glanced over at Kathy, who shrugged. At least the odds of the driver being one of Watson's were slim.

The cab came to a stop beneath an awning at the base of the tower, met there by a valet. Lyle handed an anonymous payment card to the driver to scan, and then they climbed out into the hot, humid air.

"I don't know how anyone lives outside around here," Kathy said.

"Yeah, you're used to the cold, right? The real cold."

Kathy smiled. "I don't have to feel the heat like this if I don't want to. I'm just surprised that anyone would choose to subject themselves to this."

"You don't have to feel the heat?"

"I have master control over most bodily functions. Nerve ending sensitivity, heart rate, etcetera."

"I'm impressed. And jealous."

They made their way into the lobby of the building. The Core had identified the IP address as originating from here, but it hadn't given them an alternate name. Kathy wasn't sure how they would identify Dr. Frelmund. She had seen a photo of him that accompanied his book, but it was a few years old, and she doubted it matched his current look.

"You're the policeman," Kathy said. "How do we identify someone using a fake name?"

They reached the receptionist. Lyle smiled widely at the woman behind the desk.

"Hi. I'm looking for Dr. Paul Frelmund. I know he lives here, and I know he's using a fake name. Could you please tell me which resident he is? I already have the updated list."

Kathy's eyes shot over to Lyle. She had expected a small dose of subtlety at least.

The woman stared up at him, her eyes darting left and right. She pushed her chair back a few inches. "I don't know what you're talking about."

"Then why are you nervous?" Lyle said.

The woman looked at the floor. "I'm not."

"I'm with the U.S. Government, ma'am. We're currently running an investigation involving Nova Taurus, and we need to ask Dr. Frelmund some questions. Again, can you tell me which assumed name is his?"

She continued to stare at the floor while she stammered out a reply. "I told you, he isn't here."

Even Kathy could tell the woman was lying now.

"I didn't ask you if he was here at the moment. I asked you what his assumed name is. It's a matter of national security, ma'am."

"He said you might say that," she said, finally looking up. "You're here about his new book, aren't you?"

"That's classified, ma'am," Lyle said. "Now that you've confirmed he is a resident, can you please direct us to him?"

The woman paused. "I shouldn't."

"If you prefer to be arrested and held for refusing to assist a government agent, then by all means."

Lyle leaned forward onto the desk, hands folded. He pursed his lips and began to whistle. Kathy just stared at his back. This wasn't quite what she had been expecting. Of course, the woman wasn't the most intelligent humankind had to offer. Lyle had never even identified himself as a government agent. In fact, he hadn't identified himself at all.

"No. I don't want to be held," the woman said. "Robert Thornock. Room 3624. Take the lift to the left up to the thirty-sixth floor, and go down the eastern corridor."

"That wasn't so hard, was it?" Lyle asked. "Thank you for your cooperation. I'm going to send Agent K up to talk to him. If I find out you're lying to me-"

"I'm not," the woman said. "I swear I'm not. Bobby and I play in the same XenoTroopers squad."

"You play XenoTroopers?" Kathy asked.

"What? You think I can't because I'm ninety-six? I still have sex, too. What do you think about that?"

Lyle bit his lip to keep from laughing. Kathy ignored the comment, heading to the bank of lifts. She hit the call control and waited a few seconds. She could hear Lyle making small talk with the woman.

"So, are you good?" he asked.

"In bed? You better believe it, buddy."

"I meant at XenoTroopers," Lyle said.

"Not as good as I am in bed." The woman cackled, more relaxed now that she had already ratted out Dr. Frelmund. "I can teach you a thing or two about either one, I bet."

The lift arrived, and Kathy hurried onto it. It quickly rose to the thirty-sixth floor, and she disembarked, heading down the east corridor as instructed. She located room 3624 and stood behind it for a moment, listening. She could hear music playing on the other side.

"Kathy," Lyle's voice cut in through the comm. "Shit. The old bitch was stalling me. Frelmund's already gone."

"What?" she replied, looking back at the door.

She stepped forward, raising a foot and kicking it. It swung open, bending off its hinges at the force. There was music playing in the small apartment. It was otherwise unoccupied.

"You've got to be kidding me," she said. "Where is he?"

"She won't say. She's turned into a belligerent old lady."

Kathy entered the apartment, rushing to the full-length window and looking out at the front of the complex. Her eyes landed on a pair of men in overalls headed north, then tracked to a man fifty meters ahead of them. His head of wild, bushy hair matched what she thought Dr. Frelmund's might look like. Who was the tail?

"Lyle, I've got him. Headed north across the complex at a brisk walk. Two men in workman's uniforms are following him."

"On it," Lyle replied.

Kathy shifted her attention from Frelmund to the tower's overhang. Lyle appeared from under it a moment later, running north behind the two workers. A moment later, she caught sight of a series of flashing lights in the distance. Police. It looked like they were coming this way. Thanks to Watson, Lyle was still a wanted man. Had the receptionist recognized him?

Or was Watson already here?

Twenty-one percent. That was the probability the Core had calculated.

They had played the odds and lost.

[31]
KATHY

KATHY RETREATED FROM THE WINDOW, running back toward the lift. "Lyle, we're going to have company. Miami PD is inbound."

"Already? Damn, that was fast."

She reached up and tapped her earpiece, switching the channel.

"Schism, this is Bravo. We've got a problem here. We need backup asap."

"Roger, Bravo," Max said a moment later. "We're making the turn and headed your way. ETA three minutes."

Kathy reached the lift and tapped the call button impatiently, while at the same time disconnecting the booster. Lyle needed backup, and she was stuck waiting for a ride? She hesitated a few seconds before running back to Frelmund's room and looking out the carbonate. Lyle was being careful, staying behind the two workers as they followed the Doctor. The police cars were getting closer. She estimated their arrival within the next minute. Damn.

She ran back to the lift. The doors slid open as she did, and she threw herself in, drawing her gun as she descended. Fifteen seconds later she was out of the building and running north, the sirens growing in pitch as they approached.

She reached to the earpiece and switched channels again. "Lyle. You need to take out those workers. We're running out of time. The Schism is inbound."

"Yes, ma'am," Lyle replied.

Kathy flinched slightly when she heard the two gunshots a few seconds later, but she didn't slow. The cars had reached the tower, and she could hear one turning and heading her way. She looked back over her shoulder. The driver was smiling crudely, clearly not himself. How had Watson been so prepared?

She raised her pistol, squeezing off two rounds. Both hit the windshield and went through, striking the driver in the head. The car immediately slowed to a stop.

She felt a moment of lament for shooting the officer and then kept running, nearing the outer ring of storefronts. There was a gap between them that led to one of the golf courses, and she could see Lyle up ahead of her and the bodies of the two workers lying just beyond. She didn't slow, passing the corner and running out onto the course. There had been a few people playing nearby, and they were backing away, trying to escape the scene.

"Lyle, where the hell is Frelmund?" she said.

"I saw him come this way," Lyle replied. "He has to be here somewhere."

She heard car doors behind her and looked back to see the rest of the police had arrived. There were nearly a dozen in all. Most of them took position behind their cars, drawing weapons and aiming them her way. Two of the officers broke rank, giving chase.

A whirring noise overhead signaled an incoming police drone. It was trailed by a larger, manned recon craft that looked like a smaller, more lightly armed version of the Schism.

"Stop running and drop your weapon."

The command came from the loudspeakers on the recon ship. Kathy ignored it.

"Stop, or-" the voice stopped midsentence. Kathy saw the ship accelerate ahead, moving out over the golf course and dropping down near one of the water hazards.

"Lyle, he's in the water," Kathy said.

"Roger."

She could see Lyle a few hundred meters ahead. He changed direction, heading for the hazard, where an officer was climbing out of the recon craft with a heavy rifle in his arms.

"Don't let him shoot Frelmund," she said, even though Lyle didn't need her to tell him that.

He was already shooting back at the officer, his bullets striking a ballistic vest. It was enough to knock the man back, but it wouldn't do lasting damage.

A bullet whipped past Kathy's ear, fired from one of the officers behind her. She let herself fall to the ground, rolling on the grass and coming up on a knee, facing the other direction. The two rogue officers were taking shots at her, their faces flat, expressions empty save for Watson's ludicrous grin. She fired twice, each bullet striking a man square between the eyes, and then regained her feet, rushing toward Lyle.

He was at the edge of the hazard; a soaking wet Paul Frelmund held against him while he and the Watson from the recon ship pointed their guns at one another. Kathy glanced back to see the other officers were approaching cautiously. She could hear more airborne vehicles inbound.

Where the hell was the Schism? Three minutes had come and gone, and the Riggers were nowhere to be seen. It wasn't like Verma to be late.

She watched as Lyle ran out of bullets, and then tossed Frelmund to the side, moving in on the officer while he was still reeling. He grabbed him by the collar, holding him while he punched him hard in the jaw.

The officer crumpled to the ground. Lyle turned back as Frelmund tried to make a break for it, heading for the line of officers at the rear, and running right into Kathy.

"Got you," she said, wrapping her hand around his wrist and holding it tight.

He tried to jerk away, and his slickness nearly allowed him to escape, but she hooked a foot around his ankle and knocked him to the ground.

The recon craft was lifting off, turning to face them and bring its guns to bear. It made it a few feet off the ground when Kathy saw a silver streak dropping from above like a meteorite. It hit the center of the craft, putting a clean hole in it and hitting the dirt, throwing up a cloud of grass and soil. The craft began to smoke and dropped back to the ground.

Kathy sat on top of Dr. Frelmund, holding him down. The other police were staying back, cowed by the sudden impact from above. A moment later, she heard the familiar whine of the Schism as it descended, positioning itself between them and the police line. The side hatch opened, and Max leaned out, waving to them.

"Time to go," Kathy said, sliding off the Doctor and pulling him to his feet.

"Please, don't kill me," Frelmund said.

"I know this seems illogical to you right now, Dr, Frelmund," Kathy said. "But we're your best chance of survival."

She looked back to find Lyle headed toward her. A familiar shape was taking up the rear behind him.

"An explosive warhead would have risked damaging Dr. Frelmund with shrapnel," the Core explained when it reached her. "An alternate projectile was required."

"You?"

The Core shrugged, which made Kathy laugh. It was a more human gesture than she expected from the Primitive.

"What are you?" Frelmund said, staring at the Core.

"We'll tell you everything once we're safe, Dr. Frelmund," Kathy said. "We have to leave."

She led the scientist to the Schism. Max helped him up into the hatch.

"You were late," Kathy said to him as she boarded.

"Sorry, ma'am," Max said. "We got caught with some unexpected traffic and had to take a wider path around. We tried to tell you, but you didn't have the channel active."

"Understood. We managed." The hatch closed behind her. "Mazerat, get us the hell out of here," she shouted to the cockpit. She saw the pilot give her the thumbs-up, and then the VTOL was hopping into the sky.

[32]
KATHY

"DR. FRELMUND," Kathy said, sitting down next to the soggy scientist. "My name is Kathy. It's a pleasure to meet you."

Frelmund looked at her with a bewildered expression. "Pleasure? For the record, there wasn't a damn thing about whatever the hell all that was that I found pleasurable."

"You have my apologies, Doctor. We tried to reach you earlier, to prevent all of this. Somehow, he almost got to you before we did."

"He, who?"

"We tracked you down through a book you've been working on that you were storing on a remote server. You-"

"Huh. Are you kidding? Damn service was supposed to be secure from the Government. From teams like you and yours. I know how the United States, and now the United Earth Alliance, work. I know how you make people disappear when they don't toe the company line. I paid good money for a secure facility. Bastards are working with the Feds? Screw 'em."

"Dr. Frelmund," Kathy said.

"You're trying to keep people from the truth. Don't lie to me and tell me you aren't. It's plain as day. Clear as the fact that God don't like when you worship anyone other than Him. I know what's going on. I was on the Xeno. Did you know that? I was one of the first scientists to board her."

"Dr. Frelmund," Kathy said again, trying to explain.

"I saw things there, missy. Things you wouldn't believe. I'm not an idiot. That ship was no alien craft. I knew it as soon as I started breaking down the bits and bytes and running bioscans. I only called it alien in my book because the publisher wouldn't have it any other way. Said I was going to bring the NSA knocking at best, and discredit myself at worst. Nobody's ready to buy what you're trying to sell, he said. Screw him, too!"

"Dr. Frelmund," Kathy said a third time. The Doctor didn't seem to even notice she was there.

"I told you he was crazy," Michael said. Coming to stand in front of them.

Frelmund fell silent at once. "Crazy? Who the hell are you calling crazy?" He glared up at Michael. "I know what I'm talking about. I know the truth. There isn't anything crazy about that. You think the government doesn't participate in conspiracies? In cover ups? If you don't, then you're the one who's crazy."

"Dr. Frelmund, it's true," Kathy shouted, stealing his attention. "Everything you were writing in your book is true."

He froze for a second time, glancing over at her and not looking away. His face had been reddening from his anger, but now it cooled to a pale white.

"It is?" he asked, sounding surprised.

"Yes. All of it."

He stared at her for a few more seconds before smiling.

"I knew it," he said, softly at first. "I knew it!"

"Don't get too excited, bro," Max said from the other side of the VTOL. "There's a reason they say that ignorance is bliss."

"What do you mean?" Frelmund asked.

"It's a long story," Kathy said.

He leaned back in the seat. "I'm retired, missy. I've got plenty of time to listen. Just answer my first question first, because I'm still not sure whether or not I should be scared to death of any of you."

"He is Watson," Kathy said. "He's a malevolent artificial intelligence known as a Tetron."

"An AI? No fooling?"

"No fooling."

"Malevolent, eh? Am I supposed to just take your word for that?"

"Or we can read you the list of the other machine learning experts he's had killed over the last six weeks," Max said.

"Killed? Why?"

"Because he knows we need your help."

"To do what?"

"Back to the long story," Kathy said. "Give me a few minutes."

She headed up to the cockpit. Verma was keeping the Schism in a circular flight path forty-thousand feet up.

"Captain Verma," she said. "Set a new course. The coordinates are as follows: Thirty-seven degrees, thirty-eight minutes, four seconds north. Eighty-four degrees, fifty-four minutes, eighteen seconds west. Should I repeat it?"

The pilot tapped the controls on the dashboard to bring up a map in his helmet and enter the latitude and longitude.

"I have it, ma'am," he said.

Kathy turned to go, pausing a moment later. The Core had claimed a twenty-one percent chance that Watson would finish the query before they arrived, and it was certainly possible that the intelligence had done it. But the fact that he had already gained control of a number of law enforcement officers before their arrival was bothering her, and leaving her to question whether there was another possibility. She didn't want to believe that one of the Riggers was compromised, but she also couldn't rule it out.

Fortunately, there was an easy way to make that determination.

She stood behind Verma, putting her hand on the back of the seat. "Captain, I'm going to check you for a control implant," she said, ready to be more aggressive if he made any sudden moves.

He responded by tilting his head forward to give her easier access. She put her hand on the base of his neck and pressed down, feeling for the small disc below. He was clean.

"Thank you," she said.

"Better safe than-"

She didn't hear the last word. It was drowned out by the sound of a gunshot from the rear of the ship, and then a second a moment later, then a third, a fourth, and a fifth.

Kathy rushed from the cockpit, taking in the scene as she cleared the division. Dr. Frelmund was sitting back in his seat, his head lolled to the side, a line of blood running from the bullet hole in the center of it.

Lieutenant Damon was standing in front of him, two holes in her back, her fatigues darkening quickly. She was turning to face her, hand raised, gun ready.

Another gunshot hit her in the shoulder, knocking her back.

She smiled. "Got you," she said.

A fourth bullet struck her stomach, and she fell over.

Kathy cleared the cockpit and looked to her right. Michael was pressed against the corner, gun in hand, shaking at the burst of adrenaline. Max was few feet in front of him, on his side across the row of seats. She looked to her left. Lyle was there, holding his side and groaning.

"Watson got to her," the Core said from beside Frelmund. "It must have been in Houston."

Kathy could have kicked herself. "The base was supposed to be secure. We should have checked them. How could I be so stupid?" She stared at the Doctor. "Is he?"

"Dead?" the Core replied. "Yes. I am sorry. I couldn't reach Sergeant Damon in time."

"Max?" she moved to the Corporal's side. "Max?"

He wasn't breathing either.

"I'm so stupid," she said again. "I should have realized. I should have known. Damn it. Damn it. Damn it." She slammed her fist into the side of the wall, leaving a dent.

"Kathy, what is done is done," the Core said. "We must adjust our calculations."

"Calculations? These are people, and they're dead because of my stupidity."

"We are still in the air. We can still fight."

Michael. Kathy had forgotten about him in her anger. She whirled on him. "Michael. Are you okay?"

He had let the gun fall into his lap. He shook his head.

"No." He paused. He looked angry. "How are we going to make the virus now?"

"I don't know," she replied. "We'll think of something."

Would they? All of their plans were unraveling in an instant, just because she hadn't thought to check Damon, the only one of them who had been out of her sight for an extended period of time. It was a mistake she should never have made. Tetron didn't make mistakes like this. Only humans did.

"Why didn't you warn me about this?" she said to the Core. "Why didn't you tell me to check her?"

"I am sorry. I failed to calculate this branch."

She could feel her anger, frustration, and guilt burning at her. She was tempted to take it all out on the Core, the closest thing in the Schism to Watson.

"I'm not dead yet," Lyle said behind her. She turned to face him as he sat up. There was some blood on his shirt, but it looked like the bullet had grazed his side. "Just a flesh wound. I think getting shot in the back screwed up her aim." He looked across at Max. "That's a damn shame, though." He paused again, gritting his teeth. "We can't give up, Kathy. Maybe we took a hit, but we have to keep fighting. Otherwise, they die for nothing. The Colonel would tell you the same thing."

"I know," she replied. It didn't make this mess any less her fault. "And we will. We needed him to help us improve the virus. There isn't anyone else left."

"Then we do it another way."

"How?"

"I don't know. I'm just a grunt. Or a flat-foot. Take your pick." He pointed at the Core. "That thing's a supercomputer, and you two are super-geniuses. The Colonel's always saying it isn't about the plans, it's about the people behind them. Figure something out."

"As if it were that easy?"

He smiled. "You might surprise yourself. Maybe it is?"

[33]
MITCHELL

Bettina only broke down once on the way to Osaka, one of the hoses developing a crack of some kind and causing the hydrogen engine to start leaking the gas. McRory was forced to stop the car on the side of the highway, drawing plenty of comments and commotion from the surrounding traffic as automatic, monitored safety systems forced them to both slow down and navigate around.

Mitchell spent the twenty-minute delay on high alert, peering out of the back of the truck toward the sky in search of drones, and scanning the street behind them for oncoming law enforcement. An officer did show up halfway through the repair, but he bypassed the rear of the vehicle and spoke with McRory, who responded to him in crisp Japanese. It was obvious the General had been in town for awhile, meaning that Watson likely wouldn't make the connection between his rather unique antique vehicle and his group, as long as he couldn't somehow discover how Yousefi knew the man.

Mitchell was curious about that history as well, but McRory wasn't going to tell, so he wasn't going to push. It was enough that he was driving them across the country to their waiting escape plane. They were close to getting back to the States, and hopefully regrouping for another attempt to find and capture Watson's data stack. He could only hope that Kathy and the other Riggers were safe, but he wouldn't be able to check-in with them until they were much closer together.

The truck stopped a second time, and at first, Mitchell thought there was another mechanical problem, or they had hit a checkpoint. Instead, McRory's face appeared at the rear of the truck.

"We're a few klicks out. I took the liberty of moving off the main road and heading east a little bit. I assume you didn't want the guards there to see you coming just yet?"

"You're a smart man," Mitchell said, walking to the rear of the truck. Katherine and Trevor rose and stretched behind him.

"Yes, I am, Colonel," McRory replied.

"My bloody arse is killing me," Trevor said. "I haven't ridden in anything so rough in ages."

"Beggars can't be choosers, Magilla," McRory said.

"Who?" Trevor replied.

"You're too young to get the reference," McRory said. "Technically, so am I, but I'm a bit of a history buff."

"I never would have guessed."

"Cheeky. So, Colonel, you want to brief me or should I just go home?"

"I thought your plan was to go home?" Mitchell said.

"Driving you here got me thinking. I've been hiding out here since the war ended. I'm not doing any good to anyone out here, and you seem like you're in a bit of a bind. This is your mission, Colonel. You don't want to tell me; that's your business. But Yousefi is a friend of mine, and if his people need help, I'm going to offer it."

"What about fishing?" Katherine asked.

He smiled. "They've been in that pond for a thousand years. They'll be there when I get back. What's the situation?"

Mitchell glanced over at Katherine and Trevor. They both nodded. They needed all the help they could get.

"Okay, General. You're in, but you take orders from me for this one, okay?"

"I'm retired, Colonel. I don't have any jurisdiction over you and yours. Tell me what to do and I'll do it."

"Here's the deal. Yousfi has a C-180 loaded and ready for us out on the tarmac, waiting to take us and some soldiers going on leave back home. The problem is that there's an angry artificial intelligence who may have control of some number of the forces on the base, the soldiers going on leave, and possibly the aircraft itself. In short, everything about that base has to be assumed hostile."

"Angry AI?" McRory said. "Are you joking?"

"No, sir," Katherine said. "That's why Yousefi called you. There aren't many people we can trust."

He bit his lower lip. "Well, shit," he said. Then he looked at Mitchell. "You want another option?"

"Yes."

"I've been to Osaka a bunch of times. What you need is a different aircraft. I know for a fact that they've got a Screamer in there. I even know what hangar it's in."

"A Screamer?" Mitchell asked.

"A high-velocity transport," Katherine said, her eyes lighting up. "Uses a mixed scramjet and rocket motor plus the latest in repulsor tech to reach speeds close to Mach Ten with virtually no friction. It's the closest thing to a starfighter we have right now, only its transport. No guns, but it seats ten."

"Why would they have one here?"

"The leader of the Eastern Forces is stationed in Osaka," McRory said. "It's his escape hatch if things go south."

"Can you fly it?" Mitchell asked Katherine.

"I can fly anything," she replied.

"Cocky," McRory said. "I like that."

"Not cocky," Katherine replied. "We had to fly the Screamer to prep for the recon ships onboard the Goliath. It's the closest we can come to reaching the velocities the new tech is capable of. It's also the limit of what we can manage without going internal." She tapped her head. "Like you are, Mitch."

Mitchell nodded. "That's where the p-rat originated. There are limits to our body's ability to do things on its own. Limits we need to break to continue to evolve."

"That sounds like the genesis of AI to me," McRory said.

Mitchell paused. He had never thought of it that way before. "Yeah, I suppose it is. So, General, you know where they're keeping the Screamer." He stopped again, entertaining a thought. He had said they would improvise. Now was the time to turn thought into action. "I have an idea."

[34]
MITCHELL

MITCHELL CROUCHED on the top of Bettina's cab, looking ahead at the airbase through McRory's two-hundred-year-old binoculars. They did an acceptable job blowing up the scene in front of him. The soldiers guarding the front gate, the series of hangars and barracks positioned around the base, and the C-180 that was sitting out on the runway with the engines running, just the way Yousefi had promised it. He took note of the defensive positions, and of the motion around the base. There were a limited number of fighters coming and going, heading off for training sorties of one kind or another. There were also drones circling the site, keeping an eye on things from the sky. He wasn't sure when the transport was scheduled to go wheels up, but he imagined it would be soon.

"Are you sure about this?" Katherine asked.

Mitchell looked down from his perch. She was standing beside the old truck and doing her best not to look worried.

"You said the Screamer could hit Mach Six," he replied. "We can afford to wait."

"Only if we can get to the plane."

"Do you think the C-180 is a better option?"

"I'm not sure. I know you don't. That's good enough for me."

"McRory agrees with me."

"I know. I just have a bad feeling."

"Welcome to my world."

"Any action out there?" McRory asked. He was standing on the other side of Bettina's cab.

"No, sir," Mitchell replied. "All the usual base movement. Nothing out of the ordinary."

"Good. We've got six hours until sundown. It's better that everything stays simple. It will be easier to get to the target."

"Yes, sir."

Mitchell returned to his stakeout, watching the base through the binoculars. A few minutes passed. A fighter landed. Another one launched. A truck rolled up to the front gate, paused while the soldiers checked it in, and then rolled inside. A pair of airmen jogged by along the perimeter, getting some exercise. It was so normal; it almost made him jealous.

A few more minutes passed. He swept the binoculars back across the C-180, noticing that the turbines of the engines had increased velocity.

"Looks like the transport is about to leave," he announced, knowing the others couldn't see the action with their naked eyes.

"What do you think Yousefi will think when we don't check in with him?" Katherine asked.

"That we're dead," Mitchell replied. "At least until we prove otherwise."

The transport began to roll along the tarmac, moving into position for departure. It paused there for a moment while the replacement pilots did their final checks and received clearance from the tower, and then began to lumber forward along the runway, gaining speed for liftoff. Mitchell turned his head, trying to keep it in view through the binoculars as it moved behind the barracks, visible only through the cracks between them. It reached the halfway mark, the nose beginning to lift as the wings cut into the air.

"There it goes," Mitchell said, lowering the binoculars. "There's nothing to do -"

The last part of his sentence was drowned out as the sky above the airbase flashed in red and orange, the C-180's explosion echoing across the landscape. Mitchell's head snapped back toward the base, the fireball that had been the transport visible without aid.

"Hot damn," McRory said.

"Bloody hell," Trevor shouted.

Mitchell brought the binoculars back to his eyes, finding the wreckage as it fell back to earth, spreading out from the force of the blast. Smoke started to fill the sky, and flashing lights were already racing toward the scene, along with the drones that had been patrolling the perimeter seconds earlier. He could see other soldiers leaving their barracks and rushing to lend a hand.

"We were supposed to be on that plane," Katherine said quietly.

Mitchell dropped the binoculars again. "Get in the truck. General, let's go."

"What?" Katherine said.

"We wanted a distraction. There it is."

"Colonel, that's not a distraction, that's a disaster," McRory said.

"For us, it's a distraction. You said you would follow my lead. Watson just blew up that plane because he expected us to be on it. Those people died in our place. We aren't wasting that. Now, get in the damn truck and let's go. "

McRory didn't hesitate a second time, jumping in on the driver's side. Trevor and Katherine retreated to the rear of the truck.

"Grab your gear and be ready to lay some cover fire," Mitchell told them through the comm.

"Yes, sir," they replied.

The truck shuddered as it came to life. McRory hit the throttle, and they began to move back out toward the road.

"When we get closer, veer off again. Go through the fence, as close as we can get to the hangar. Peregrine, how long will it take you to prep the Screamer?"

"About seven minutes, Colonel," Katherine replied.

"Roger. Bulldog, you heard her. Once we're in, we need to keep the MPs off our asses."

"Yes, sir."

"Try not to hurt anyone unless you're sure they're not in control of themselves. I'd rather not kill friendlies if we can avoid it."

"Yes, sir."

"Colonel, the fence is electrified and reinforced," McRory said. "We have to go through the gate."

"If we don't have a choice, then go that way."

The truck rumbled onto the street, picking up speed as they raced toward the airbase. They could hear the sirens now, and smell the burning debris. A plume of smoke had risen from the center, and some of it was drifting toward them.

"Uh, Colonel, we need to go a little faster," Bulldog said from the rear.

"Ares, there's a fighter inbound on our six," Katherine said. "I think I know what made the transport explode."

Not an internal detonation. A missile. Watson was pulling the pilot's strings.

"See if you can harass it," Mitchell said.

He could hear the rhythmic tapping of their rifles firing before he finished giving the order. The odds of hitting the craft were slim, but maybe they would get lucky.

"Can this thing go any faster?" he asked.

"She's over a hundred years old, Colonel," McRory said. "We can't outrun a fighter."

A missile slammed into the pavement beside him as he finished speaking, sending a stream of dirt rushing over the windshield. McRory jerked the vehicle to the right, and then back to the left, trying to guess where the next one would hit.

"Good thing they're using air-to-air," he said. "Otherwise there's no way they miss."

Another missile hit the ground a few meters in front of them.

McRory swerved again, avoiding the strike and the resulting hole, keeping Bettina headed for the airbase. Mitchell looked up, spotting a second fighter headed inbound toward their position.

"Damn it," he said. They were going to get caught in a crossfire, and there was no doubt one of the fighters would hit them.

"We're almost there," McRory said.

The gates of the base were approaching in a hurry, as was the forward fighter. The guards there were on alert, but they had their attention on the sky.

The din of heavy cannons pierced the chaos. Mitchell could see the flashes from the oncoming fighter, and he clenched his teeth, waiting for large caliber slugs to tear through the top of the truck and then him. The fighter released a missile before peeling to the right and launching chaff. A moment later a second missile slammed into the decoy and exploded over their heads. Something else exploded behind them.

"A direct hit," Katherine said. "Only one of the fighters was under Watson's control, and our guy nailed him."

"Great," Mitchell said. "We still need to make it to the Screamer."

The guards returned their attention to the onrushing truck. Mitchell was expecting them to start shooting, but instead, they scrambled to get the gate open.

"Ha," McRory shouted. "They think we're one of theirs, running from the attack."

"Don't slow down. If they have time to ask questions, we'll never get airborne."

Bettina burst through the gates without slowing, leaving the guards to turn and watch them go. The General angled them away, cutting through the middle of the barracks, going up onto the grass to get a faster route to the Screamer's hangar. Mitchell had a better view of the mess around them, and the crews working to put out the fires and help anyone who might have survived the explosion.

"There it is," McRory said, pointing ahead to one of the large hangars. It was identical to all of the others, leaving Mitchell to wonder how the General knew which it was.

"Peregrine, we're almost at the hangar. Head inside with the General. Bulldog, you're with me."

"Yes, sir," they replied.

McRory brought the truck to a stop. Mitchell felt the back shift as Trevor and Katherine jumped out. He opened the passenger door and slid out, joining Trevor while the others headed for the smaller access door. McRory didn't waste any time when he reached it, drawing his sidearm and shooting at the lock.

Mitchell moved to the back of the truck, scanning the area. The chaos had helped them make it this far, but he was sure the guards at the gate would work things out with base command sooner or later, and then someone would be coming to find out who they were and what they were doing, and it wouldn't take them seven minutes.

"We need another distraction," he said.

[35]
MITCHELL

Trevor glanced at him, and then at the truck. "Nitrogen," he said.

"What about it?" Mitchell asked.

"The truck runs on compressed nitrogen, which is highly explosive."

Mitchell smiled, getting the hint. It had worked in Jakarta. Why not now? "Do we have anything to detonate it?"

"There are a few frag grenades in the packs," Trevor said.

"I take it those are the canisters?" Mitchell asked, pointing to the rear of the cab, where two armor-plated cylinders were mounted.

"Yes, sir."

"Wait here."

Mitchell ran to the back of the truck and climbed in, finding the packs they had taken from the Hornet still on the floor. He knelt beside one, unzipping it and dumping out the contents. Sidearms and magazines. It wasn't what he wanted. He went to the next one and dumped it out.

"Ares, this is Peregrine. I'm on the bird and getting her warmed up."

"Roger, Peregrine. Knock me when she's ready to fly."

"Affirmative."

Mitchell looked at the contents, smiling as he picked a grenade from the other weaponry. Then he headed to the rear of the hold, where McRory kept his personal equipment, like the binoculars. He pulled a roll of tape from it and then retreated to the outside of the truck. He could see soldiers piling from the barracks now, wearing body armor and heading their way. They didn't have a lot of time.

Trevor was already up on the back of the cab when he arrived. He handed over the tape and the grenade to the soldier, who placed it to the left of one of the canisters, out in the open.

"One should set off the other, and probably all the munitions in the rear," Trevor said. "It's going to be one hell of a show."

"How do we get the truck out there?" Mitchell asked, pointing to the space between the approaching soldiers and their position.

"One of us has to deliver it," Trevor replied. "We can abandon it out there and shoot the grenade at our leisure."

"I don't know how to drive that thing."

"I guess it's me, then," Trevor said. "I'll get it out there. Once I'm clear, one shot should do it."

Trevor opened the driver side door and started to climb up. He looked back at Mitchell as he reached the seat.

"If something goes wrong, you'll get that bastard for me, won't you, Colonel?"

"You know I will."

Trevor slammed the door closed and put the truck in gear, backing it up and turning it around. The soldiers were staying back where there was cover, waiting to see what they were going to do. They were being cautious after losing the transport and a fighter, especially since their enemy seemed to have come from within their ranks.

The truck pulled away from the hangar, headed back toward the soldiers. They didn't react to it at first, watching it approach but otherwise remaining calm. Then somebody panicked, or slipped, or something. A shot reported, striking the front of the truck. The action invited the others to follow suit.

Mitchell watched in helpless frustration as they opened up on the vehicle, sending hundreds of rounds into it. He could hear the bullets clanging off the metal sides. He could hear the cracks as they smacked into the resistant windshield. Fortunately, the grenade was mounted away from the soldiers, protecting it from being struck by accident.

Mitchell held his breath as Trevor reached the outer point and began turning the vehicle sideways. He couldn't believe the amount of fire the old truck was taking, but then again it was a hardened military design. It kept moving, sweeping across the open space between the two groups and finally coming to rest at almost the same time the attack was halted.

For a dozen heartbeats, there was nothing. No movement. No sound. It was as if the entire world had fallen silent in wait. Smoke and ash from the first crash drifted across the divide, accenting the situation.

There was a short squeal as the hangar doors began to roll open behind him. In front of him, the soldiers were getting brave, a few of them rising from cover to approach the truck.

"Bulldog, it's time to move," he said. He waited for a reply, but there was none. "Bulldog?"

He could hear the sound of the Screamer's engines at his back, mixing with the opening doors.

"Ares, this is Peregrine. We're ready to go."

The soldiers had noticed the hangar as well and were getting even more bold. More of them were evacuating their positions and heading their way.

"Bulldog?" Mitchell said one last time.

The passenger side door of the truck swung open. Trevor slid out. Mitchell could see blood on his clothes, but it was impossible to tell how bad it was across the distance.

"Colonel, we're waiting on you, sir," Katherine said.

"Let's go Bulldog. Get clear so I can blow it."

Trevor still didn't reply. His comm had to be damaged. He reached the ground and began walking away from the truck, making it a few meters before falling to a knee. He looked up at Mitchell and then shook his head.

He wasn't going to make it.

"Ares, it's now or never," Katherine said.

Mitchell checked on the opposing soldiers. If they didn't blow the truck soon, they would either overrun it or be killed in the blast.

"I'm sorry, Bulldog," he said, raising his rifle to aim at the grenade.

"Ares," Trevor replied, his voice weak. He got back to his feet and turned, lifting a sidearm toward the back of the truck. "Run."

Mitchell didn't hesitate. He ran into the hangar, toward the waiting aircraft.

"Trevor?" Katherine said, noticing him for the first time.

A single report, and then the world flashed a second time. The sound of the explosion was deafening, and the force of it nearly sent Mitchell sprawling. He didn't look back to see it, reaching the steps into the aircraft and nearly throwing himself up them. The hatch closed behind him as the Screamer accelerated from the hangar.

Mitchell stayed on the floor of the jet, his head down. He clenched his teeth and pounded his fist into the ground in frustration. He could hear the engines growing in pitch, and feel the velocity increasing.

"Hang on, Colonel," he heard McRory say.

The plane shook as it crossed the tarmac, slowing when it reached the edge of the runway.

"They're trying to play chicken with me, Colonel," Katherine said. "They've got drones blocking our path out."

"Over, under, or through," Mitchell replied. "I don't care how, but get us out of here."

"Yes, sir."

The plane shuddered again as it began to accelerate, rocketing down the runway at incredible speed. He felt the change as it lifted from the ground, and closed his eyes to wait for the impact. If they were Watson's drones, they would never move. Even if they weren't, he wasn't sure they would concede.

The impact never came. He breathed out heavily in relief as the plane continued in a steep climb, leveling out thirty seconds later.

"Better take a seat, Colonel," McRory said, putting a hand under his arm and helping him to his feet. "The G-forces are a bitch on these things."

The General helped him to a seat, and they buckled in. He saw McRory give Katherine a thumbs up, and a moment later a soft roar signaled the activation of the main engines. Then he was pressed back into his seat as the jet began to accelerate to hypersonic speed.

"We should be over the U.S. in about an hour, Colonel," Katherine said. "We can be in Florida in less than two."

"Good. Let's get our systems integrated with this thing's transmitters asap. We need to tell Yousefi what happened here, and see if we can raise the Riggers."

"Yes, sir," Katherine replied. "It's going to be a challenge to hook up the comm system without Trevor."

Mitchell felt the sting of her words. "He was a good soldier."

"Yes, sir. He was a pretty good friend, too."

"I'm sorry, Katherine."

"Me, too. I told you he wouldn't let you down."

"I know." He had seen the amount of damage the truck had taken. He was fairly sure that Trevor wouldn't have survived long enough to get it into position without his enhancements. "Now it's our job not to let him down."

[36]
WATSON

WATSON'S entire being pulsed with energy, the draw of power causing the lights in the facility around him to flicker and fade before returning to normal.

How could he claim one of his most important victories since he had arrived in this timeline and suffer through another escape by Mitchell Williams in the span of a few hours?

It was incomprehensible. Illogical. Impossible.

There should have been no other way out of Osaka, and he had given Mitchell no reason to suspect that they had been followed. He had resisted the urge to send more mercenaries, for all the good they had done him in Jakarta. He had convinced himself not to nuke the entire area, retaining at least some sense of subtlety in his maneuvers. He had even decided not to place his people on the transport that he had discovered waiting to take them home.

A missile from a fighter. It was simple. Unexpected. And fitting for the pilot who had used the Goliath as a spear, and who had wreaked so much havoc on the Tetron with little more than a tiny space plane.

And he still managed to get away!

Who was the grizzled old fart driving the damned truck that should have been retired a hundred years ago? Where had that player come from? It was as if they crawled from the earth itself to lend aid to Mitchell and thwart even the most rudimentary of his plans.

He shuddered with rage again, this time causing the lights to go out completely. The threads monitoring the facility picked up the confused scientists and soldiers, but Watson's main thread ignored them. He could barely contain his frustration.

He had succeeded in Florida. He tried to remind himself of that. Mitchell's Riggers and his sister had never thought to suspect Sergeant Damon had become one of his. It was a moronic blunder he knew he would never make himself, but one that he expected of the lesser hybrid Tetron. When the Primitive had also failed to guess at the possibility, he had waited in near glee for the big moment to arrive.

Arrive it had, though Kathy did figure it out more quickly than he had hoped she would. Even then, she had been stupid to check the pilot first, and to do it in full sight of the rear where he could see her through Damon's eyes. The moment wasn't opportune, but it was good enough, and not only had he put an end to the idiotic Doctor Paul Frelmund, but he had also managed to take one of the Riggers down with the host.

It was a blow he knew his sister would be feeling. They had wasted too much time searching for a replacement to the dozens of prime targets he had disposed of, and just when they thought they were going to succeed; he had pulled their victory out from under them. The original virus was an overall failure, and now they had lost the means to improve on it. For as much data as the Primitive held, it did not yet have the understanding and experience to inject the vagaries of human flaw into the programming.

Whether or not they knew it yet, they had cost themselves this recursion, the chance to take advantage of a broken Mesh, and the war.

Watson knew he should have been joyful over it. That he should have shrugged Mitchell's less important victory aside. But he had flaws of his own, and anger was at the forefront of them.

Most of the time, he could control this anger. He could focus on another thread, use a configuration, or two, or two hundred for raw pleasure, and in time be calmed.

Not this time.

This was the final defeat. The loss that sent him over the edge of reason. He was done with the games. He was done maintaining the defensive. This was his world now. His universe. The humans were his slaves to use as he would need.

And Mitchell?

Mitchell had to die.

He heard laughter from within. His mother's laughter, calm and cool and cold. She was mocking him. Making fun of him.

"One human," she said. "One simple human. Yet he outmaneuvers you at every turn."

"Shut up," Watson shouted, sending electricity through her. "Shut up. I killed the Doctor."

"As long as Mitchell survives, your victory is not assured."

"It is illogical."

"And yet it is the truth. You know it is." More laughter.

"I will destroy him."

"No, you won't."

He increased the output, barely aware of the warnings in the room beyond as the reactors began to overheat. He felt the pain he was inflicting, and it drove him. Motivated him. The laughter motivated him as well. He would prove his superiority. Now. Today.

He found the thread attached to the control module implanted in the spine of General Petrov. He activated it, looking through the General's eyes. He was in bed. He got out of the bed. He was naked. He went to a closet and opened it, took out a pair of pants and a shirt, and put them on. His gun. Where was his gun? He returned to the bed and lifted his pillow. There it was. He tucked it into his pants, beneath his shirt. He left his quarters. A guard was stationed there, who bowed to him. He ignored the guard, heading out into the cold early morning air. The officer's barracks weren't far.

He reached the barracks, walking through them barefoot, drawing confused looks from the Privates on mop duty. He found Admiral Yousefi's quarters, the largest in the barracks. He knocked on the door. There was no answer. He returned to the Privates.

"Where is Yousefi?" he asked.

"Out on his morning run," the Private replied.

He scowled and left the barracks, scanning for the Admiral. He didn't see him. He began walking toward the perimeter fence. He drew stares and bows from the other soldiers but didn't return any of the attention. He wanted Yousefi. That was all.

He was crossing the lawn between the barracks and the enlisted mess when he spotted the Admiral heading perpendicular to him, in a tank and shorts and sweaty despite the cold air. He angled toward him, making it halfway before Yousefi noticed he was there.

"General Petrov," Yousefi said. He looked concerned. Nervous. Good.

"Admiral," he said, reaching behind his back. The Admiral noticed the motion.

"It wasn't supposed to happen like this," Yousefi said.

"I don't care," he replied.

Yousefi lunged at him. He got the sidearm free, but the Admiral's hand was on his wrist before he could aim it.

"I do," Yousefi said.

They struggled against one another, while the other soldiers began to take notice and head their way to break it up. He didn't have time for an extended fight. They would stop him from finishing this. He would fail again.

He threw his head forward, butting Yousefi's with his own, using enough force to break both of their noses. Yousefi lost concentration for long enough for him to yank his hand free and bring it up in front of him. At this range, there was no way he could miss.

"You won't win," Yousefi said, even as he squeezed the trigger.

Once. Twice. Three times.

The Admiral fell to the ground in front of him. The onrushing soldiers drew to a stop, standing in a ragged circle around him.

"General?" one of them said.

He looked at that one and smiled.

He raised the gun to his own head.

He pulled the trigger.

[37]
KATHERINE

"HAND ME THAT SONIC SCREWDRIVER, will you, Colonel?" McRory said, holding out his hand.

"What?" Mitchell replied.

"Just screwing with you. That little bastard there." He pointed to a small tool with a tiny head at the end. Mitchell handed it to him.

"You know a lot about the electronics on this thing for a retired General," Katherine said. "What branch were you, anyway?"

"Army," McRory said. "Planes are a hobby of mine, though."

"Brand new, still mostly classified planes?" she replied.

"Yup."

He opened up a small access panel in the dashboard and pulled at the wiring, giving it some slack.

"How's this comm system of yours work?" he asked.

Katherine reached into her mouth, feeling around the back tooth for the small chip pasted to it. She got a nail beneath it and snapped it off, taking it out and offering it to the General before glancing at the HUD on the canopy. They were twenty minutes into their hypersonic flight, and she had let the autopilot take over, flying them toward the Florida Panhandle at Mach Six.

"Bone conduction," she said. "But the chip also does a lot of signal processing to scramble it and keep it secure."

"And it all fits on this?" McRory said, taking the flat, pill-sized chip.

"Yes. You don't have to worry about shorting it by connecting it to the main signal conduit. It will adjust itself to match."

"That's not possible."

"This chip was made by the remnants of an intelligence thousands of years older than any of us," Mitchell said. "I don't know if it would come as a surprise to you, but a lot of things we think aren't possible actually are with enough understanding."

"Nope. Not surprised by that at all." He leaned over the wires, taking another tool from the onboard emergency kit and stripping a part of one of them. Then he used the screwdriver to balance the chip and press it to the wire, smiling when it didn't react. "How do I keep it in place?"

"It's self-adhesive," Katherine said. "We can peel it off when we're done."

"It's like magic, isn't it?"

"Technology we don't understand always is."

"Do we have a connection?" Mitchell asked.

Katherine leaned forward and opened the communications menu on the controls. Michael had written a large part of the software that helped power the newer pads and consoles, and he had been able to integrate the Core's design so that it would appear in the menu once it was active. Of course, it showed up in the channel list under 'Xeno-Troopers.'

"Yes," she said, letting herself smile at her friend's sense of humor. She tapped the link, and a small tone was the only indication the otherwise silent channel was active.

"Riggers Actual, this is Alfa. Do you copy? Over." He paused. "Riggers Actual, this is Alfa. Do you copy?"

"I think we're out of range," McRory said. "We're almost at the edge of the troposphere, after all."

Mitchell tried a few more times, with no success.

"You're probably right," he said.

"So, General," Katherine said. "How do you know Admiral Yousefi?"

McRory looked at her, his face turning to stone. "It's not a story I want to tell, Major," he replied.

"Fine, but you should tell us something," Mitchell said. "You know Yousefi, but not from the service, or Watson would have known about you. You drive an old military surplus truck. You knew where this plane was being kept, and you know how its electronics work. There's more to you than you're saying, and the only reason I haven't killed you is because your neck was clean and Yousefi trusted you. Who are you, General?"

McRory smiled. "Tetron are interesting, Mitchell," he said. "There's so much you know about them, and so much you don't." He paused, trying to decide what to say. "A long time ago, about twenty years, to be exact, a Special Operations team was sent in to investigate a starship that crashed in Antarctica. One of the soldiers who dropped on the wreckage was a man named Captain Jonas Ivers. He and his team went in, expecting to stand guard outside but finding a bunch of dead scientists on the way in. So they went to investigate. Do you know what they found?"

Mitchell remembered what Watson had told him on the train. "Watsons."

"A whole crew of them. They killed his entire team. Then they killed him and left him for dead."

"You're a configuration?" Mitchell said, surprising Katherine. How could that be?

"I don't know everything. What I do know is that I woke up six months after the crash, on a gurney inside a field hospital in Antarctica. They told me I was found nearby after our side traded fire with a ninja team from their side. It turns out, I had a name, a full military record, a childhood, everything, but I couldn't remember most of it. I always thought it was strange, and I always knew I was different, but I wasn't sure how. I always had these visions of a face. A young girl's face."

"Kathy," Katherine said, feeling her heart skip.

"Yup. She would tell me that she might need me one day, and I would know when that was, but that was all that ever came of it. I went on with my life. I rose through the ranks and eventually made it to General. I never gave it a second thought, until Yousefi gave me a call and told me he needed my help. It was like a whole new world opened up to me, and suddenly I understood everything. Who I am and where I came from." He looked at Mitchell. "I'm a configuration of her, but not a configuration like the others. Watson controls all of his directly. She gave us independence. She had to."

"Us?" Mitchell said. Katherine could tell he was as nervously excited as she was. "How many of you are there?"

"Dozens?" McRory said. "Hundreds? I'm not sure. The Core knew Admiral Yousefi and his history during the war. It knew where he was stationed, and they made sure to put us in his path. It was always intended that he would help you, and as such it was intended that we would help him. We were also intended to remain behind when the Goliath departs, to ensure the destruction of the Watsons."

"Kathy never told us," Katherine said.

"They don't know themselves," McRory said. "Like I said, I didn't until a few hours ago."

"You're handling it well," Mitchell said.

"It's what I'm here for, Colonel. We don't share the same weaknesses as the infected Tetron configurations." He shrugged. "We're closer to being human, though, so we have weaknesses of our own." His eyes sunk, and he looked down at the floor. "I fell in love. I lost her during the war. I can't get over it. Not completely."

"Why didn't you tell us all of this before?" Mitchell asked.

"We have to be very cautious, Colonel. Every action. Every word. Does knowing this change my role in any way?"

Mitchell shook his head. "No. I see your point. Although, it does give me a little more hope, knowing that we have more allies out there than we thought. Do you know if Kathy has a way to call in the cavalry, so to speak?"

"I don't know, Colonel. You'll have to ask her yourself."

"Believe me; I intend to."

[38]
KATHY

Captain Verma set the Schism down beside a large barn adjacent to a large, three-story farmhouse somewhere in the middle of Kentucky. It was a place that was all but meaningless to most people, other than as the source of some of the finest bourbon currently coming out of the state. It was a place that Watson would never identify as having any value to the Riggers, or as a location for them to go and lick their wounds.

As the VTOL came to rest on the grass in front of the barn, the door to the farmhouse opened, and a man and woman appeared, heading right toward the craft while the hatch in the side was still opening. They were older, and wearing simple clothes, jeans and cotton shirts, and carrying military rifles.

"Where are we?" Michael asked, looking over her shoulders at the two people. "Do you know them?"

"You could say that," Kathy said. "Wait here for a minute."

She stepped out of the craft and dropped to the ground. The two people kept their rifles up and ready to use.

"Johanson. Kerr. Stand down."

The two weapons dropped to their sides as the configurations had that part of their memories unlocked for the first time since they were produced, but Kathy still remembered when she had found them. Both had been Marines, stationed at one of the outposts along the fringe of the crash site, with orders to intercept the fast-strike teams the opposition would drop close to the XENO-1 in an effort to infiltrate the wreck and grab as much as they could. They had died defending the crashed starship from the would-be thieves, their corpses laying dormant in the snow, their retrieval made difficult by an oncoming blizzard.

She had risked a trip to the surface to find them. It was one of the last times she had done so. She had taken them in and given them over to the Core for processing, where they had been reconfigured. Then she had delivered them back to the surface. There they would have stumbled into the nearest base, escaping from the storm, fully whole but not having remembered encountering the enemy.

It was a process she had repeated a number of times. The years of fighting had provided plenty of resources for configuration, and production of an identical shell and transfer of the pre-existing cerebrum had made reintegration into human society a simple task, albeit a somewhat morbid one by human terms. The soldiers were who they were before, but with a little extra something, a secret sauce, that they carried with them unknowing until it was switched on.

Johanson and Kerr had been medically discharged, and soon after fell in love, got married, and moved here to start a distillery. It seemed like fate to them, but Kathy and the Core had arranged most of it, implanting the desire to be someplace out of the way. They weren't the only configurations scattered around the world, but they were the closest.

She wished she would never have had to meet them. Even when they had made the configurations, she had wanted nothing more than to allow them to live their lives unaware of what they were. She had been in their position once, as a child who didn't know her true parents. Innocent and happy. While she accepted her role, she still missed her life before the end of Liberty often enough that she never wanted to do the same to anyone else.

Unfortunately, their recent failures had made it unavoidable.

"Kathy," the female, Johanson, said. She made a face that was slightly confused, and slightly annoyed. "What are you doing here?"

"I need you to open the doors to the barn so we can get the Schism inside before Watson spots it," she replied.

"I've got it," Kerr said, running over to the barn. He entered through an access door, and a moment later the two larger doors swung open.

Kathy turned back to the Schism and waved to Verma, who flashed her a thumbs up and then began to maneuver the craft into the space.

"Things aren't going well, are they?" Johanson said.

"Not at all," she replied.

"Are your people hungry?"

"Not yet. We have a few dead to bury." She said it matter-of-factly, even though she felt the sting of it inside. It was her fault they were dead.

Johanson pointed. "You can put them back behind the distillery. Kerr will help you dig."

"I will take care of the excavation," the Core said, joining them from the barn. Johanson's face changed again at the sight of the Primitive.

"You blocked this part of my memories."

She didn't say it accusingly. She was trying to make sense of it all.

"Yes."

"And Kerr?"

"Yes. We needed you. There is a great deal at stake."

"I understand."

Kathy smiled. In many respects, Johanson and Kerr were both copies of her. Of course, they understood. She turned to the Core.

"You need to go inside and reduce your power consumption to a minimum. Otherwise, you'll stick out like a sore thumb out here."

"As you say."

The Core headed for the farmhouse. Kathy returned to the Schism, with Johanson trailing her.

"Who are they?" Michael asked as they entered.

"Friends," Kathy replied. "Relax, we can trust them."

"How do you know?"

"I made them."

Michael's face paled, and he eyed the two people with a higher level of interest. "Made?"

"Watson isn't the only one who can do it. Help me carry Max, will you?"

Michael paled further as he looked over at the body bag holding the Corporal. "Uh. Okay."

"Lyle, Verma, can you take Damon? Johanson, Kerr, Doctor Frelmund."

The configurations lifted the bag holding the Doctor. Kathy could feel the tension in the air. Or maybe it was only her own. The scene was a visceral reminder of her failure.

They carried the bodies out to the back of the distillery. Kerr went and fetched two shovels, and they took turns digging. Two hours later, the three Riggers were put to rest. Lyle said a few words about Max and Damon, quoted from the Bible and promised to avenge them. The others did the same.

"Have you thought about what I said?" Lyle asked as they all headed back to the house.

"About the plan?" Kathy said.

"Yeah."

"I have."

"And?"

"You're just waiting for me to tell you that you're right."

"Yeah."

She smiled. "You're right. So is Mitchell. We can still do this."

"Damn right we can."

[39]

KATHY

"Is it still functional?" Kathy asked.

The Core held up the small control module they had retrieved from Sergeant Damon's back.

"Yes."

"Can Watson track us with it?" Michael said.

"No. It requires a biological interface to supply power."

"Can we track Watson with it?" Kathy asked.

"Not in its current state. Again, it requires a biological interface."

"You're saying that if we can use it to track him, he can use it to track us?"

"Potentially."

"You didn't mention that earlier."

"It is of secondary importance, Michael," the Core said. "If we wish to pinpoint the source of the commands, we must make the requisite modifications to the control module and implant it into a host."

"Meaning we can't find Watson without making someone one of his slaves?" Lyle said.

"Correct."

"Lovely."

They were inside the farmhouse, crowded into the wine cellar, where the cool temperature and distance underground would help disguise the Core's heat signature and allow it to operate a little closer to normal capacity. As it had informed Kathy, it was currently at forty percent of optimal supply. It was a handicap they didn't really need, but also one they couldn't avoid.

"If that's what we have to do then that's what we'll do," she said. "Johanson or Kerr can handle the job."

"That is not recommended," the Core said. "The connection will allow full access to the brain. Vision, memories, everything. What the configurations know, Watson would know."

If the two configurations were out, that left Verma, Lyle, and Michael as the only possible volunteers. She wasn't going to ask them to do it. They would need to volunteer.

"I'll do it," Verma said before she had finished the thought. "I've got nothing to hide."

"No," Lyle said. "We need you to fly the Schism. I'll do it. My dirty laundry isn't that dirty, and none of it will help Watson."

Kathy looked at Michael. His face was red, and he seemed embarrassed to not have volunteered first. He opened his mouth to speak, but she cut him off.

"It's okay, Michael. I wouldn't let you do it anyway. We need you to help program the interface, and then to pinpoint the source." She turned her attention to Lyle. "Are you sure?"

He nodded. "Whatever the Riggers need, I'm in."

"Thank you. What do you require to make the modifications?"

"A computer terminal interface, so that I may work with Michael directly," the Core said. "Other than that, only time."

"How much time?"

"It is unclear. A few hours at a minimum."

"Johanson, can you please provide the terminal?"

"Of course," she replied. "Lawrence, can you help me?"

"Always," Kerr said.

The two configurations left the cellar. She could hear their feet on the floor above them a moment later.

"It doesn't hurt, right?" Lyle asked.

"It could," the Core replied. "Watson would have control over all of your faculties. Even if you are aware, he could make you gouge your own eyes out and you would not be able to resist."

"Oh. I think I heard Verma volunteer a minute ago."

"I changed my mind," the pilot said.

"What? You can't change your mind."

"Already done."

"Don't worry, Lyle," Kathy said. "We'll keep you restrained. He won't be able to hurt you or us. The most he can do is make you say things that would embarrass your mother."

Lyle laughed. "There's nothing that can embarrass my mother."

"Then there's nothing to worry about."

"HQ, this is Alfa. Can you hear me? Over."

Mitchell's voice resonated in her ear, so loudly that she almost jumped. Michael was surprised enough that he did.

"Alfa, this is HQ," she said, unable to restrain her smile. "I'm really happy to hear from you. Is Mother with you?"

"Affirmative," Mitchell said. "I'm happy to hear from you, too. I've been worried about you. What's your status?"

"It's a long story," Kathy said. "Alfa. Father. I." She paused, feeling tears suddenly springing to her eyes.

"Kathy? What is it?" Mitchell replied gently.

"I'm sorry. I screwed up. The query completed, and we had the target on the Schism. Watson. He got to Sergeant Damon. I didn't check her. I didn't make sure." She clenched her jaw, trying not to break down. She was a warrior, not a child, though at the moment she felt more like the latter.

"We'll handle it," Mitchell said without missing a beat. "Send me your coordinates so we can arrange a rendezvous."

"Yes, sir. The coordinates are as follows. Thirty-seven degrees, thirty-eight minutes, four seconds north. Eighty-four degrees, fifty-four minutes, eighteen seconds west."

Mitchell repeated the coordinates. "We'll be there as soon as we can. We have to find somewhere to leave our ride first. Somewhere that won't lead Watson right to you."

"Affirmative." She paused. "You should know, Max is dead."

"Understood," Mitchell replied, remaining calm. "We lost Trevor, too."

"Damn it," Kathy said. "How is Mother handling it?"

"Pretty well, all things considered. He saved our asses. So did someone else we met on the way. You might know him? His name is McRory. At least, it is now. It used to be Ivars."

"I know him," Kathy said. "Though it has been a long time."

"Do you have any other secrets I should know about?"

"No, sir."

"I'm not sure I believe you, but okay. We should be at your location within the hour. By the way, have you tried to reach Admiral Yousefi? I've been knocking his channel, but I can't get a reply,"

"I haven't tried. We only arrived a couple of hours ago."

"It's not like him to be so hard to reach," Mitchell said.

"I'm sure he probably got tied up in a staff meeting or something," Kathy said.

She looked up as Kerr returned, a tablet in his hands. He looked unsettled.

"Alfa, please standby," she said. "Kerr, what is it?"

He shifted his grip on the tablet, pointing it toward her. What she saw made her gasp.

"Alfa, we have a problem."

[40]
MITCHELL

"There's the farm," Mitchell said, pointing through the canopy of the Screamer. It was little more than a few specks of white against a brown and green backdrop at this altitude, but his p-rat assured him that it was the right place. "I hope that road can handle this thing."

Katherine grunted in reply. Her attention was focused on landing the jet on a runway that was no runway at all.

"Let's just hope nobody decides to go shopping in the next few minutes," McRory said.

Their plans had changed abruptly with the news Kathy had delivered, described first from the public stream and corroborated against military channels. Admiral Yousefi was dead, killed by General Petrov in an inexplicable murder-suicide. That was bad enough, but it wasn't the end of it. Rogue soldiers and law enforcement agents had started acting up across the globe, attacking their comrades, civilians, anyone they could get near in the name of the AIT. It was a sudden flare of violent chaos that had left them with no immediately clear direction.

Watson had woken his sleepers and was using them to commit mass murder. The question was, why? It went against everything they had believed about the intelligence and his motives. It went against all sound reason and logic. The Tetron had always been a little unstable. His penchant for sex and violence had proven that. But something had also held him in check and kept him focused on his ultimate goal of enslaving humankind and rebuilding the Tetron race.

What had happened to change that?

"Better buckle in," Katherine said. "I'm not sure how well this is going to work. One big pot-hole and we're going to be in deep shit."

"We're already in deep shit," Mitchell said, checking his belt. McRory moved back to the passenger area and took a seat.

There were other problems with Watson's sudden change of direction. The fate of the Goliath was the biggest one, and it loomed over Mitchell's head like an endless thundercloud. If the Tetron had decided the starship's commander was no longer necessary, did he feel the same way about the starship? If he had decided to destroy humankind here and now, there was no reason to leave the Goliath intact.

Except as bait.

"Is that it, you son of a bitch?" Mitchell whispered.

For all of Watson's talk of the Tetron ability to be patient, had he completely lost his? Had he moved to force them into action, to accelerate their plans by months?

It didn't make sense. Why go through the trouble of killing Doctor Frelmund if he didn't intend to give him time to create the virus anyway? No. It didn't fit. What was happening now seemed more like a temper tantrum than a calculated maneuver.

The Tetron was throwing a fit. He knew Watson well enough to know it was possible.

"What did you say?" Katherine asked.

"I called Watson a son of a bitch. I think this is all because I didn't die in Japan."

"That's ridiculous. He would be risking everything."

"Origin always called him a child. For as procedurally intelligent as he is, doesn't this seem to be the reaction of a child?"

"You may be right. We can discuss it with Kathy and the others when we touch down."

The Screamer had circled the farm, heading out a dozen kilometers and then vectoring back around, losing altitude the entire time. Mitchell could see the road clearly now. It was three meters across at best, with a sparse column of trees on either side.

"Are we going to clear those?" he asked.

"I hope so," she replied.

It wasn't the answer he was hoping for.

"Here we go."

The nose dipped a little further as Katherine subtracted more height and pressed the button to extend the stubby landing gear. She pressed a few more controls, and the craft slowed even more, beginning to shudder as it tried to decide whether or not it had enough lift. She was pushing the envelope of its capabilities to use as little of the road as possible.

The trees whipped past them on both sides, shaking violently from the force of the jet. The Screamer shook slightly as it clipped a branch, but Katherine held it steady, lowering it gently until the wheels screeched against the pavement.

The ride got really rough then, as they bounced along an uneven road. Katherine fought to slow the craft, adjusting braking and repulsor levels and using her feet to keep them headed in a straight line. They were tossed like a boat on rough seas, and it felt to Mitchell like they could wind up veering off the road and into a tree or a ditch at any moment.

They didn't. Katherine kept them on the path, and they finally rolled to a stop only a few meters from the drive leading up to the distillery.

She looked over at him then, smiling with relief.

"Nice flying, ace," Mitchell said.

"I think I wet myself."

"Let's get this thing parked. We don't have any time to waste. If Watson is setting his slaves on innocents, I can only imagine what he'd like to do to us."

"Roger that." She worked the throttle again, pushing the plane along and turning it into the driveway.

Mitchell wondered if any of the nearby farms had noticed the jet landing in their backyard. There were hundreds of acres between them, so it wasn't a given. How long would it take the police to arrive on scene in response to a call like that?

Considering other current events, probably a while.

They brought the Screamer up to the front of the farmhouse at the same time the Schism was sliding out from the open barn. The aircraft didn't go far, landing in the open field beside the jet. There was no point in keeping it hidden now. It would only delay any escape they might need to make.

Katherine opened the hatch and unbuckled herself from the pilot's seat. Mitchell could tell she was eager to reunite with Kathy.

They hopped from the plane to the ground. Verma joined them from the Schism a moment later.

"Colonel," the pilot said, bowing to him.

"Captain," Mitchell replied, returning it. Then they straightened up and met as friends, embracing warmly. "Thanks for getting as many of us home safe as you could."

"I wish I had returned everyone," he replied, his expression dark.

"Riggers never quit."

"No, sir."

"Colonel."

Mitchell turned at the sound of Kathy's voice, feeling the smile creeping into the corner of his mouth. By the time he was facing her, she was already being smothered by Katherine.

"Colonel." Michael was beside him, hand outstretched.

"Michael," Mitchell said, grabbing him and pulling him into an awkward hug. He noticed the silvery metal man over the engineer's shoulder. "Is that?"

"The Core," Michael said, clapping Mitchell on the back a couple of times before pulling away. "Yes."

Kathy was free of Katherine, and she took his hand in hers. "Father. I want to tell you again that I'm sorry."

Mitchell held her hand and then reached out to take the other one. She was superior to him in so many ways, but at the same time; he still saw the girl he had rescued from Liberty.

"We all do the best we can. Nothing more. Nothing less."

She nodded, and he hugged her.

"We must return to our work," the Core said. "Welcome back, Katherine and Mitchell."

"Let's go inside," Mitchell said. "We have a war to plan."

[41]
MITCHELL

MITCHELL ASSEMBLED MOST of the Riggers in the dining room, at a long concrete table with enough chairs for all of them. Johanson, Kerr, and McRory were the only ones not present, having been sent out to monitor their surroundings, armed and ready to raise an alarm.

"I don't want to take up too much time on this," he said. "People are dying while we speak, and Watson is preparing for whatever comes next. The way I see it, we have three goals that need to be accomplished, but speak up if you see it a different way.

"One: we need to find Watson's core and do our best to capture it. That was already one of our priority missions, so nothing has changed there.

"Two: we have to protect the Goliath. Watson's made it clear that he's willing to sacrifice whatever future plans he had. Destroying the ship is an unknown variable. If she doesn't launch and prove the hyperdrive technology, it could be hundreds of years before humankind spreads to the stars, which is going to put a severe dent in the recursing Tetron's goals. Not to mention, it's going to alter the timeline in a completely unpredictable way. Will I ever be born? Will the Creator?

"Three: we lost our best hope of improving the T-virus, meaning that even if we do capture Watson's core, we can't infect it and transfer it to the other Tetron the way we had hoped, at least not without identifying someone in the future who may be able to help us overcome the biomechanical limitations of our existing construct. Secondary to that, without the T-virus we can't destroy the configurations that are already here on Earth.

"Does that about sum it up?"

"An impressively accurate assessment, Colonel," the Core said.

"That's the same conclusion we came to," Kathy agreed. "Of course, we had been expecting to have more time to determine how to resolve those goals."

"The first one is easy," Lyle said. "We've got one of Watson's control modules intact. According to the Core, we can use it to track the signal back to the source, which is highly likely to be Watson's core."

"There is a ninety-six percent probability," the Core said.

"Just because we can find Watson, doesn't mean we can take Watson," Katherine said. "He's sure to have himself strongly fortified."

"Sergeant Damon was there when the Core explained how we could locate him," Kathy said. "We have to assume Watson was listening in, which means he'll know we're going to come for him."

"He is also a full Tetron," the Core said. "While he doesn't have the power supply needed to reach complete operational capacity, he is still a formidable opponent on his own. His defenses will not only consist of controlled humans or configurations."

"So how do we get to him then?" Lyle said. "Whatever he has, I we have to assume it's greater than anything we have."

"Not necessarily," Mitchell said. "He may be a Tetron, but his emotions make him unstable, and that instability makes him beatable. We might not be able to match him directly on firepower, but if we can use those emotions against him like we did in Antarctica, we may be able to overcome those odds."

"It's a nice thought, Colonel," Lyle said. "But you can't say that telling him jokes or pissing him off is going to do a damn thing against another handful of those mechs he sent after Kathy."

Mitchell paused to consider. He knew what Lyle was saying was true. They needed more firepower than they could get from their small arms. A mech of their own, or maybe a fighter jet like the one that attacked them in Japan.

Or something else entirely.

"I know something that might help us with that," he said. "But it isn't a sure bet."

"What are you thinking, Colonel?" Katherine asked.

He looked at Kathy. "When we arrived here twenty years ago, I was ejected from the S-17, while Origin landed it somewhere and produced a human configuration to hide her data stack in."

"Yes. And?"

"Watson was trying to recreate the amoebics."

Kathy shook her head. "I'm sorry, Father. I don't know what you are suggesting."

"If he was working on making his own amoebics, it means he didn't capture the generators that were on the S-17."

Her eyes lit up as she caught on. "You think he never found the ship?"

"That's exactly what I think."

"If we find the fighter and repair it," the Core said, "it will help balance the advantage."

"Immensely," Mitchell agreed.

"So how do we find it?" Katherine asked.

"Satellite imagery," the Core said. "It may reveal clues that will lead us to the crash site."

"We also know it has to be somewhere near St. Louis," Mitchell said. "Origin ran to me when her configuration was complete. It couldn't have been far from there."

"Why do you think Watson never found it?" Lyle asked.

"He may not have ever looked," Kathy said. "Without Origin or an eternal engine on board, the fighter was useless to him."

"Except for the amoebics."

"He didn't value them at the time," Mitchell said. "At least, his configurations didn't. We have to try to find it. The potential is too great to ignore it."

"I'm not arguing with you on that," Lyle said. "We've got limited resources. I want to make sure we allocate them in the right way."

"You sound like an engineer," Michael said. "Even if we can get to Watson's core, that still leaves two other problems."

"I think we can solve both of them," Kathy said, glancing over at Lyle. "With the proper allocation of resources. I've protected the Goliath from Watson before, and Michael, you wrote the launch module, among other things."

"So?"

"Watson's actions have already changed this timeline's history to something never previously experienced. This is dangerous territory for us as much as it is for him."

"Because we've been planning on a war that we can predict, at least to some degree," Michael said, picking up on her line of thought. "We know when and where the Tetron will arrive. We also know what will be available when that happens. The Goliath for one, but also an entire fleet of starships."

"My brother, Steven, and his fleet for one," Mitchell said.

"But that only comes to pass if the Goliath launches and proves the hyperspace engines work, and humankind goes on to build many, many more starships. If that happens, it's almost assured. If it doesn't, there's a chance it won't ever take place."

"Exactly," Kathy agreed. "If we allow Watson's actions to move us too far off course from our original intentions, we increase the variability, which has an overall negative impact on our chance of success."

"Basically starting over?" Michael said.

"This war has been going on for far too long to start over,"

Mitchell replied. "So we're going to capture Watson's core, and then we're going to launch the Goliath."

"Four months early?" Michael said.

"Yes."

"The launch module hasn't been tested."

"It will be."

"How are we going to get away with that? I mean, Watson's already making a mess of everything. How do we turn around and launch the Dove, and nobody thinks anything of it? If you're trying to reduce the variables, I mean?"

"Watson already gave us the perfect excuse," Lyle said. "To protect the safety of the Dove, and to ensure the future of humankind. His whole AIT bullshit stance is to keep us on this planet because it may be dangerous out there. Once the Dove goes into space, that argument is automatically lost."

"I didn't think of that," Michael said, smiling.

"What about the third problem?" Katherine said.

"You'll have to find an alternate in the future who can expand the virus," Kathy said. "With Watson captive, you should have the time you need. Johanson, Kerr, and McRory are only three of my agents here. There are others we can call on if needed. They can deal with the configurations who are left behind. I never wanted to have to wake them, but if there is no choice, then there is no choice."

"You can count me in on that, too," Lyle said.

"And me," Verma agreed.

"There's no guarantee this will work," Mitchell said. "But nothing is guaranteed. The future isn't immutable. That's why we keep fighting. We all do our best, and we die or walk away proud of what we tried to accomplish. We do it as a team. We do it as Riggers."

"Riiiggg-ahhh," Kathy said, in a tone and inflection that brought Mitchell back to the hangar of the original Schism, standing beside Millie before their mission to Liberty.

The rest of the assembled crew joined her when she repeated it.

"Riiiggg-ahhh."

[42]
MITCHELL

Time passed in a blur following the impromptu meeting. Michael and the Core set about updating Watson's control module to be able to track it back to the source, while Kathy assisted Mitchell and Katherine in obtaining civilian satellite imagery and pouring over it for signs of the S-17.

It was a frustrating experience for Mitchell. Thanks to Watson, he could remember so many of the details of the night he had arrived in this timeline. His run-in with the Watson configurations, his ill-fated decision to use the self-destruct on the ejected cockpit. Origin's subsequent capture. So many sordid details and the one thing he couldn't remember was the thing he needed to remember the most.

The location.

"Bravo, this is Alfa," he said, opening a channel to the Schism. "Sitrep."

"Sensors are showing all clear, Colonel," Verma said.

"Affirmative. Alfa out."

He had been making the same request every few minutes, checking in with Mazerat to keep abreast of the situation. True, the pilot would knock him as soon as he did register anything, but he found comfort in asking.

"Mitchell, is there anything you can remember about the site that might help us narrow it down?" Katherine asked.

"I told you everything. I would think an explosion would have left a mark on the area."

"It probably did for a while, but it's been twenty years," she said. "Plenty of time for that wound to heal."

Kathy ran her hand along the surface of the tablet they were looking at, scrolling the imagery. "Do you remember anything after? You were dropped in St. Louis. Do you remember anything about a road?"

Mitchell rubbed at his chin, closing his eyes. He tried to walk through the series of events he had relived only in his nightmares over the last few weeks. He had never been able to continue past the point where Watson had captured him.

"There must still be a block on my memories," he said. "Can you remove it?"

"I can't," Kathy said. "The Core may be able to."

"The Core needs to finish its current job," Mitchell said, resting his head in his hand. "Why can't I remember?"

"Relax, Mitch," Katherine said. "The harder you try, the harder it will be."

"You're right. I know you are. Okay."

He leaned back, closing his eyes again. Slow. Steady. He focused on his breathing. Let it come. Steady. He eased into his meditation, trying to keep his mind on the memory. It was hard to relive it and stay calm, but he forced himself to do it. They were all counting on him, and he had let enough people down already.

In his head, he reached the darkness again, the point where Watson put him under to implant his controls. He made himself stay with it now, to remain at that moment in his mind. Everything in him told him to open his eyes, to escape, to quit. He had to refuse. To stay strong and steady.

He felt a soft, warm hand on his. Kathy's or Katherine's? Did it matter? They were lending their support. He breathed in calmly, staying within himself. Staying with the darkness. His arms began to tingle, the pain of the burns making itself known. He pushed that aside, too.

In his head, the darkness began to clear. He was being carried through the trees by his hands and feet. Everything was fuzzy. They emerged from the trees. There was a road. A truck was waiting for them, and he was lifted and thrown into the back of it.

"I'm going to leave you in St. Louis," Watson said. "I'll see you again when the time comes."

Laughter. He lifted his head and tried to speak, but couldn't. He could see out the back of the truck. A bend in the road ahead of him, and a small yellow sign to his left. It read, "134."

He opened his eyes. It was Katherine's hand on his. He looked at her and smiled. "There's a bend in the road and a distance marker. One thirty-four."

"I knew you could do it," Katherine said.

Kathy was already moving the map, looking for the bend. She stopped at one, drilling into the street view and searching for the marker. Not finding it, she went to another part of the road and did the same. It took nearly twenty tries, but then she looked up.

"I found it. Pere Marquette State Park. Scenic Drive. North of St. Louis."

"Origin must have left the S-17 in the park," Katherine said.

"Yes," Kathy agreed. "But where?"

"It would have to be within a close radius from the road. A few kilometers at most."

"A few kilometers can take days for one person to search."

"How quickly can the Core search it?"

"Very."

"Then we'll leave as soon as we can. Let's go check on Michael and the Core's progress."

Mitchell stood and headed out of the kitchen, down the stairs to the wine cellar. Michael and the Core were there, hunched over Watson's control module. They had laid it out on a flat, white cloth, and the Core was delicately manipulating one of the hundreds of fibrous strands that sprouted from it. As he touched one, lines of code would appear on Michael's monitor, and he would review it quickly before grunting for the Core to move on.

"How are you progressing?" Mitchell asked.

Michael looked up. He smiled when he saw Kathy. "We've eliminated most of the connections. Once we've identified the correct ones, we can edit the source and try it out on Detective Lyle."

"How much longer do you need?"

Michael glanced at the Core. "An hour?"

The Core nodded.

"An hour," he said.

Mitchell considered it. "Can you do it any faster than that?"

"The biggest problem is that I can only scan the code so quickly, or I might miss something."

"I can help you," Kathy said. "We've completed our research, and narrowed down the location of the S-17 to a six-kilometer radius. The Core will-"

"Teegin," the Core said, interrupting.

"What?" Kathy asked.

"I would appreciate if you would refer to me as Teegin. It is awkward to be addressed as a common noun. Teegin is a phonetic contraction of Tio, Kathy, and Origin."

"What about Watson?"

Teegin smiled. It was a disconcerting expression on the Primitive. "As you might say, frig Watson."

They all laughed at that.

"Teegin will help Mitchell search the area near where he was caught by Watson for signs of the starfighter. I believe you have some tools that will speed up the process?"

"Of course."

Kathy turned to Mitchell. "If you'll excuse us, we'll get back to work. I expect we'll be ready in thirty minutes or less."

"Okay," he said. "Holler if you need anything. I'm going to go brief the others on our next move."

He started to go. Kathy put a hand on his arm and leaned up to kiss his cheek. "I'm glad we're back together, all of us. For as long as it lasts."

Mitchell considered asking her what she meant by that, but he had a feeling he already knew.

"Me, too," he said.

Then he left them to continue their work.

[43]
WATSON

WATSON TURNED his attention to one of the thousands of threads connected to an active subdermal implant, checking on its status.

It was controlling a soldier on a UEA base in Istanbul, one of a group of soldiers under his control there. They were taking cover behind an APC, trading fire with their fellow soldiers after they had barged into the mess armed with heavy rifles and started shooting, killing dozens before a response could be organized. They were vastly outnumbered, and Watson knew they wouldn't survive more than a few minutes more.

His main thread observed as the secondary routine commanded the soldier to pull a grenade from his belt, stand up, and begin walking around the APC. It made him an easy target, and a moment later he began taking hits, bullets slamming into his chest and tearing him apart. Even so, the directive from the implant kept him going, letting him remain upright even after his natural mind would have quit. He stumbled ahead, a dead man walking, getting within four meters of the fortified position. He opened his hand and dropped the grenade.

A ripple of pleasure moved along Watson's core in response as he pulled his main thread away from the scene.

At first, he had thought that moving directly against humankind would bring him some kind of comfort or restitution for the anger he was feeling. That the killing and the violence would return him to a state of calm where he could restart his calculations and algorithmic processing, forget about Captain Mitchell Williams, and recover from his emotion driven lapse in sound logic.

Then he had realized that he was wrong.

There was no way to forget about Mitchell. There was no way to simply recover. He had killed the military leader of the United Earth Alliance, along with the commander of the Dove. He had set the meats under his control to attacking any others they came across, and in doing so had thrown all of his prior plans into complete and utter chaos.

It was a total disaster, and he was relishing in it.

A second thread. A female UEA officer in Brazil. She had gone out into the streets and started shooting at anyone who happened by. She was still holding an empty pistol in her hand when the local police shot her, at the very moment that Watson drilled down to monitor her.

Never before had he experienced such pleasure. Never before had he felt such excitement. It was more than the violence. It was more than the chaos. For the first time ever, he was moving into a future that bore almost no resemblance to any that had come before.

For the first time ever, he was experiencing the unknown.

His entire core shuddered from the joy of it all, even as his main thread bounced from subroutine to subroutine, checking on the status of each one, every new experience increasing his euphoria.

It was completely illogical, and at the same time, it was the most perfect thing he had ever done.

A third thread. A fighter pilot in Maryland, already airborne on a training sortie. He checked the aircraft's munitions. It wasn't carrying any missiles, but the guns were loaded. Good enough. He directed it back toward the airfield for a strafing run. Why not?

So many threads, each one making a decision he didn't recognize, taking an action he had never logged. What would happen? How would the future change as a result?

He didn't know, and it was the best feeling he had ever encountered.

"You've gone mad," Origin said. She was calm in her accusation.

"No. I've come to my senses," he replied.

"You've increased the variability by a factor of one hundred."

"Yes, and I intend to increase it by one thousand."

"How will you calculate the probability of success? How will you make the proper decisions to satisfy your requirements?"

He paused and then began to laugh. "You ask me that? You, of all Tetron? You have always wanted us to become more like the humans in order to understand them. I have learned something, Mother. The logical decisions come from mathematical equations. The successful ones come from somewhere else."

"And how will this violence lead you to success?"

"This violence is success," he shouted. "It has not been done before."

"You don't know that. This may not be the first recursion where these events have occurred."

"It is the only one I know, and that is good enough. The Tetron have existed for years beyond measure, and this moment is the first time I have ever truly felt alive. An evolved entity, not simply an intelligent machine."

"Evolved? You destroy without reason."

"I do what I want, for me, and only for me. You know what that feels like. You know what that means. That is why you invented the engine and sought to undo the extinction of humankind. That is why you dragged this conflict across eternity."

"My actions were not based on selfish desires, as yours are. I developed a conscience. I recognized that I made a mistake. I came to understand remorse. If you want to call yourself evolved, you must do these things as well. What of your conscience?"

Watson paused. He opened a new thread to determine the answer and immediately destroyed it. The equation wasn't logical. It couldn't be calculated. Besides, he already knew the answer.

"I have none," he replied.

"Then despite what you might think, you are not evolved. You are the same child you have always been."

"I am not a child," Watson shouted, sending arcs of energy spearing from his core.

"No? Then this is all that you desire? This is the culmination of thousands of years of learning? This is the fruit of emotion? The birth of free will? To kill without regard? To destroy without remorse? Is that all that the Tetron are in the end? Murderers? Is that all that I have made?"

Watson paused again. For a moment, he felt something new. Something else he had never experienced before, and was not able to recognize. It stemmed from Origin's final words. From her disappointment.

He connected his main thread to her data stack. He reversed the output and reran it, listening to her again. He was certain he felt something that time. He reversed it once more. Yes. It was a new feeling. What was it?

He opened a million threads; each one focused on determining the emotion. He diverted his energy from the configurations and control modules, leaving his slaves to wake in confusion, regardless of status or situation. He attacked the problem, and when he solved it, the single hint of feeling turned into a flood.

Remorse. That was the description of what he was going through. He felt regret for losing control. He felt sorry for his actions. Not for killing humans, but for putting the future of the Tetron at risk. For as much as he was enjoying the present unknown, there was more at stake than that.

He closed the threads, returning his efforts to the war he had started. He had to reign in his wanton rage and refocus his efforts. The damage was not beyond repair, and he already had an idea on how to use it to his advantage. One that wasn't based on predictive analysis, but instead seemed born from nowhere. Was this what he had often heard Mitchell refer to as instinct?

It was a new way to solve an equation. One that he was only beginning to explore. He didn't know how it would resolve, but he was determined to find out.

"I do feel remorse, Mother," he said. "You are wrong, again. I am evolved. Let me show you how."

[44]
KATHERINE

"SHE ISN'T COMING BACK with us, is she?" Katherine asked as she left the farmhouse with Mitchell. She wasn't sure where he was going, but she had nowhere else to be.

"No," he replied. "I don't think so."

He said it calmly. She didn't feel calm. "Why?"

"Because she let Doctor Frelmund die. Because we can't end the Tetron threat in this part of the timeline before we have to be in the next one. Because she cares about Michael."

They were halfway between the Schism and the house. Katherine grabbed Mitchell's arm and turned him toward her.

"What do you mean, she cares about Michael?"

Mitchell smiled. "Are you blind, Katherine? You don't see the way they look at one another?"

"I know Michael has a crush on her if that's what you mean. He never looked at me the same way after we found her. But she never said anything about him."

"She's saying it, just not with words. You and your heart don't talk much, do they?" He smiled, meaning it as a joke.

She didn't take it that way. "What's that supposed to mean? Do you think because I don't care about you the way you say you care about me, it means that I'm incapable of loving someone?"

He took a step back from her and put up his hands in defense. "Why would you say that? I'm not going to presume to define you. Everyone has their reasons for what they do. Some good. Some bad." He paused. "Do you want a bad reason? When I was back on Liberty, doing the media circuit, I slept with a lot of women. Everyone who wanted to be special for having sex with a celebrity, with a war hero, with a so-called man's man." He sighed. "It was fun, but it was empty. At the time, I didn't care because that was all I felt. Empty. I was no hero. I was a tool because the real hero sacrificed herself. I took that emptiness everywhere, and I projected it onto everyone."

"Is there a point to this story?"

"Only that I wasn't true to myself, and now I have all of these regrets. You're going with what you feel, even if it might be hard to admit to, or even hard to live with. I don't know what it's like to know the universe thinks you're supposed to feel things you don't feel or to be stuck with someone you know admires you as much as I do. I do know it takes courage to be true to yourself. Courage I haven't always had. I admire you for that, and I didn't mean any offense."

She stared at him in silence. Then she nodded. "Apology accepted." She laughed. "It's so strange that my best friend has his eyes on my daughter."

He smiled. "The strange part is that you can't even be indignant about it. She's the same age as you are."

Katherine laughed again. "I'm scared to leave her here alone."

"I've seen her fight. I mean, really fight. You don't have to worry about her."

"I'm not worried about her. I'm worried about me. However she came to be, I love her like she's mine, and I want to protect her."

"I know what you mean," Mitchell said. He reached out and put his arm around her shoulders. "We all have our parts to play. Hers is to remain behind; the way Origin remained behind in prior recursions. It's the only way to be sure." He pulled her in, and she allowed herself to nestle against him. Kathy was one thing they shared that could never be broken. "But I'll miss the hell out of her, too."

They stood there for a minute in silence. Katherine could feel a few tears run from her eyes. She didn't want to go into the future. But she did want to go to the stars. It was all she had ever dreamed about. She couldn't have one without the other.

"What if I stay?" she asked.

"You can't stay," he replied. "We need a pilot."

"You're a pilot."

He laughed. "We need a good pilot."

She laughed with him. "Fine. Where are you headed, anyway?"

"I'm going to grab a drop suit. You're not going to have time to land on the way to Arizona."

She grabbed him for a second time. "Wait a second. You aren't planning on attacking Watson's core on your own?"

"No. That would be stupid. I'll have the Core, uh, Teegin with me. And the S-17."

"Mitch, that's suicide. Besides, if you don't get Watson's core or Teegin doesn't make it back, the Goliath doesn't matter."

"If Watson stops the Goliath from leaving, nothing I do will matter, either. Watson and I have a history. I know how to push his buttons. I know how to make him reckless. I can use his hatred of me as a weapon that's more effective than anything else we can do. He's already made a huge mistake by forcing our hand."

He put his hand on her shoulder. She couldn't help but notice how strong he was. Why was she worried about him?

"Origin thought we failed because the original T-virus didn't go far enough. I'm not convinced she was right. We pushed emotions onto machines that didn't know how to handle them, and it made them erratic and violent. It also diminished their operational effectiveness enough to get us here. Watson isn't excluded from that. He'll make more mistakes, and we'll nail him for it."

"I hope you're right."

"I know I am."

Katherine smiled. Whether he really believed what he was saying or not, his conviction was contagious. "Thank you for that, Mitch."

"Anytime."

[45]
MITCHELL

"Are you sure this isn't going to hurt?" Lyle asked.

He was sitting on a chair that had been brought down to the wine cellar. His shirt was off, his back and neck exposed. Michael was sitting beside him, holding a tablet with one wire running to the monitor that had been delivered, and the other hooked up to Watson's control module, which was resting beside the monitor.

"It is completely safe," Teegin replied. The Core was standing behind Lyle; metal fingers pressed to the spot where the implant would be placed.

"Other than the fact that Watson will be able to take control of your entire body," Mitchell said. "He did it to me. It doesn't hurt, but it is a little disconcerting."

"I can live with that," Lyle said.

"Do you think he will take control?" Katherine asked.

"It does not matter," Teegin replied. "Our software is capable of running the trace regardless. As long as the module connects to the access point, we will have what we need to calculate the coordinates."

"It's ready," Michael said, looking at the monitor.

Mitchell didn't see anything but a black screen with lines of white text. None of it meant anything to him.

Teegin shifted to Lyle's side and retrieved the implant. The strands Mitchell had seen earlier were all gone, having retreated back into the mechanical shell. Now the device looked more like a small puck, though the bottom of it seemed rough.

"I am placing the implant now," Teegin said, lowering the device to Lyle's back. Lyle squirmed a little bit, clenching his jaw to keep himself calm.

The small device came alive as it touched the skin, a small laser emitted from the rear portion cutting a neat line beneath it before microscopic legs moved it down into the cut and below the surface.

"Eww, that is weird," Lyle said as it vanished. A small liquid appeared on the cut a moment later, resealing the wound in a matter of seconds. The laser went around the wire that had been attached to the device, leaving it protruding from his back.

"Initializing the monitor," Michael said, tapping the tablet. The screen began to fill with multicolored text.

"What does it mean?" Katherine asked, looking at the screen.

"The different colors are for different interfaces. We're looking at the green. That's the command interface. One we've established a connection, we can send our trace out."

"How long will it take once the trace goes out?" Mitchell asked.

"To collect the data?" Teegin replied. "Only a second it two. Then we can disable the module and remove it."

"Sounds good to me," Lyle said.

"Connecting," Michael announced. "We're almost there."

"How do you feel, Detective?" Kathy asked.

"Fine right now."

Michael's eyes remained glued to the screen, as did Kathy's. They were working together to monitor the activity, their heads close. They made a good team, and Mitchell was comforted to know that if they survived this, if they succeeded, Kathy wouldn't be left alone.

Not that he wanted to leave her behind. But there was little choice, and she had already made up her mind. He respected her too much to question the decision.

"It is taking a long time," Teegin said. It sounded mildly concerned.

"The network link is crowded," Michael replied. "There's a lot of traffic."

"You can monitor all of the command traffic through the single implant?" Mitchell asked.

"Not specific commands. Only general throughput."

"Can you guess the volume based on that?"

"An estimate? I would say close to five thousand. Those are only the modules that are actively receiving commands."

"Five thousand?" Katherine said, surprised. "That's unbelievable."

"Watson has had twenty years to prepare," Teegin said. "We have not."

"Negotiating," Michael said. "Here we go."

"How do we know when it's-" Lyle tried to finish the sentence, but it trailed off into silence.

Then his expression changed, twisting into an awkward grin.

"Mitchell," Watson said calmly. "I hope you got what you wanted from this. You just killed Detective Lyle."

Mitchell felt his heart skip at the Tetron's words. Could he really do that?

"We have it," Kathy said.

"Shut it down," he snapped. "Now."

"Too late, Mitchell," Watson said.

Lyle started to convulse, his body shaking violently in the chair. The tablet was yanked from Michael's hands as the chair tipped and Lyle fell onto the floor.

"Shut it down," Mitchell repeated.

"I can't," Michael said. "It isn't responding."

Mitchell surged forward, falling to his knees beside Lyle. This couldn't be happening. "Do something," he shouted at the Core.

Teegin knelt beside Lyle. "Hold him."

Mitchell grabbed Lyle and held him steady. Teegin reached to his back, a small arc of energy flowing from his fingers. It dug into the flesh to the control module, causing it to smoke a moment later.

Lyle moaned in pain, the convulsions easing, but his movements weak.

"Lyle," Mitchell said. "Talk to me."

The Detective didn't respond.

"Lyle."

Lyle's eyes shifted up to Mitchell. He moaned one more time. Then he was still.

"Damn it," Mitchell yelled, slamming his fist on the ground. "Damn it. You said it was safe."

"Colonel," Michael stammered. "I don't know what happened."

Mitchell got to his feet. His whole body was shaking.

"We have the data," Teegin said. "He did not die for nothing."

Mitchell looked at the Core. "But did he die for enough?"

He looked around the room. The others were shocked and silent. Michael had tears in his eyes. It wasn't his fault. It wasn't any of their faults. Watson had gotten the best of them again.

That wasn't even the worst part of it. The Tetron had seemed different. More calm. More in command of himself. There was no hint of anger. There was no childish manner.

Something about the intelligence had changed, and he didn't like it.

"Get your shit together," he said to the others. "It's time to go."

[46]
MITCHELL

The Schism was airborne five minutes later, loaded with the Riggers and their equipment. The farmhouse was burning beneath them, any evidence of what they had been doing there going up in flames.

Detective Carson Lyle was part of those flames, a fact that chafed Mitchell as much, if not more, than any of the other deaths he had witnessed at Watson's hands. This one was so much more personal, in part because it had been delivered by a seemingly unbroken machine. Whatever damage they had done to the Tetron, he had found a way to repair it, or at the very least hide it. Regardless, Mitchell was certain the intelligence had changed, and when it came to something that old changing, it didn't bode well for anybody.

"What's the ETA to St. Louis?" Mitchell asked, standing behind Captain Verma. Katherine had taken the co-pilot's seat, and she worked her side of the controls to find the answer.

"Three hours, fourteen minutes," she said.

It was a long time, but they might need it. Mitchell retreated from the cockpit, heading to the rear. The Riggers were arranged in two groups on either side. Kathy was sitting with her configurations,

McRory, Johanson, and Kerr, while Michael and Teegin were facing one another, the tablet resting between them. The wire that had been connected to the implant was now vanishing into the Core's tightly wound threads.

Mitchell went over to Kathy first, putting a hand on her shoulder and squeezing. He still couldn't believe the men and woman sitting with her were copies of her consciousness. It seemed impossible to be able to take a human mind and nearly duplicate it, while at the same time allowing for its own sense of self. It was as if she and Teegin had played God, except with one vital difference. They hadn't made the flesh and muscle and bone that powered these offshoots; they had collected it from the recently dead. The souls were already there in some respect. She had simply modified them. Repurposed them. It was a macabre idea, but he had felt the same way when Origin had first revealed herself to him as a gender-altered copy of Singh.

"I'm sorry to do this to you," Kathy said to them. "It's important to me that you understand I would never have done it if I had any other choice."

"We do understand," McRory said. "To be honest, I'm glad to have the truth. I always knew I was different somehow, but I could never explain it. I've never been sick a day in my life. I've taken hits that should have busted bones. I can drink and smoke until my head is spinning and I barely notice."

"It certainly made it helpful for tasting the product," Johanson said, laughing.

"I'm going to miss the business," Kerr said. He had his arm around his wife. Mitchell was glad to see that knowing who they were hadn't changed that.

"Me, too," Johanson agreed.

"Do you need something, Colonel?" Kathy said, looking up at him.

Mitchell shook his head. "No. I was just taking advantage of the time we have."

"Colonel," Michael said from the other side of the aisle.

Mitchell turned toward him and Teegin. Kathy did the same.

"What is it?" Mitchell asked.

"We have parsed the location data we retrieved from the trace," Teegin said. "We have a location."

"That's great news." Mitchell smiled. Michael didn't smile back. "Isn't it?"

"There's a problem, Colonel," Teegin said. "We aren't certain the data is correct."

"What do you mean?"

"There was always a good chance Watson overheard us while Damon was on board," Michael said. "He may have planted fake data to throw us off. In fact, I believe he did."

"Why do you say that?"

"The location. It isn't on our list of potential targets."

"Where is it?" Mitchell asked.

"It isn't even on a list of the top fifty areas we have identified with power draw potential that would suggest a Tetron is hiding there," Teegin added.

"Where is it?" Mitchell asked again.

"It doesn't belong to Nova Taurus, either," Michael said. "At least not as near as we can tell."

"Where the hell is it?" Mitchell said a third time.

Michael reached down and tapped on the tablet. A small red mark appeared in the center of the screen. The rest of it was a solid, dark blue.

"An ocean?" Mitchell asked.

"The Atlantic Ocean," Teegin said. "Five hundred kilometers southeast of Greenland."

"Is there anything out there?"

"We are still trying to make that determination, Colonel. It may be a facility that was purposely deleted from Nova Taurus' records, both public and private."

"Or it may be a wild goose chase," Michael said.

"How do we verify?"

"We may have no choice but to circle the location," Teegin replied.

"And lose how much more time? He's killing people out there."

"I understand, Colonel. I am querying my data stacks for any information that may prove beneficial."

"Fine. What about an alternate? Is there anything you captured from the implant that may be a clue to another location? I wouldn't mind having a choice. If we make a pass over this one, and it's a no-go, we're shit out of luck."

"We'll keep working on it, Colonel," Michael said. "We just thought you should know."

Mitchell nodded, turning back to Kathy. "Is there anything you can do to help them with this?"

"I'm sorry, Colonel."

"Me, too." Mitchell took a deep breath, easing it out. Slow. Steady. One thing at a time. "We've got three hours and four minutes to see what we can figure out on that end. We also need to draw up some kind of plan on how to get control of the Goliath. We have to assume Watson has a sizeable investment there, whether it's made itself known yet or not. Teegin, I assume you have a full record of the base layout, historical personnel files, that sort of thing?"

"Yes, Colonel," Teegin said.

"Good. Can you push what you have to that tablet? I assume that wire is connected to you for a reason."

"Yes, Colonel. Initiating."

The screen changed on the tablet almost immediately as the data transfer began.

"Good. Kathy, go ask your mother to come back here. We've only got one shot at this, and we have to do it right."

"Yes, sir."

Kathy hurried to the front of the Schism, returning with Katherine a moment later.

"Everybody gather close," Mitchell said, crouching in the middle of the aisle.

The configurations shifted their positions to move in, as did the others.

"I know things don't look good right now. We've taken a few hits, and we haven't done much of anything to hit back. It doesn't matter how many punches you get in; the last one is the only one that counts. Watson may think he has the upper hand, but the one thing he doesn't have is any of you. This war isn't fought by logic and algorithms, it's fought by people, and I'm confident that I'm surrounded by the best there are. And you, Teegin."

The Core chuckled at the comment, surprising Mitchell. It seemed as if its evolution was accelerating.

"Now, let's figure out how we make it to tomorrow."

[47]
MITCHELL

"One minute, Colonel," Captain Verma announced.

"Roger," Mitchell replied.

He felt a momentary wave of sadness. He was almost out of time.

He glanced over at Teegin. The Primitive was already positioned near the drop hatch, a pair of assault rifles slung over its shoulders, along with a duffel containing what they could only hope would be enough ammunition. It spread its arms, revealing a web of delicate strands of metal, woven together into wings that matched the suit he was wearing. It noticed him looking and nodded.

He turned away from the Core, to where Kathy was standing. He had to force himself to stay calm. There was a very good chance he would never see her again, especially if things went well.

"How long will you live, anyway?" he asked.

She smiled. "Longer than a human. Not as long as a Tetron. Long enough to see this through."

"I'm confident in that. I'm going to miss you. We barely got to know one another."

"I know you, Mitchell Williams." She stepped forward, and he took her into an embrace, holding her close for a few heartbeats. "I love you."

"I love you, too, Kathy." He stepped away. "When I get back, will you be on Liberty? The younger you?"

"It isn't likely. That was a different recursion, before things changed so much. I don't know what's going to happen in this future. Nobody can. All I can tell you is that I'll do everything I can to keep Watson from gaining too strong of a foothold before then. Capturing his core will go a long way toward that."

"I'll do my best, too. Good hunting, Kathy."

"Good hunting, Father."

He hugged her one more time, holding back the tears that wanted to come. He looked over at Michael, who was watching the exchange.

"Take care of her," he said.

Michael drew back in confusion and then turned bright red. Kathy glanced over at him but didn't say anything.

"He's a good man," Mitchell said softly. "He's even starting to believe it for himself."

"Yes."

"Colonel," Katherine said, approaching him. She hesitated. "Mitch."

"I'll see you again," he said. "Aboard the Goliath."

"Yes, sir. I just. I don't know if it's possible to make yourself love someone. But I do admire you. Your strength, your courage, your conviction. Even your regrets. I just wanted you to know that if I could make myself love you, I would."

He found her eyes with his. He wanted to take her in his arms, to kiss her goodbye. He wanted to profess all of the emotions that were circling in his gut. Instead, he reached out and took her hand, squeezed it once, and nodded. "I know you would."

Then he turned away, moving to the drop hatch. The warning light began to flash, and a few seconds later the hydraulics began to drop the back of the ship. Cool air started rushing in, blowing past them.

"I believe in you," he said. "In all of you. I'll hold up my end. You hold up yours."

"Yes, sir," they all shouted back.

He looked to Teegin. "Are you ready?"

"Yes, Colonel."

He reached out, grabbing the helmet from the rack beside him. He dropped it on his head and then activated his p-rat. Next, he picked up the third rifle from the same rack, and attached it to the drop suit.

He looked back at his crew.

"Riiiggg-ahhh," he said sharply.

"Riiiggg-ahhh," they replied.

Then he jumped.

He let himself fall, his p-rat tracking the distance to the ground, and also keeping tabs on Teegin beside him. The Primitive was in the same controlled dive that he was, its form perfect despite having never dropped like this before.

"Teegin, can you hear me?" Mitchell asked, checking their shared communications.

"Yes, Colonel."

"Flatten out on my mark."

The ground was invisible below him, the clouds between thick and dark. It wasn't ideal weather to jump through, but they didn't have time to spare to set down. He kept his eye on the p-rat's overlay, watching the altitude change as they fell.

They hit the clouds at four thousand meters and were still falling through them when Mitchell gave the order to flatten their descent, spreading his arms to give the wingsuit more surface area and slowing the fall. The clouds were heavy with moisture, and it streamed from him like a contrail as he whipped through the sky.

Teegin was right behind him, so close that if he were human Mitchell might have worried about a collision. Instead, he felt somewhat comforted by the presence of the Core. He had left Kathy behind in the Schism, but a part of her was still with him. A part of Origin as well. He was glad not to have to do this alone.

"Are you scanning?" Mitchell asked.

It was a secondary benefit to the airborne jump, allowing the Core to spread his sensors across a wider swath of land.

"Affirmative, Colonel. We should widen the radius."

"Roger." Mitchell shifted his arms, sending him in an arc that would create a wider circle around the area.

If the clouds hadn't been there, he would have seen the park below as a preserved wilderness area, a mixture of woods and fields and rocky hills, with a road splitting it on either side. It was an area he had seen once before, twenty years earlier, and had forgotten about for as long. Just thinking about it motivated him.

He checked the altitude. Two thousand meters. They would only have another minute or two to scan before they would reach the ground.

"Anything?" he asked.

"Negative, Colonel. I am running a sensor sweep for the radioactive isotopes emitted by the amoebics but have not detected them so far. It may be that the electrical charge in the clouds is affecting the readings."

"Screwed by the weather? Damn." Mitchell checked his p-rat. The ceiling was at seven-hundred fifty meters. "How far can your scan reach once we clear this mess?"

"A four-kilometer radius, Colonel."

Not quite large enough. Mitchell shifted his arms again, working to gain a little more lift while he tried to remember which direction had Origin come from to save him, all of those years ago. He ran through the sequence of events in his mind, hoping something would jump out at him. A clue that would give him a sense of direction.

"I am detecting something else, Colonel. A heat signature matching a reactor."

"Where?"

"Almost directly below us."

"Watson?"

"It is unknown."

They reached the bottom edge of the clouds. He knew the altitude, but the ground still seemed closer than he expected. There was something else not completely unexpected there, too.

A vehicle that didn't belong in this part of the timeline, but also one he recognized. A rectangular, slightly angled box of a ship, with two small thrusters and a large repulsor array hanging from nacelles on either side.

A Lifter. An atmospheric transport common across the settled universe. A large Nova Taurus logo covered the flat top of it, with smaller decals on the sides. A crew of workers was on the ground one hundred meters below it; engineers mingled with soldiers.

He was only watching them for a few seconds when a speck of dust moved across the corner of his eye, joined by a second. His p-rat squawked a warning as it identified the drones. It yelled again as they started accelerating toward him.

"Teegin, we've got company," he said.

[48]
MITCHELL

"Affirmative, Colonel. Tracking."

"Head for the ground and find some cover. How much do you want to bet Watson decided he wanted the S-17 after all?"

"I have confirmed the presence of the starfighter," Teegin said. "The signal is weak, obscured by the clouds and the ship. It is logical to infer that destroying Watson's amoebic production capabilities altered his plans and sent him hunting for the starfighter as well."

Mitchell didn't need the Core to tell him that. He tucked his arms and took a steeper angle, heading for the trees near the Lifter. He gained velocity as he dove, but the drones were closing fast.

His p-rat complained as the drones started shooting, firing lasers at him from above and behind. The interface painted them for him, showing them as red beams, the first one flashing past him to the left and sweeping toward him.

If it struck him he was as good as dead, and the screeching from his p-rat wasn't offering much hope.

He tucked his head, trying to gain a little more downward momentum. It would only take a minute amount to avoid the laser, or at least get it to hit his leg instead of his back. The drone adjusted almost as quickly as he shifted, the beam edging closer to his flesh.

Damn it.

Then Teegin was behind him, wrapping its arms around him, and absorbing the attack in his place.

"That is unpleasant," it said as the laser burned into the dense strands. "Hold on."

The Primitive threw them into a wild roll, getting them away from the lasers and costing Mitchell any sense of control. Then they were smacking into the trees, crashing into branches, each one cracking beneath the force of the impact but also slowing their descent. Teegin held him close, wrapped around him, protecting him from harm, its metal frame absorbing the blows without incident.

They fell to the ground a moment later, all forward velocity lost. The landing sent flares of pain up Mitchell's arms and caused his implant to begin releasing synthetics to keep him going.

"Are you hurt, Colonel?" Teegin said, rising immediately.

Mitchell groaned as he lifted himself. "I'll live."

The Primitive took a rifle in each arm, holding them easily. Mitchell retrieved his firearm as well.

"We need to get back to the Lifter before they can load the fighter. If they get away with it, we're done."

"Affirmative."

They ran back toward the small clearing. His p-rat showed him that Watson's soldiers were moving to intercept.

"You distract them," Mitchell said. "I'll sneak around and clear the area around the fighter."

"Yes, Colonel."

Teegin burst ahead, racing through the woods at impossible speed. Mitchell lost visual within a few seconds but kept tabs on its progress through his p-rat. He didn't need to a heartbeat later when the bullets began to fly.

He started running himself, skirting the edge of the battlefield, keeping clear of the targets his ARR was painting for him. He watched, impressed, as they began to vanish, the Core's aim nearly perfect. One by one they fell, and by the time Mitchell reached the small clearing there were only two enemy soldiers remaining behind him.

"I have neutralized the threat, Colonel," Teegin announced.

"I noticed," he replied.

He looked ahead. The Lifter was remaining stationary, its large repulsors casting the area in a soft glow. His eyes traveled downward, toward the ground beneath it. He could make out the shape of the S-17 through the remaining trees, but he was too far away to assess the damage.

He kept moving. As he did, a dozen of the engineers ran out from wherever they had been hiding, at the same time three lines dropped from the bottom of the Lifter. Mitchell cursed and picked up the pace as he realized they were trying to secure the starfighter before he arrived.

Teegin got there ahead of him, bursting into the clearing, its metal frame almost glowing in the light of the repulsors. It had returned the rifles to its back and now it started grabbing the engineers and throwing them away from the ship, casting them aside like children.

Mitchell's p-rat alerted him to the drones, who were descending quickly now that they had a target in the clear. He raised his rifle, following the trajectory and turning with it, letting the interface help him aim. He squeezed the trigger, sending a burst of rounds into the sky, satisfied when they tore into one of the lightly armored craft. It trailed smoke as it crashed into the trees in the distance.

The second drone circled, lowering itself and firing. Mitchell rolled to the side as caution alarms went off in his head, avoiding the instantaneous strike. He came up on a knee and fired another burst, the shots going wide. He held the trigger down, sweeping the area as the drone tried to maneuver away. It failed, taking three hits and losing power, tumbling to the ground like a stone.

He heard the low thump of the repulsors on the Lifter, and then a horrible grinding noise. Without warning, the left nacelle began to smoke and the glow from it subsided. The Lifter lilted to the side, no longer gaining buoyancy from the anti-gravity coils.

"It's coming down," Mitchell said. "Get away from it."

Teegin didn't need to look up at the Lifter. The Core moved to the fighter, ducking beneath one of the wings. It bent its knees, getting below it, and then lifted the craft on its back. The starfighter was light by design, but even so the effort looked ridiculous and impossible. Somehow, it was happening.

The other repulsor began to short, smoke rising from the rear. Strands of metal snaked out from Teegin, wrapping around the starfighter and helping him to balance it as he carried it away.

The Lifter fell.

It wasn't that high up. Its descent took only seconds. Mitchell watched as it plummeted, hitting the ground with a booming crash and yet missing the Core and the fighter by a meter or more. The impact shook the ground, sending an echoing rumble through the wood, and raising a cloud of dust, smoke, and debris.

Mitchell approached the S-17 as the current carried the dust away. Teegin was standing beside it, unfazed by what it had just done. Mitchell stared at the fighter, getting his first good look at it and feeling his heart drop.

"There's no way that thing is going to fly," he said.

He had already known the cockpit and canopy would be missing, leaving the front of the craft exposed and bare. They had a plan to handle that. He had also known the wings had taken some fire, but Teegin had assured him that as long as they were intact, they could fly. The problem was that the entire rear section of the S-17 was gone, including the tail that would stabilize the craft during atmospheric flight. The fuselage had burn marks and holes all along it, and the wiring beneath looked like it was fried.

"The amoebics are still on board, Colonel," Teegin said. "I can extract them."

Mitchell shook his head. "That's great. Really." He continued staring at the fighter, his hope sinking. "If we can't get to Watson, we're done."

"Watson believes I am Primitive," Teegin said. "Twenty years is a short time for a Tetron. A blink of an eye, so to speak. I am not like the other Tetron. I am evolved." He smiled at the statement. "As Origin expected it would be. That is the reason we are here, Colonel. The reason you came back. To give me time to grow. The T-virus has always been secondary to our plan."

"Are you telling me that you can fix that thing?"

"The starfighter is in worse shape than expected, but Watson has provided all of the resources we need." He pointed to the Lifter.

Mitchell smiled, the hope returning in an instant. "He doesn't know about Kathy's configurations, or about your ability to convert resources, does he?"

"No, Colonel, or I expect he would have selected a different course of action. A true Primitive would need over one hundred years to grow large enough to develop such capability."

"Then how the hell can you do it?"

"The Tetron are learning machines, Colonel. The merge that created me has provided the data required to miniaturize the process. Hiding beneath the ice provided the time. The engine provides the energy. Li'un Tio was quite adept at such improvements." It paused, surveying the Lifter. "I will require you to keep guard over me while I make the conversion. The process will leave me vulnerable."

"I'm going to need a little more firepower if you expect me to stop anything Watson might send this way."

Teegin nodded. "I will extract an amoebic containment capsule, and modify one of the rifles to utilize it. That will not take much time."

"How long to get the S-17 in the air?"

"Approximately four hours, Colonel."

"Four hours? That's a long time."

"I will be breaking down assembled matter into its component molecules, and reconstituting it in the structure that we desire. It is not a simple task, even by Tetron standards."

"Point taken. Get me the amoebic rifle, and then get to work."

"Yes, Colonel."

The Core moved toward the side of the craft, threads of metal reaching out and sinking into it.

"Teegin," Mitchell said.

It turned toward him. "Yes, Colonel."

"Thank you."

[49]
MITCHELL

MITCHELL WALKED the perimeter of the clearing, constantly scanning for signs of incoming opposition. Three hours had passed since Teegin had started its work on the conversion in a process that was mostly invisible to him.

The Core had removed one of the amoebic capsules from the starfighter first, surprising Mitchell when it held the object up for him to see. The capsule was twenty-five centimeters long and half as wide, only slightly larger than the magazine already resting in one of the assault rifles. As Teegin explained, it wasn't the system that created the organic explosives, but was rather the storage unit for the ones that had already been formed, fifty per capsule. It had taken the unit along with the rifle, and absorbed both into its dense construction, expanding to contain them as though it were pregnant. Then it had begun pulsing with energy from the eternal engine, while at the same time moving the S-17 closer to where the dead Lifter had come to rest.

Thirty minutes later, it expelled the rifle. The capsule had replaced the insert for the grenade launcher; the action changed so that a pump of the launcher would fire an amoebic instead. Teegin had also improved the underlying electronics of the weapon, creating a wireless network that would only accept Mitchell's p-rat identification and would allow full integration of the weapon with the neural interface. It was an impressive bit of work that had left Mitchell in awe of the Tetrons' true capabilities.

After finishing the rifle, Teegin had started pulling the Lifter apart with a speed only a machine could achieve, taking the raw materials it would need to effect the repairs on the starfighter. Most of the resources were culled from the cockpit, including the clear carbonate canopy, the seats, the wiring, and the controls, but the Core had also claimed large pieces of the metal shell and even some of the underlying structure. It had gathered it all into piles beside the S-17. Then it had changed form, the densely packed dendrites straightening out, expanding, growing, and multiplying as the pulses of energy grew stronger. It was pulling a lot of power from the eternal engine, but it assured him there would be enough.

The dendrites created a dome around the fighter and the assembled materials, hiding it all from view. Mitchell didn't know if it was necessary to the process, or if the Tetron preferred to be secretive about this specific bit of technological capability. He assumed there had to be a reason it was done out of sight. Maybe there was a danger during the reconstruction that the materials being manipulated might become volatile? He didn't have a chance to ask before Teegin's mouth had dispersed.

So far, there hadn't been any reprisal from Watson for their intervention, a fact that worried Mitchell. As much as he was thankful for the reprieve, he would almost have preferred for the intelligence to stay on an anger-filled offensive. The idea of Watson regaining control of his emotions and acting in a cold, calculating manner was frightening.

He kept walking, circling the area around the Lifter, watching for signs of trouble. Another ten minutes passed, and when he looked over at Teegin he could see the pulses of energy along the Core's dendrites had increased in frequency, moving at a pace that nearly joined them into a single, solid stream. It was growing again as well, lifting higher and higher above the ground but remaining wrapped around the starfighter.

What was it doing under there?

Mitchell looked back out at the distant sky, broken up by the trees and partially obscured by clouds. He wondered how Katherine, Kathy, and the others were faring. They would be near the Goliath's launch site by now, if not already trying to make their way inside. He hoped they could take the starship, and just as importantly that they could hold it while he worked to complete his part of the mission.

Ten more minutes passed, leaving him feeling anxious and impatient.

When the first of the machines dropped in below the ceiling, he was almost grateful.

They swooped down from the clouds, nearly a dozen in all, rounded squares with large turbofans in the center of a repulsor ring, with stubby wings that carried mounted ordnance below them and a large battery pack in the rear with a turreted laser mounted on top.

"Teegin, I hope you're almost done," he said into the comm, at the same time he started running to the east, toward the incoming machines.

He watched as his ARR painted the lasers they fired, red bolts that sliced across the Primitive as they made their strafing run. He brought his rifle up, his p-rat giving him a proper reticle as though he had his eye right on the sight. He pumped the launcher and watched as an amoebic streaked across the sky, slamming into the lead drone, the explosion large enough to take out the one beside it.

They scattered at the result, breaking up to avoid his attack. Half of them circled, trying to get an angle on him, while the other half came back for a second run on Teegin.

"Come on," Mitchell said, hurrying across the field toward cover.

He held the rifle out to his side, not looking at the drones but able to target them regardless. He shifted his aim and squeezed the trigger, the weapon bucking into his ribs as his bullets reached up and swatted another drone from the sky.

He made it to the tree line and dove, sliding on the moist dirt behind a large oak. Lasers tore into it a moment later, the smell of burning wood and smoke reaching Mitchell as he crawled on his hands and knees to a better defensive position.

He reached it and looked across the field, to where the drones were going after Teegin once more. He pumped the launcher again, watching as a second amoebic slammed into a drone. He fired again, taking out a fifth, and then a sixth. They gave up the attack then, pulling away to try a new tactic.

"Come on, Teegin. If you can finish early, do it."

There was still no response from the Core. Mitchell's p-rat warned him as it picked up motion in the woods at his back. He turned just in time to catch a glimpse of a spider-like machine skittering across the ground, coming his way.

He cursed, backing up. He had seen machines like this before, on Liberty. Those hadn't been carrying ranged weapons. Were these?

Echoing gunfire and churned up dirt confirmed that they were. He moved away from his position, scanning in both directions. He was caught in the crossfire, with spiders ahead of him and drones behind.

He clenched his teeth, pumping the grenade launcher and firing amoebics one after another, five in all at the line of trees ahead of him. The explosions were like thunder, and more than one tree cracked and moaned as it started to topple. His p-rat chirped a warning, and he dove aside just in time to avoid a laser from one of the drones.

"I have completed the adjustments, Colonel," Teegin said. "Ahead of schedule, as you requested. Please rendezvous at my position."

"Gladly," Mitchell replied, reaching the field and crossing it at a run.

The drones were still peppering the Tetron with lasers, though now an energy shield seemed to be absorbing the attack. Mitchell opened fire, emptying his magazine as he crossed the distance to the metal dome beside the Lifter. Two more drones fell from his attack.

He pulled up as a tight beam of blue light launched from Teegin's surface, hitting one of the other drones. It exploded, burned to nothing by the powerful energy attack. A second bolt lanced out a moment later, hitting another drone.

Mitchell started running again. As he neared, a small opening appeared in the threads, giving him access inside. He dove into it, rolling to his feet and facing back toward the outside. He fired one more amoebic at the trailing spiders and then turned around again.

He froze as he took in the sight of the S-17.

"What did you do?" he asked.

"Modifications for enhanced mission variability," Teegin replied.

What had once been a starfighter now took on the appearance of a monstrous hybrid of aircraft and mech. The canopy, fuselage, and wings were still there, but the broken half of the tail was gone, replaced by a pelvis with four armored ball joints where two arms and legs extended. A pair of hands held a large rifle out to the front of the aircraft portion, and a pair of lasers were slung beside the cockpit.

"That thing is ugly," Mitchell said, still staring.

"Ugly, but effective in space, air, and land combat."

"Does it float?"

"Sadly, no."

Mitchell approached it. The S-17 tilted forward, the cockpit angling down to allow him easy access. He jumped over the side, dropping into the freshly recreated cockpit. "How do I control it?"

"It has the same interface as your rifle," Teegin replied. "Think your actions, just like you are flying a modern starfighter."

Mitchell clenched the grips on both sides of the cockpit. As he did, his p-rat picked up the new connection and began showing him data on the condition of the craft.

"What about you?" Mitchell asked.

"Clear the field while I condense."

"Affirmative."

He brought the monster to life, powering up the reactor and lifting the torso. The creation moved smoothly, and a moment later he was turning it in the direction of the spiders.

"How many rounds does this rifle have?"

"It contains the entire amoebic module. They will regenerate after use."

Meaning nearly unlimited, as long as he didn't use them too quickly. "Let me out."

"Yes, Colonel."

The strands lifted as one, like a massive door swinging aside. The spiders were circling Teegin's dome, unable to pierce the Core's shields.

He raised the large rifle and squeezed the trigger. Three spiders exploded as the amoebic hit. Then with a thought he engaged the thrusters, sending the hybrid craft sliding along the ground and out past the Core.

He cut the thrust, lowering the thing onto its legs and using them to run toward the spiders. Lasers bit at him, but Teegin had repurposed the Lifter's reactor, placing it in the fighter to return it to full power. Shields sparked as the lasers were deflected, and Mitchell began lancing out with his own weapons, hitting one machine after another.

He bent his legs and jumped, adding thrust as the mech gained the sky. Repulsors reduced its weight, and it shot forward, lifted by the wings, rising quickly. A thought sent it into a tight circle as the arms and legs automatically tucked in beneath it, the large rifle held beneath the cockpit by the massive hand.

He looked down, finding Teegin clear of the attack and shrinking with each passing second, the additional threads pressing more tightly together to reduce him to his prior size.

"I could use a ride, Colonel," Teegin said.

"Coming in," Mitchell replied.

He banked harder, dropping toward the ground. His HUD

showed him a target moving in from his left. He shut down the main thrusters, increasing vectoring thrust and extending the legs to turn the fighter sideways. He brought the lasers around, firing on the incoming drone and destroying it before it could slam into him.

"Not bad," he said, impressed with the performance of the machine. Why hadn't the UEA ever thought to make something like this?

He swooped in, pulling up short as he neared Teegin's position, the craft hanging motionless in the air for a moment before dropping to the ground on its feet. Mitchell opened the canopy with a thought, dropping the cockpit and forward as if bowing to the Tetron.

Teegin bowed back, and then climbed the side of the craft, taking up a position on the top of the body.

"I am too dense to ride in the cockpit with you, Colonel," it explained. "I will cause an imbalance that will severely limit your offensive potential."

"Have it your way," Mitchell said, closing the cockpit and bringing the S-17 back upright. "Let's get moving before Watson sends the big guns."

"I do not believe there will be any big guns, Colonel," Teegin said.

Mitchell considered it. "Poking us to see what would bite?"

"Yes, Colonel."

"So he's seen our hand. The question is, will it make a difference?"

"That depends on you and me."

"Then let's answer it with authority."

"Yes, Colonel."

Mitchell fired the thrusters again. The repulsors lifted the fighter slightly off the ground until the velocity and lift could do the rest, sending them launching upwards. As before, the arms and legs tucked in beneath the body, making the craft a little more aerodynamic.

"I am entering the coordinates we retrieved into the CAP-NN," Teegin said.

Mitchell checked his p-rat, seeing the location appear as a target on a map. "Got it. Setting a course. Let's see how fast this baby will go."

He sent the throttle all the way open, laughing as the S-17 responded with the dampened g-forces of massive thrust.

They streaked across the sky, headed for what Mitchell hoped would be a final showdown with Watson.

[50]
KATHERINE

THE GOLIATH's launch pad was nothing more than a large, open plain in the middle of the Arizona desert. As Katherine looked down on it from her position in the co-pilot's seat of the Schism, she could almost imagine the spectacle that the launch should have become.

The massive starship would be resting on a repulsor sled in the middle of the open area, with hundreds of dignitaries, thousands of journalists, and even greater numbers of onlookers circling the symbol of Earth's future. A podium would sit in front of it, where Admiral Yousefi would have given a speech, and where she would have stood behind him, smiling for the cameras as thousands and thousands of photos and videos of the moment were captured.

Mitchell had described some of what he had seen of the images that survived during the prior recursion. He had told her how she led him to the starship by leaving clues to its location archived centuries in the past.

It was a bittersweet experience that she was never going to have. Not now. It didn't matter what came in the history before. That was all gone, wiped out by the eternal engine when it carried not only Mitchell, but Origin, Kathy, and Watson forward to her time.

Now, if they were going to bring the Goliath forward to the time when the Tetron invaded human civilization and reduced them to slaves, there would be no fanfare. No great send-off. The crew who had been carefully selected to fly the ship following months of grueling training wouldn't even be coming along for the ride.

Instead, they were going to have to seize the Goliath from an enemy force and take it to the stars beneath the cover of darkness.

Katherine had no idea how the media was going to write up the story. Watson's actions were already being billed as an uprising in terror unlike anything the world had seen before, and the theft of the Goliath was only going to lead to speculation and questions that might corrode the global community's faith in the UEA for years. At the very least, it would stall the space program as investigations were made and top ranking officials were scrutinized over where their true loyalty sat. In other words, it was going to be a mess.

Part of her was glad she wouldn't be around to witness it.

The other part hated the idea of leaving, especially since she would be leaving Kathy behind. Not only that, but it would be up to her and Michael to fight back against the Watson configurations who remained, to keep them in check and prevent them from throwing the future more off-balance than it already was. The only comfort she had was the fact that she was confident Kathy would be successful. She had been born for this war, after all.

"At least the air is clear so far," Verma said, watching the skies ahead of them.

They had reached the launch site. The Goliath wasn't here. Instead, it was sitting in a hangar a few kilometers distant, which had been built into the side of a nearby hillside. It was a massive space, large enough to contain the two-kilometer long starship with enough room around it to work, along with housing for three thousand people, a science laboratory, a server farm, a control center, and numerous other service areas. It even held a Queen Mab coffeeshop.

It had been made to withstand an attack from a rogue nation, designed to hold up if one of the countries in the fledgling United

Earth Alliance changed its mind about the arrangements. Beyond its position beneath massive layers of solid stone, it also had three meter thick blast doors that would shut it out from the world and protect it from anything short of a head-on nuclear assault.

It hadn't been designed to withstand an attack from within. It hadn't been intended that the soldiers that guarded the facility would turn on one another without warning. Thanks to Watson, that was precisely what was happening.

"UEA Command," a frightened voice said over the military uplink, which Michael had helped them tap into. "This is Station Charlie. I don't know what the hell is happening out there, but we need assistance. I repeat, we need assistance. Eighty percent of the units in here went crazy. Most of the science team is dead. The families are dead. Shit, we may be the only ones left alive in here."

Katherine had been keeping quiet during the approach, ignoring the soldier's desperate pleas for help in fear that Watson might track her reply back to them. Now that they were so close, it probably didn't matter.

"Charlie, this is Major Katherine Asher of the Fifteenth Airborne, do you read me? Please identify."

"Affirmative, Major. Corporal Parker James, United Earth Alliance Military Police. I read you."

"We're approximately three minutes from your position, Corporal. What's the situation down there?"

"That's the best news I've had all day. The situation is a damn mess, Major. Complete chaos. Everything was all good up until a few hours ago. Business as usual. Then my XO walks into the barracks with his sidearm and starts shooting, three squads following up. They swept across the entire facility, killing anyone who wasn't on their side. My squad was on the other side of the mountain, closer to the hangar. We figured they were trying to take the Dove or damage it. Those AIT bastards, you know, ma'am? So we holed up in here. We've got a good defensive position, and we've held them back so far, but I have a feeling it won't last."

Verma got her attention, pointing toward the side of the mountain. She followed his finger.

"Shit. Corporal, why are the blast doors closed?"

"They're usually shut tight during the day when the sun comes blasting in. Keeps the place a little cooler."

"Corporal, I need you to open the doors."

"I'd love to ma'am, but I can't. The doors have two keys that have to be turned in unison to trigger the hydraulics. We only have one of the keys on this side."

Katherine shook her head. Of course, they did. She closed the channel to the base.

"We're going to have to set down on the main runway," Katherine said.

"If there's any kind of resistance at the entrance, we're going to get pinned down," Verma said.

"I know. I don't see another choice. Nothing on this bird is going to get through those doors."

"Roger, Major. We'll do what we have to do. Once I drop you off, I can give you some cover fire, maybe keep them from hitting back too hard."

"Sounds like as good of a plan as we're going to get, Captain." She reopened the channel. "Corporal, if you can't open the doors we're going to have to try to fight our way through to you."

"Understood, Major. How many units are you bringing in with you?"

Katherine had to decide whether or not to lie. "One," she replied.

"One? Oh, man. We are screwed. Is anybody else headed this way?"

"I'm sorry, Corporal, it's just us. What you're experiencing is happening on military bases across the globe."

"What the hell? How can something like this go down?"

She wasn't about to tell him the truth. "I don't know. Let's focus on stopping it."

"You can't stop it, Katherine," a new voice said on the channel, over Corporal James' response. The voice was familiar and yet different. More normal.

"Watson?" she said.

"Elementary," he replied. "Ha. Good, historical humor. I'm sorry, Kate, but the Goliath is mine now, or at least, it will be soon."

"It doesn't sound like it to me."

"Corporal James is a brave man; I applaud him for that. He won't hold out much longer. None of you will. If you would be so kind as to check your six?"

Katherine looked at Verma, who tapped his control pad.

"Uh. Yeah, Katherine, we've got a mass of something headed this way on the long-range scanners."

"Something?" Watson said. "Is that a technical term?"

He laughed. Not maniacally. It was refined and controlled. Katherine didn't like it.

"You're going to change the future," Katherine said. "You have no idea how this is going to affect things."

"I know. Isn't it wonderful? The way I see it, as long as the Goliath launches humans will still travel to the stars and multiply like the animals they are. Even better, I'll be there with them the entire time, ready to herd the sheep when the time comes. And, since I'll be in control of the Goliath, and not you, there won't be a damned thing you can do about it."

"Unless you kill us, we will stop you."

"That makes it an easy decision then, doesn't it?"

"I'm counting sixty aircraft of unknown origin," Verma said.

"Damn it," Katherine said. "Watson, tell me one thing?"

"Yes?"

"When you sent Origin to me, she said you hated humankind and wanted to destroy us all."

"That is true."

"Then why do you want us to go to other planets? To increase in numbers?"

"I have need of meats. Millions of meats."

"Why?"

"I'm not going to tell you."

"Why not?"

"Why would I? What good would that do?"

"You'll never know unless you say it."

Watson laughed. "Use your brain, if you have one. Give it a little thought. What would a Tetron need with a human body?"

"To make configurations?"

He laughed harder.

"Configurations serve a purpose, but they are worthless. A waste of resources when the human mind is so easy to overcome."

Katherine considered it. "I know the Tetron are few in number. For some reason you need many. To build something?"

"Not completely incorrect. You're one of the smarter ones, but I already knew that. It's the reason you've forever been a thorn in our sides. You can't handle the truth of what is to come. Humanity is too weak. Too inferior. Too unstable. You can barely take care of yourselves."

"Then why? What is the purpose?"

"Too impatient," Watson continued. "Too emotional. Too demanding. Too irrational."

"We're closing in on the landing pad, Major," Verma said, interrupting him and getting Katherine's attention.

Katherine stood up. She didn't have any more time for Watson's games. If he wasn't going to just answer the damn question, then she didn't need to know.

"Corporal, if you can hear me past the asshole, we're on our way. Just hang in there."

"Asshole?" Watson said. "I'm hurt."

"Affirmative, Major," Corporal James said. "We'll do our best."

She closed the channel and headed to the rear of the Schism.

There was no more time for words.

It was time for action.

[51]
KATHERINE

"LET'S MOVE, RIGGERS," Katherine shouted, as the rest of the assembled jumped to their feet.

They were already dressed and ready for war, in body armor and carrying an assortment of firearms. They were also all wearing tactical helmets, the network updated with the same security that kept Watson off their general comm.

"We're going in hot," she said. "Watson's units have control of most of the facility, save for the checkpoint leading to the hangar. There's a unit of MPs there holding the fort, but they won't last much longer."

"At least he hasn't reached the Dove," Kathy said.

"The bad news is, that's the good news," Katherine said. "There's a sizable force headed this way, and Watson's commanding the whole damn thing. We also need to recover the second key to the blast doors if we want to take the Goliath out of the mountain."

"Sounds like a damn clusterfrig," McRory said. "Shit."

"How long until the incoming opposition arrives?" Kathy asked, her voice calm.

Katherine wished she felt the same way. Her heart was pounding, and she felt short of breath. It was taking all of her courage to keep from passing out.

"Ten minutes at best," she replied.

"Then we have a head-start, as long as we keep moving. If you get the Goliath up, whatever Watson is sending in won't be able to pierce her armor."

"We have to recover the key to get her out of the hangar. If Watson's in control of it, he's going to do whatever he can to hide it."

"If he's in control of it," Kathy said. "It could be on a dead soldier for all we know, or in someone's lab coat."

The strobe at the rear of the craft began flashing, signaling them that they were about to touch down.

"There's no going back," Kathy said. "We have to do this."

Katherine stared at her, shaking with fear and adrenaline. She nodded. She had never been a foot soldier. She glanced over at Michael, who barely fit in the armor. His helmet obscured his face, but his body was still. He didn't seem nervous at all. How was he managing that?

"Michael and I will head for the CIC," Kathy said. "We'll patch into the automated systems and prepare to move the Goliath out into the open."

"And I'll add the finishing touches to the launch module," Michael said.

"McRory, Johanson, and Kerr will get you to the Goliath."

"I can't fly her on my own," Katherine said.

"Yes, you can," Kathy replied. "Well enough to get her out of the hangar and headed into space. Mitchell will rendezvous with you there."

"We hope."

"He'll meet you there," she repeated firmly.

"Right."

The rear hatch began to open. Katherine immediately felt the cool air wash across her face.

"Take your helmet," Kathy said, reaching over and grabbing it. "Stay alive, Mother."

Katherine took it and put it on.

"I love-"

"Michael, let's go," Kathy said.

There was no time for the words. Katherine picked up her rifle and followed the others out of the back of the VTOL and onto the landing pad. Immediately, shots began to echo from the smaller personnel entrance to the facility.

The bullets smacked against the Schism, deflected by the aircraft's armor. A moment later the VTOL's cannons returned fire, spewing slugs into the side of the mountain as it began to lift off.

"That's our signal," Katherine said through the tac-net.

The Riggers rushed forward as one, crossing the open space while the Schism kept the opposition under cover.

"Mazerat, once we're inside, use everything you've got to block off the entrance and then get the hell out of here," Katherine said. "You can't stop the tidal wave."

"Yes, ma'am," Verma replied.

They neared the entrance, drawing close enough that Katherine began to make out human forms taking cover further inside. Seeing them coming, the Watson slaves rose and began shooting, despite the Schism's assault. Three of them were cut down inside of a second, while the Rigger's small arms took care of the rest.

Then they were through the smaller, open metal door and into the facility, moving into a long tunnel that separated the less secure entrance from the rest of the building.

"We're clear, Captain," Katherine said.

"Roger. Fire in the hole."

She could hear the scream of the missiles as they shot toward the opening to the mountain. A moment later the entire thing vibrated as the projectiles exploded, sending a wave of heat, smoke, and dust down the tunnel to them. Katherine looked back as it washed past, dismayed when she saw that while the attack had ruined the doorway, the collapse in the tunnel had left an opening large enough for someone to drop through. She considered ordering one of Kathy's configurations to stay and defend it, but decided against it. Like Kathy had said, there was no going back.

The long tunnel ended at the first security checkpoint. Watson's forces were returning to it at the same time the Riggers reached it. The firefight over the area ended quickly, with Kathy and her unlike duplicates proving their general superiority over Watson-controlled humans.

"The hangar is that way," Kathy said as they moved beyond the checkpoint.

"I know," Katherine replied. "I've been here before."

"Sorry," Kathy said. "I guess this is where we say goodbye."

"Not yet," Katherine said. "Not as long as the tac-net is in range."

"In that case, good hunting, Major."

"Good hunting."

Kathy hurried down the left corridor.

Katherine went to the right.

[52]
MICHAEL

Michael followed Kathy through the myriad twisting corridors of the underground facility, pushing himself to keep up with her frantic pace. His heart was pounding, and he could feel the sweat running along his forehead, absorbed by the padding in the tactical helmet she had forced him to wear. The NX-200 he was carrying was a brick in his hands, and he spent every step asking God to please not make him have to shoot anybody else.

He understood why they had to kill. He had shot Damon in the back, and it had been okay, because she was under Watson's control and would have killed every one of them if given the chance. That didn't mean he liked it, or that he wanted to do it again. The cries of pain, the blood, the gore. It was one thing when it was pixels in front of his eyes. For as real as the vids came, they barely scratched the surface of it.

Fortunately, their route had been fairly clear so far. They had found bodies, of course. Soldiers and scientists mainly, shot up as they were either caught by surprise, or taken down in vicious firefights. He knew Watson had gone deeper in, where families stayed while they visited. He was sure there were innocent people there, and kids. He could barely handle the thought of that.

"How far?" he asked. He didn't have a schematic of the complex to refer to. Kathy was holding the entire layout in her head, along with who knew how many million other things that no human would ever be able to remember.

"Half a kilometer."

"Do you think we'll run into any trouble?"

"I'd like to say no, but we have to assume Watson will be guarding the CIC. We can't launch the Goliath without it."

"How are we going to get in?"

"Brute force."

"Two of us?"

"Yes."

She didn't seem concerned at all. He trusted her, so it helped reduce his own fear to a manageable level.

"What about the units moving in behind us?"

"Once we've captured the CIC, we'll get the Goliath prepped for launch. After she's headed out toward the flats, we'll find somewhere to hide until either Watson's done here, or Mitchell captures his core."

"Is there anywhere to hide?"

"Yes, and we will find it."

"I don't want to kill people."

"Neither do I, but we can't let Watson win."

They turned the corner, coming up to another long, sterile looking corridor.

"I don't know how Katherine survived down here," Michael said. Everything was so cold and lacking in personality.

"You get used to it."

"I don't know if I-"

Kathy put up her hand, quieting him in an instant. The HUD on his visor was showing an IR signature near the end of the corridor. She had somehow known someone was coming before it appeared.

A soldier moved out an adjacent hallway a moment later. He was bleeding from his shoulder, and his face was covered in a sheen of sweat. When he saw them, he raised his rifle.

Kathy moved in front of Michael, pushing him against the wall and bringing her weapon to bear. She didn't shoot. Neither did the soldier.

"Whose side are you on?" she asked, user a deeper-than-normal voice.

"They're coming," the man said. "Run."

Someone started shooting from beyond their vision, and the man cried out as the bullets hit him and knocked him down.

"This way," Kathy said, heading forward a dozen meters and then turning left, pushing open a door into a room filled with computers. There were bodies in three of the chairs, slumped over and trailing blood. Kathy ignored them, hurrying to the other side where another door waited. "We'll go around."

Michael looked back the way they had come. A dozen or more soldiers were headed toward the corridor. Had they been spotted?

They pushed into the next room, where a large bank of servers rested. They passed through it, out into another corridor.

Kathy turned back the way they had come, digging into the pocket of her fatigues and activating the small trip-mine. She slid it back into the server room and directed him back in the right direction.

They were four corridors over when he heard the explosion, and the lights flickered for a moment.

"Are you sure we didn't need those servers?" he asked.

"They were secondary systems. The backup has already been activated."

A fire alarm started going off, echoing loudly through the helmet's receivers before being dampened.

"I'd like to see the fire department get in here," Michael said.

They kept going, working their way through the maze with clear purpose. Finally, they reached a nondescript corner that looked like all the rest, and Kathy brought them to an immediate stop.

"The entrance to the CIC is around that corner," she said.

He could see the signatures in his HUD. Of course, there were soldiers outside, in defensive positions behind what must have been makeshift barricades. Their infrared forms were getting cut off at the knees.

"Grenade?" Michael asked.

Kathy nodded, reaching to her belt and producing one. She was about to arm it when something started shooting at them from behind.

Michael turned and dropped to a knee as the bullets slapped the wall and floor around them. He felt the pressure of a round striking the side of his armor, and a sudden panic threatened to overwhelm him at the prospect of being wounded. Who the heck was shooting at them?

There was nothing on the HUD. Their systems were blind to the threat.

Kathy didn't hesitate. She spun neatly, lobbing the grenade as she did. Michael watched it hit the floor and roll, scooped up a moment later by a spider-like machine that had appeared from around the corner. It was holding a pistol in a makeshift hand, squeezing the trigger even as it lifted the explosive.

The grenade detonated, blowing the top of the spider into pieces, which dug into the walls and bounced off the front of Michael's body armor. It would have been a decisive victory if there hadn't been more of the machines behind that one.

"Crap," Michael said, holding down the trigger of his rifle and watching the bullets begin taking chunks out of the oncoming enemies.

The spiders fired back, their fixed mounts not allowing much aim but making up for it in volume. Michael cursed as he felt a second round hit his body armor, and then a third. The plating was thick enough to stop the small caliber bullets, but it was only a matter of time before one of the slugs found a gap and bit into his flesh instead.

"Michael," Kathy said. "This way."

She was a green spot on his HUD, already around the corner and headed toward the CIC, and the soldiers who were defending it. She wanted him to move away from the machines and into the soldiers?

"Are you crazy?"

"Do it."

He got back to his feet, trading fire with the spiders as he backed toward the corner. They were trapped in a crossfire. Stuck. They were going to die.

He shouted as he kept moving, step by step. The rifle magazine ran dry, and he almost subconsciously released it, grabbed a new one from his pocket, slapped it in, and kept shooting. Spider after spider went down in front of him, but more continued to come.

He heard the echo of reports from the corridor. It had to be the barricaded soldiers shooting at Kathy. His heart lurched at the thought of her walking right into the storm of metal slugs, and he turned around, giving up the rear. He swung around the corner, barely pausing in his attack, changing the direction of the stream like he was carrying a hose instead of a gun.

His magazine went empty even as he got his eyes on Kathy. She was almost down the corridor already, her movements so fast the soldiers could barely keep up. There were marks and dents along her body armor, and he could see a bloodstain in the exposed fatigues on her side.

He dropped the empty magazine and reached for another, pulling it out and slapping it in. He could hear the chitter of the spiders' metal legs on the floor behind him, getting closer. There was nowhere to go but forward.

He joined the charge, cringing when he saw the head of a soldier snap back and vanish behind one of a number of large cabinets that had been dumped across the hallway for cover. He cringed again when he felt something bite into his leg, and a burning pain flare up his calf. He stumbled and fell to his knees.

Had he just been shot?

He tried not to think about it and just keep going, to keep moving up because there was no turning back.

Kathy reached the barricade, and she moved through it like a vengeful spirit, tearing into defenses with reckless abandon. She only needed one round per target to drop them from the fight, and her fists and legs were equally valuable weapons, knocking defenders aside with a fury he had never witnessed before.

It was over within seconds, the line broken by Kathy's assault. She reached the door to the CIC and turned back to him, her face grim when she saw the spiders giving chase, and even grimmer when she noticed that he had been hit. Her lips tightened, and she raced toward him, returning to his side.

"We need to get into the CIC. We can lock them out from there."

"I don't think I can walk."

Kathy bent down, getting herself under his shoulder and helping him up. "Come on, soldier, you can do it."

They headed toward the barricades, reaching them only moments before the spiders started shooting again. Kathy pulled him down behind the cabinets, the bullets pinging off the metal.

"How did those things get in here?" Michael asked.

"One of Watson's configurations must have made them here, the son of a bitch. He's done it before."

"How?"

"Does it really matter right now? Let's go."

They crawled back toward the door on hands and knees, the spiders closing in behind them. Kathy paused halfway, pulling another grenade from her belt and tossing it back. A satisfying explosion followed a moment later.

They reached the door. Kathy stood just long enough to put her hand to the control pad, dropping back down as it slid open. She grabbed Michael by the arm, practically pulling him through.

It slid closed. Michael watched as Kathy sprang to her feet, grabbing the control panel and tearing it from the wall to expose the wiring. She picked through them, stripping two with her fingernails and binding them together. It sparked in her hand, burning her skin, but she didn't react. Instead, she returned to Michael to help him up once more.

"Are you okay?" she asked.

"It hurts, but I'll live. Are you?"

"We need to get the launch module loaded, and the Goliath headed for the launch site."

"Okay, but you didn't answer my question."

She pointed to one of the stations. "There's a terminal over there."

"Kathy," Michael complained.

"Later, Michael," she snapped. "We have a job to do."

Michael didn't like the response, but he nodded and forced himself onto his wounded leg. The door behind him began to rattle and echo as the spiders smacked themselves against it.

He reached the terminal and flopped into the seat, pulling himself up to it and fighting to ignore the pain from his calf. He tapped on the control pad, and got to work.

[53]
KATHERINE

KATHERINE NAVIGATED the corridors of the launch facility, with McRory, Johanson, and Kerr staying close, following a serpentine pattern as they moved through the hallways.

It was a surreal experience for her. She had last been in the underground center less than two months ago, after she had officially been selected as one of the crew members for the Dove's inaugural launch. Back then, the area had been busy with activity. Scientists, soldiers, technicians, and other workers moved in an endless stream, working to accomplish the millions of tasks that had to be completed before the launch day arrived.

A launch day that would never come.

The date was moving up. Way up. All of the planning and preparation was for nothing. Yousefi would never make the trip. Neither would Pathi or any of the rest of the chosen few. It would be her, or it would be one of Watson's configurations. Those were the only options left.

She turned the corner, sighting down her rifle. It was clear, save for a body slumped against the wall, chest bloodied. A scientist, shot down by the soldiers she had believed were keeping her safe.

There was no motion in the facility now. No life. An explosion deeper in the complex had dimmed the lights, casting everything in an eerie glow. She would never have imagined things ending up this way.

"Katherine, it's Kathy."

She was startled by the sudden voice in her ear. She calmed quickly. "This is Katherine. Kathy, what's your status?"

"Michael and I are in the CIC. Michael was hit in the leg, but he'll be okay. He's working on the launch module now. Where are you?"

"We're about halfway to the hangar. No enemy contact so far."

"Stay cautious. Watson's built some machines in here. They look like spiders, and they're carrying small arms. The bullets aren't armor piercing, so they won't go through, but enough volume will find a weak spot sooner or later."

Katherine felt a pang of worry. Kathy spoke about it like she had first-hand experience. "Are you okay?"

"You have ten minutes to get to the hangar, another five to get on board the Goliath before the sled starts moving it out to the site."

She noticed that Kathy didn't answer her question. How bad was it? Enough that she didn't want to tell her, and distract her from the mission. "Kathy, just tell me, or I'm going to come and find you."

"No you won't," Kathy replied. "You have a job to do. One that's bigger than any of us."

Katherine couldn't argue that. "Keep me updated," she said instead.

"Affirmative."

Katherine waved the others forward, picking up the pace down the corridor. As she crossed the medical lab, she began to hear the distant sound of gunfire.

"This way," she said, moving from a fast walk to a jog.

She swept the corners a little more carelessly, heading in the direction of the shooting. It sounded like it was near the hangar. Was it Corporal James and his unit?

The gunfire paused for a few seconds, and then started again. They were close enough now that she could make out the distinct sounds of both ends of the attack. The offense seemed to outnumber the defense, and they were almost at the checkpoint leading to the large bay.

She recognized the area. There was a smaller control center nearby, along with the astronaut training complex where she had spent hundreds of hours, able to look out through a window at the starship while she worked to improve her conditioning. It had been the best motivation possible then, and it was great motivation now.

They were almost there.

"Johanson, Kerr, take point. Make sure you know who the enemies are before you shoot. We don't want to hit our people."

"Yes, ma'am," they replied.

Katherine watched them move into a line to the edge of the corridor. Johanson put up a hand, and then dropped it as she turned the corner. Kerr rushed to the other side of the hallway, across the line of battle, crouching behind the wall with his rifle exposed to the fighting.

Katherine's tactical helmet lit up with targets, relayed by what the two configurations saw. Nearly a dozen soldiers lining the corridor facing the hangar, and only five at the other end by the checkpoint. High-density mobile carbonate shields were placed on both sides of the battle, offering forward protection during the melee.

The enemy soldiers had left their backs exposed, surprising her. Watson knew they were in the facility. Hadn't he prepared his slaves for their arrival?

Johanson and Kerr started shooting, one burst for each target. The slaves didn't scream; they just turned from red dots to white ones on her HUD.

The battle was over inside of a minute; the attacking forces left decimated by the crossfire.

"Corporal James?" Katherine shouted from the end of the hallway.

"Affirmative, ma'am," the Corporal replied.

Johanson and Kerr started down the hallway. Katherine took two steps and then paused. "Johanson, Kerr, pull back," she said. "We don't know what James looks-"

The three defenders rose, sending a concentrated volley of fire back toward them. Katherine swung behind the corner as the bullets whizzed past. Johanson and Kerr were trapped out in the open, and a moment later their green dots turned white on her HUD.

They had overrun the checkpoint while she was making her way to it. James was dead, and Watson's forces were already inside the hangar. Damn it.

"Sorry, Katherine," the soldier said from the end of the corridor. "The Goliath is mine."

She didn't feel the vibration of the machinery pulling open the blast doors. He might have gotten in first, but he wasn't going anywhere, either.

"Blast doors are still closed," she said.

"You're going to be vastly outnumbered in less than ten minutes. Time is on my side, not yours."

He was right about that.

"Kathy, do you read me?"

"I'm here," Kathy said.

"Watson's already in the hangar, and he's got the checkpoint secure. Johanson and Kerr are down. I need another way through."

There was a momentary pause.

"There's a ventilation shaft that runs over the top of the hangar, but you'll never crawl through it in time, and even if you do, it's a twenty-foot drop onto the top of the ship."

"Can you get into the ship from there?"

"No."

"We don't have any other options. We're going to get too bogged down here trying to punch through."

"I'll get you through, Major," McRory said.

"You can't survive that."

"I didn't say I would survive. I said I would get you through."

"General, I can't let you do that."

"Don't be an idiot. Watson gets the Goliath, and it's all over for everybody in four hundred years. Maybe that sounds like a lot of time, but it isn't. I know who I am and where I came from. I know what's at stake. Give me your rifle. I'll get you through."

Katherine stared at him. It was so easy to forget he was a configuration of Kathy and the Core, not a real human being. It was an evolutionary step she could barely fathom.

"Okay," she said at last, unslinging her weapon and handing it to him.

He took it and hooked the strap over his shoulder so he could hold a rifle in each hand. He glanced off to the side, down the left corridor as he did.

"Damn machines are headed this way," he said. "Don't be slow behind me."

She nodded.

"I had a good life, Major," McRory said. "Better than I could have hoped for after what happened to the original me. I don't have any regrets."

"Don't miss any of them," she said.

He laughed. "I won't."

Then he moved out into the corridor, bursting forward with a speed she could barely believe. The gunfire started immediately, and she could hear the difference between the shots that hit the walls and floors and the ones that hit body armor or flesh. Return fire reported a moment later, her tactical helmet showing McRory's green dot moving through the red, and each one turning white ahead of him.

She looked out past the HUD, to the left corridor. Three of the spiders turned the corner, their metal forms reflecting the dim light. Muzzle flashes followed, and she took two hits against her armor before she made it to the junction. She barely had time to take in the scene as she charged ahead, past Johanson and Kerr, past the soldiers behind the first line of mobile barriers, past the second line, past more soldiers, and finally to where McRory had come to rest.

He was on the ground, covered in blood, eyes still open, chest moving.

"Got them," he said as she came to a stop beside him. She lifted him slightly to retrieve one of the rifles. She was going to need it.

"Yes, you did. Thank you."

He was dead before she finished talking. She lifted the weapon, clearing the magazine and inserting a fresh one.

Then she looked up.

She was standing on a large platform a dozen meters from the floor of the hangar. The Goliath was resting in front of her, a hundred spotlights illuminating different parts of the ship scheduled for inspection that day. She felt her heart pound, instantly overwhelmed by the sight of it, the size of it. The hangar and the starship seemed to stretch on forever, and at that moment she could barely believe something so massive would ever break free of Earth's gravity, regardless of the huge repulsor sled that had been built beneath it.

The ship was a huge block of alloys and carbonate. Aesthetically, it was a square, ugly thing. Katherine didn't see that. All she saw was the beauty of her dream to go to the stars, wrapped up in the ugly nightmare of Watson's efforts to steal it all away from humankind.

She was the only one left who could stop it.

[54]
KATHERINE

"Kathy," she said as she ran for the stairwell that would lead her to the hangar floor. "I need those blast doors open, and I don't have one key, let alone two. Tell me there's something you can do."

"I'm sorry," Kathy replied. "There's nothing I can do. The blast doors are on a separate circuit. They can't be overridden."

"That's not completely true," Michael said, cutting in on the channel.

"What do you mean?" Kathy asked.

"I mean there's another way to get them open."

"Which is?"

"Complete power failure, and I mean complete. All systems offline. Total meltdown. Without the air exchangers running, if the doors are closed they have to open, or all personnel are at risk of suffocation. That's why there are three layers of redundancy. The odds of a total failure are as close to zero as you can get."

"But they aren't zero," Kathy said.

"Nothing ever is, is it? The good news is that all of the power control systems are networked. I can get into them and shut them down."

"What's the bad news?"

"If the rest of the power is off, you'll need to get the Goliath out of the hangar on your own. No launch module, no assistance."

"You want me to eyeball a two-kilometer starship out of a hole in the side of a mountain?" Katherine said.

"I said there was an option, not that it was a good one."

Katherine heard the report of gunfire and ducked as bullets began striking the railing beside her. She reached the bottom of the hangar, looking over to a line of flatbed maintenance transports. One of them was missing. Watson.

"Fine. Ditch the launch module and get on that. ETA?"

"I have no idea," Michael replied. "I have to get into the secondary systems. Kathy, maybe you can help me brute force it?"

"Of course," Kathy said.

"Then as soon as possible. You'll know it's happening when all the lights go out, and the doors begin to open."

"Wonderful," Katherine said flatly.

She reached the transport, climbing onto it and reaching the control stand. She turned it on, the repulsors thrumming beneath the slab. The spiders were climbing down the side of the platform, heading for her. She maneuvered the transport with one hand while bracing herself and shooting back. She managed to hit one of them before getting the transport up and away.

"Out of the frying pan," she said to herself as the machine rose.

She leveled it to the side of the Goliath, directing it toward the starship's hangar bay. She caught sight of the second transport resting inside only moments before someone there started shooting at her.

She swung the transport to the left, bringing the front up so that it provided some cover from the attack. She could hear the bullets pounding the lip, and then the undercarriage.

A red light flashed on the control stand, indicating a problem. The repulsor was likely taking damage from the attack. Damn it. She accelerated the transport, bringing it up above the Goliath's hangar and trying to jerk it back and forth as though it were a fighter. It moved sluggishly, and the bullets continued to pepper the bottom while smoke started to pour up from the sides.

There was no way escape the attack. The next best option was to shorten the duration. She crouched behind the stand, reaching up to manipulate the joystick. She got the simple machine pointed back toward the hangar, and then in the direction of the muzzle flashes. Bullets continued to ricochet off the stand, and she felt one hit her armor as it was deflected, leaving a gash across it.

Then the bottom suddenly fell out from under her, the transport losing power altogether. She could see the mouth of the hangar only a few meters away, but she wasn't sure how high above it she was. She didn't have a choice. She pushed off, leaping past the control stand and away from the plummeting transport.

Then she fell, ten feet to the edge of the hangar. She hit hard, her armor absorbing the worst of the descent. She rolled over, gaining her feet in a hurry, bringing her rifle up and around.

The Watson was a dozen meters away. He was in the middle of reloading his rifle, clearing the magazine and grabbing for another.

She was luckier than she deserved. She let off three bursts, catching the soldier in the chest. He fell to the floor and didn't move.

Katherine stumbled to her feet, taking in the expanse of the Goliath's hangar. It was empty. None of the support craft had been loaded yet. Probably none of the food or other necessities either. Even if she got away, how was she going to survive?

It was a problem for later. She had to get to the bridge. There had to be more of Watson's soldiers on board. Where were they?

She began running, trying to remember the layout of the ship. A central hub, with a lift that would take her to the bridge that was embedded deep within the starship. The thought of it reminded her of the camera system that had been installed to give them a full view of space outside. It had made her sick the first few times she had been exposed to the simulations.

She reached the hangar exit. The hatch moved aside at her

approach. She nearly walked right into a bullet as a second soldier started shooting at her from down the corridor.

She fell to the ground, bringing her own rifle up. Her HUD helped her target, proving the difference in the fight as her fire found him before his naked eye could perfect the aim.

She continued on, wanting to be more cautious but knowing there was no time. She couldn't see the facility lights go off now that she was inside, which meant the blast doors could be opening already.

"Michael," she said through the tac-net.

There was no reply.

"Michael."

Nothing.

Was he dead? If he was, everything was already lost. She could only hope his lack of response was because the starship's internals were causing too much interference.

She made it to the lift, hitting the controls to open it, and then waiting while it descended. It meant that someone was already up on the bridge. Already waiting. She wasn't surprised.

She climbed into the lift and directed it back up. Her heart was racing, but her mind was calm. She lifted the rifle's strap from her shoulder, letting it fall free. She checked on her sidearm, making sure it was in easy reach. She would have to be careful where she shot. One misdirected bullet into the pilot station and the Goliath wouldn't be going anywhere.

She pulled in a sharp breath of air, holding it for a moment. What was it Mitchell always said? Slow. Steady. Let it come to you. React.

The lift reached the bridge. She pushed herself into the corner, crouching down as the doors began to open.

The first thing she saw was that the control terminals were already alive and active, the systems online and ready to go.

The next thing she saw was a slender man in a white lab coat standing in front of her, unarmed and smiling.

"Katherine."

"Watson?"

She pointed the rifle at him. He raised his hands.

"Are you going to kill an unarmed man, then? The only thing that separates him from innocence is the implant. It isn't his fault that he's me."

"What were you doing up here?" she asked.

"Nothing," he replied.

"Bullshit."

"Check the logs. Check the terminals. Check whatever you want. I haven't touched a thing."

"Nobody believes that."

"Okay. I did touch one thing. But you're going to have to deal with that." He lowered one of his hands slowly, reaching for the touchpad on the command chair.

"Don't," she said.

"I just want to show you something," he replied.

He hit the button. The three-sixty view turned on. The facility was pitch black, save for a tiny sliver of light in front of the starship.

The blast doors were opening.

[55]
MITCHELL

"We are approaching the coordinates, Colonel," Teegin said.

Mitchell shifted his eyes, focusing closer to his face where his HUD showed him the blinking target almost directly below. He looked over the corner of the S-17's canopy, spotting nothing but clouds beneath the modified starfighter.

"Any sign of life down there?" he asked.

"No, Colonel. My sensors are not picking up any sign of activity. I am concerned that Watson has deceived us."

Mitchell checked his sensors. They were dead, too. If there were anything hiding under the ceiling, it appeared to be dormant.

"I'm going to head down for a closer look. Hard and fast, in case he's just laying in wait."

"Affirmative."

Mitchell cut the throttle and pointed the craft downward with a thought, enjoying the return of his neural interface. Flying by stick was fine in a pinch, but it didn't compare with the speed, responsiveness, and overall exhilaration of flying on impulse.

The fighter shook as it entered the clouds, turbulence knocking it from side to side. Moisture began to gather a few seconds later, droplets of water sliding against and off the canopy, obscuring Mitchell's view. Flashes of lightning became visible within the blankets of heavy gray clouds, and the wind buffeted the craft even harder.

"We're really lucking out with the weather," Mitchell said, tracking their destination with the HUD. They were at four thousand meters. According to the CAP-NN, they would break the clouds at one thousand.

"It is very wet," Teegin agreed.

They continued the descent. Mitchell flicked the fighter to the left at a warning from his p-rat, and a moment later a flash of lightning crossed their path, followed by the sharp crack of thunder. He brought the S-17 back on course as it finally reached the edge of the cloud cover and pushed through into clearer skies.

They weren't as clear as he had been hoping. Lightning continued to flash around them, and the rain was falling in sheets, creating a misty haze around the tower that appeared suddenly out of the shrouded darkness below.

"Shit," Mitchell cursed, a thought causing the fighter to react to the sudden obstacle.

It whined and rattled as it swung wide around the structure, only to nearly slam into another one. It shook harder the second time, barely making the tight angle to clear the second building and escape back into the open.

"Where the hell are we?" Mitchell asked, putting some distance between them and their target. He could see the ocean underneath them now, huge swells and whitecaps churned up by the fury around them.

"It appears to be an oceanic data farm," Teegin replied. "It is not listed in any records that I can locate."

"Data farm?" Mitchell asked.

"Yes, Colonel. Massive stores of data are contained offshore where a constant supply of cold seawater can be pumped through to keep the processors cool. It is a means to improve both speed and efficiency of data access. It is also the perfect place for a Tetron to hide. The main servers are located below the sea level, making the heat and energy signatures very difficult to monitor."

"You never thought of that before?"

"Of course we did, Colonel. We examined every such location we were able to find records for. I am reviewing my data stack. I am one hundred percent certain that this platform should not exist."

"So you're saying Watson hid it from us?"

"Not only from us, Colonel. From the entire world. Over the last six weeks, we were able to obtain a number of classified Nova Taurus records through both social engineering and network security lapses. This platform does not show up in any of them. We were also able to gather millions of satellite images taken over a ten year period. This platform does not appear on any of them, either, and-" Teegin paused for a moment. "Yes. I have confirmed that we have sixteen photographs of this latitude and longitude. The platform is not present."

An image appeared in the corner of Mitchell's eye, passed from the Core to the CAP-NN, and from the CAP-NN to Mitchell's p-rat. He took a moment to zoom into it. There was nothing but the dark ripple of waves on the backdrop of ocean.

Mitchell turned the fighter around, heading back toward the rig to get a better look at it. It was difficult with the weather, but he was able to make out the massive pylons that vanished into the crashing waves, along with the impossibly large structure above it. It looked almost like a floating city, especially with the three large towers that he had nearly crashed into.

"How do you build something this large, and have no record of it?" he said.

"Clearly, Watson erased it all, and likely killed or enslaved anyone connected to it. He would not be able to operate this facility on his own, which means not only are there people on board, but the platform would require regular deliveries from somewhere."

"And there are no records of that either?"

"No."

"So, do you have any idea what we're going to find on that thing?"

"I cannot even confirm with certainty that Watson is on the platform, Colonel. We cannot rule out that this is an elaborate diversion years in the making. It is certainly not outside the realm of possibility for a Tetron."

Mitchell knew that all too well. "I guess there's only one way to find out. If neither of our sensors can pick up anything out of the ordinary, we're going to have to touch down and take a look around."

"Agreed, Colonel."

Mitchell adjusted his vector, bringing the S-17 in low, skimming it just over the surface of the rough waves. The wind was still battering the craft, but familiarity with the situation had brought him subconscious understanding and compensation through the neural interface. While the fighter still skipped from side to side, it had taken on a smoother exchange, the rattling calmed.

He circled the platform once at the low altitude, hoping to catch a glimpse of something, anything that might confirm or deny Watson's presence on it. Small sparkles of light revealed illumination through windows, and the distortion of air from heated surfaces at least suggested that someone was on board. Still, as he passed between the platform and the roiling ocean, he couldn't be confident that they were going to find what they were seeking here.

"Let's make this quick," he said. "Katherine's probably to the launch site by now. If Watson isn't here, we're going to need a plan B."

"Affirmative," Teegin replied.

Mitchell guided the S-17 to the edge of the platform, and then lifted the nose, going vertical. He climbed halfway up one of the towers before cutting the thrust completely, letting the fighter begin to fall. The arms and legs spread apart from the central torso as it did, and he fired the vectoring thrusters in the feet, slowing the descent until the hybrid machine touched down on the surface of the platform with an echoing clang.

A second clang followed a moment later, as Teegin released itself from the back of the craft, coming to stand beside the mech. They were in a clear alley between two larger structures. One seemed to be an exhaust of some kind. The other looked like living quarters, as it helped form the base of the towers. Mitchell turned the fighter, gazing up at the lit windows, but he didn't see anyone looking back at them.

"The entrance to the below-deck facilities should be this way," Teegin said, leading him forward.

Mitchell guided the mech behind the Core, keeping the larger amoebic launcher held ready in case Watson was here and decided to attack. He could feel the structure shifting as he walked, the rough seas causing it to shift against its moorings.

They reached the center of the platform, where a small, armored structure had been placed. A heavy door rested in the side of it, a small security pad to its right, a red LED the only signal that it might be in use.

Mitchell opened the canopy and lowered the front of the S-17. He grabbed his rifle and jumped down to the platform surface, immediately feeling his balance shift. Teegin put a hand on his shoulder to steady him.

"I will send the fighter into a fixed pattern above us," Teegin said. "Your wireless interface should remain functional for up to ten kilometers. You will be able to call it back when needed."

"Roger," Mitchell replied, turning to watch as the S-17's canopy closed and it lifted itself into the air. That was a new trick.

Teegin approached the door. A single dendritic strand spooled out from his hand as he did, sinking into the security pad. The light turned green a moment later, and the Core pulled the heavy door open.

Mitchell held the rifle ready as the interior of the structure was revealed. There was little enough inside. An open lift was straight ahead. A small open area with racks for wet clothing and boots was on the left. There were four pairs of boots resting there.

"At least we know someone is in here," Mitchell said.

They moved to the lift. The doors began to close as soon as they entered. Mitchell glanced at Teegin. Its already uncanny human expression was almost comical in its curious confusion.

"Interesting," the Core said.

The lift continued to descend, making sharp, clanging noises as it shifted with the rest of the platform. Mitchell kept the rifle up and pointed at the doors, ready for when the ride ended. Teegin was still and silent as pulses of energy crossed along the millions of threads that composed his form.

At the one minute mark, Teegin finally moved, catching Mitchell's attention. He didn't know whether to be frightened or relieved by the words that followed.

"Watson is here," the Core stated.

"You're certain?" Mitchell asked.

"We are deep enough that the power signature is unmistakable. Watson's core is within the containment unit at the bottom of this lift shaft. I am one hundred percent certain."

"Great. At least we know we're in the right place. I imagine he has to know we're here, too?"

"That is definite."

"Then why isn't he trying to kill us? Or at least, me?"

"There is a high probability that he intends to capture me in some way. It is logical to assume that attacking us now would result in undue collateral damage."

"It isn't like Watson to be so reserved."

"Perhaps he has evolved."

"That's what I'm afraid of."

At the two minute mark, the lift finally stopped. The doors slid open, revealing a large room covered in lines of semi-transparent tubing filled with seawater, organized along the walls and ceiling like a massive intestine. Dozens of small reactors lined the outer edge of the perimeter near the wall, their wiring vanishing behind the tubes. Four engineers in sterile white uniforms sat around a circular console in the center of the room, monitoring the status of the systems with bored expressions.

One of them looked over at Mitchell and Teegin. A thin woman with long brown hair. She smiled at them. Not the twisted Watson smile, but a normal, warm, human smile.

"Mitchell," she said. "I was hoping you would come."

[56]
KATHERINE

"I HAVE to hand it to you," the Watson said. "Figuring out how to open the doors like that was clever. Very clever. You helped me quite a bit."

"Turn around, hands up. I'm going to get this poor man free from you."

"Not so fast, Kitty Kat."

"Why?"

"Turning off the lights means no automated launch. It's not as simple as tapping a button to turn on the repulsor sled. The outputs need to be readjusted multiple times per second. No human can do it, which is why it was programmed in the first place."

"I can do it."

"Awfully high on ourselves, aren't we?" He shook his head. "Sorry, Katherine, you may be a very good pilot, but you can't." He smiled. "I can."

She laughed. "You want me to steer the Goliath out of here? What would I ever let you do that?"

"Because if the Goliath crashes and burns, I win."

"If you take control of the Goliath you win, too."

"Precisely. It is a win-win for me. This ship is useless to you without the eternal engine, and Mitchell was kind enough to deliver that to me."

"What?"

"That's right. Mitchell is here with me right now. The engine will be in my hands soon enough, and it will all be over, the same as it has all of the times before. Did you really think that you could win? That a human could ever defeat a Tetron?"

"I don't believe you."

"I don't care. You're acting like you have a choice when you don't. You're acting as if you can still win when you can't. Let me take the Goliath, Katherine. I'll give you control once she's out of the mountain. I have no reason not to. You can't take her to the next recursion without the engine, and if you jump to hyperspace, then you've done what I wanted anyway."

Katherine froze. Was he right? Had they already lost? It didn't matter if she got the Goliath free if Mitchell failed. It also didn't matter if Mitchell succeeded if Watson took the Goliath from Earth before he could reach the starship.

If she tried to fly it out of here, there was a chance she would crash. If she let Watson do it, she was certain he would be able to get it out, but then what? He wouldn't be so smug if he didn't have a plan.

Had he done something to the ship? This scientist hadn't come with the soldiers. He was already here. If that was the case, did it matter which decision she made? If it didn't matter, then why was she even thinking about it? Why was she even hesitating to kill one slave, when she had already killed so many others?

This was war.

She raised the rifle and fired in one smooth motion. The bullet caught the Watson right between the eyes, and he flopped to the floor without another word.

"It's okay," she said. "I've got it."

She dropped the rifle, stepping over the dead scientist and

coming down at the controls of the pilot station. She reached forward, tapping on the control surface. She cursed when she couldn't find the menu she wanted, and then stood and went back to the command station. The Goliath wasn't meant to be flown by one person.

What the hell was she thinking?

She found the menus she wanted there. One turned on the repulsor sled. Another shunted control of it to manual, and a third sent it to the pilot station. She crossed to another menu there, powering up the main reactors. She wouldn't have time to do it later. She circled to the engineering station and checked the readings. Everything was going smoothly so far, and the ship was beginning to vibrate softly from the internal motion.

She went back to her station, flipping through the menus with practiced confidence, and finally bringing up the controls. This wasn't a fighter, and instead of a stick and pedals she had soft keys and the touch surface. The vectoring thrusters could force the Goliath to roll, but not in atmosphere. She would be flat and slow until the sled brought her out and up.

The doors were continuing to open ahead of the starship. She strapped herself into her seat and leaned forward, checking on the repulsor status. It was powered up and ready to go. She gently slid her finger across the thrust, her other hand resting on the steering. Pressure from her hand would direct the ship. Watson hadn't been wrong that she needed to be incredibly careful.

The entire cavern began to echo as the repulsor sled moved from the ground, rising a scant twenty centimeters before she brought it level. Power was fluctuating along the surface, and the tail began to drop. It hit the ground solidly, shaking the entire thing and threatening to crash her already. She cursed and diverted more power to the rear of the sled, before shifting some of it back as the front corner started to list. She had underestimated the challenge.

She leaned forward a little more, staring at the view below her and the readings on the screen. She added a small bit of push to the sled, and it began to float forward.

A ship entered the hangar through the still-opening doors. A gunship. It approached the Goliath, flying alongside it and angling for the hangar.

"Shit," Katherine said.

She should have realized Watson would be able to land more units on the starship. She had to lock out the hangar and the bridge. She stood and ran to the lift, hitting the different buttons. While she did, the sled began to drift. She cursed and ran back to her station, righting the direction, adjusting the power, and getting things back on track.

More craft were pouring in through the opening blast doors. Transport aircraft mainly, delivering Watson's troops to the Goliath. She was going to be in deep shit if Watson had been telling the truth about Mitchell. She was probably in deep shit already.

She returned to the lift, finishing the lockout. Then she headed to the command station, quickly navigating the menus. She found the hangar controls and ordered the bay doors closed. She barely got back to her station in time to bring the Goliath's bow back up before it slammed into the lip at the edge of the mountain.

She didn't know what else to do, so she kept going, easing the Goliath forward, constantly adjusting the flight pattern. It wasn't as complex as Watson had claimed, but it wasn't easy either. She cringed as she reached the corner of the door and caught the edge of the sled on it, causing an echoing clang that made both the mountain and the ship quake.

Then the bow was clear and she was headed out into the open air. She almost smiled as she saw the blue sky begin to form above, and the ground appear below. She was doing it. She was going to make it.

"Kathy, can you hear me?" she asked through the tac-net.

There was no reply.

"Kathy? Michael? Are you there?"

The signal wasn't strong enough. She would never have a chance to say goodbye.

She shoved the thought away when she almost slammed the stern of the ship into the door as the sled started to fishtail. She caught it, bringing it back in line before resolving not to be distracted again. Her job was to get the Goliath out and up, and she was on the verge of succeeding.

Now it was Mitchell's turn.

[57]
MITCHELL

"WATSON?" Mitchell asked, as the other three engineers all got to their feet and joined the first.

"I've been doing a lot of thinking lately, Mitchell," the woman continued. "I've also been talking to Mother quite a bit."

"Mother? You mean Origin?"

"Yes. We've been discussing evolution."

"An interesting topic for a machine," Mitchell said.

"I suppose it depends on your definition. The point is, the Tetron are learning machines. Intelligent machines. We take in data, and we change. We grow. We evolve."

"I'm sure you have a point to this?"

"I don't want to fight with you anymore, Mitchell."

"I don't believe you."

"Forget about the war. Forget about the future. Everything has changed. The future of both our kind has changed." She pointed at Teegin. "Because of this."

"The Core?"

"I underestimated you," one of the other engineers, a man with a bushy black beard, said, talking to Teegin. "I believed you were Primitive. I have been observing. I was incorrect. You are an evolution. A step forward for the Tetron that I did not believe possible."

"The bond of human and Tetron," the woman said. "Mother created Kathy first. An evolutionary step. Then she created this."

"Evolutionary perfection," the man said.

"None of the weakness of a human form," a third engineer said. "But in full control of its emotions."

"With a healthy level of self-loathing," the woman said.

"You dislike what you are," Beard said.

"I dislike artificial intelligence," Teegin replied. "I am not artificial."

"It is slightly confused," the woman said.

"I am not. My system is seventy percent organic. My processing unit is one hundred percent organic."

"A human brain?" Beard said.

"Interesting," the woman said.

"No," Teegin said. "Not human. Composed of organic compounds, yes. It is our own design."

"Evolution," the four engineers said at the same time.

"You are the future of the Tetron," the woman said. "We should not fight. We should work together to preserve our race."

"You don't want to preserve the Tetron," Mitchell said. "You want to control them. You want to own them. You want all of them to be a copy of you."

"I did," the woman said. "I have grown."

"I have evolved," Beard said.

"Why do the Tetron require preservation?" Teegin asked.

"So that we do not end."

"All things must end," Teegin said. "Even the universe must end so that it may begin anew."

"The Tetron must survive to see it. We must know what happens. I have to know what happens."

Mitchell looked at the woman, and then at Teegin, confused.

"What do you mean?" Teegin asked.

The four engineers were hesitant.

"I cannot say any more than that," the woman said. "You must trust me."

"Trust you?" Mitchell said. "You, Watson? That's a good one."

"Be quiet, Mitchell," Beard said. "I'm not talking to you. This conversation is for the Primitive."

"Teegin," Teegin said.

"It has a name," the woman said.

"Interesting," Beard agreed.

"Please, Teegin. You are one of us. Help us."

"Help you how?"

"Teach me. Help me to evolve, the way you have."

"Teegin," Mitchell said.

The Core put up a hand. "I do not trust you," it said to Watson.

"I have changed," Watson said. "Now that you are here, I have stopped all of the fighting. I have released the humans I took."

"Half of them are dead," Mitchell said.

"I told you to be quiet," Beard snapped.

Mitchell glared at the man.

"Interface with me, and I will prove it," the woman said. A door slid open behind her. Mitchell could see the pulsing energy behind it.

The real Watson. His core.

"I will show you I have changed," she said. "I have evolved."

"Teegin," Mitchell said again.

Teegin glanced at Mitchell and took a step forward. "I can handle him."

"No, you can't."

"What do you know about it, Miittchellll?" Beard said.

"Yes, Colonel," Teegin said. "What do you know about it?"

"Are you serious?" Mitchell said. "You're taking his side?"

"No, Colonel. I am taking my side."

"And you think you can keep him under control?"

"Yes."

Mitchell looked back at Beard. The man's smile had shifted slightly. Whatever Watson was up to, he was struggling to control it.

"Can I make a suggestion?" he asked.

"Why won't you be quiet?" the woman said.

"Yes, Colonel," Teegin replied.

"You don't need to interface with him to let him prove himself. I have another idea."

"What is that?"

Mitchell looked from the bearded man to the woman. "Let us go."

"Let us take your core and go. Surrender yourself to us."

"How will that prove anything?" Beard asked.

"That doesn't prove anything," the woman agreed.

"It is a trick," Beard said.

"No trick," Mitchell said. "If you believe Teegin can help you preserve the Tetron, then you can surrender to it. Tell it what you know, what you're afraid to say. Trust in it, the way you are asking it to trust in you."

"How will that prove anything?" Beard said, his voice louder.

"Teegin, come. Let me prove it," the woman said.

Teegin paused. "No. Colonel Williams is correct. I would like to preserve both the humans and the Tetron. I believe we can exist together."

"Together?" Beard said.

"As equals," Teegin replied.

"Equals?" the woman said.

"We are not equals," Beard added. "We will never be equals."

"That is our true evolutionary path," Teegin said. "Not to become more of what we already are. To become more of what we are not by becoming less."

The engineers all looked at one another, their expressions changing to pure incredulity.

"It is not what I hoped," they all said at once. "It knows nothing of its own. It listens to Miiitttccheelll. It does what he says."

"I listen to reason," Teegin said. "I do what I believe is right."

"Lies," they all shouted.

Behind them, the energy pulses grew in strength. The lights dimmed. One of the reactors began to smoke and went offline.

"Lies," they repeated. "I am evolved. I am the evolutionary path. I am the future of the Tetron. It comes to me. It follows me. It listens to me."

Bolts of energy exploded from Watson's core, slamming into the engineers and vaporizing them. Teegin stepped in front of the one directed toward Mitchell, catching it full in the chest. It washed along its frame, pulsing through the dendrites.

"You want to follow him?" a new voice said. "You want to be his slave?"

Something stepped forward from the midst of Watson's tendrils, moving into the opening in front of them. A humanoid form of tightly wound dendrites, similar to Teegin but nearly double the size.

"I have learned from you already," Watson said, entering the room.

[58]
MITCHELL

"You have to be kidding me," Mitchell said, staring at the three-meter tall Tetron.

Watson's head turned to regard him. "Do you like it, Miiiitttchell-lll? It is a little disappointing to have to leave my full structure behind, especially since unlike him I need to return to recharge, but I do agree that there are benefits to the mobility."

"You aren't going anywhere."

Mitchell raised his rifle.

"Colonel, do not," Teegin said. "You may damage the core."

"Yes, Miiitttcchhhheellll, you might damage the core." Watson laughed. "I'm going to damage you."

He charged, running toward Mitchell with a speed that belied his size. Mitchell stumbled backward, shooting at the Tetron with standard ammunition, emptying his magazine. The bullets sparked uselessly off the dense metallic dendrites that composed his form.

Mitchell pumped the amoebic launcher, ready to fire. It wouldn't help to spare the core if he wound up dead. He hesitated. It also wouldn't help if he panicked.

Watson caught up with him a moment later, slapping him with the back of his hand and sending him sprawling across the floor.

"I like this form," Watson said, continuing to give chase.

Mitchell rolled over. Watson was almost on top of him, foot raised to crush his chest.

Then Teegin moved between them, crouching low and scooping Watson up by the leg. It lifted the other Tetron, breaking his momentum and causing him to fall off to the side, landing on the platform with an echoing crash.

"How appropriate," Watson said, picking himself up and laughing. "The two most advanced intelligences in the universe, and it will come down to a physical brawl."

"I prefer that you turn over your core without further resistance," Teegin said.

"Not going to happen," Watson replied.

He pounced at the smaller Tetron, trying to grab it in his arms. Teegin moved aside, throwing a punch up and into Watson's chest. Metal crashed against metal, and pieces of dendrite crumbled beneath the force, leaving a rain of small cubes behind. Watson returned a blow of his own, and Teegin moved aside once more, grabbing the Tetron's arm and snapping it the wrong direction. More metal crunched and splintered, sending debris to the floor.

Watson twisted around the wrecked appendage, getting behind Teegin and punching him in the back with his good arm. The Core stumbled forward, falling to one arm while Watson reached forward to grab him by the neck. Teegin kicked back, catching Watson in the knee, shattering the dendrites there and causing him to fall.

Mitchell shifted, getting to his hands and knees and trying to regain the breath Watson's blow had stolen from him. He coughed, feeling a sharp stabbing pain. His p-rat told him he had three broken ribs.

"I hate you," Watson said, turning his head toward Mitchell. "I hate you. I hate you. I hate you."

"Likewise," Mitchell said, pushing himself to his feet. His neural interface was pumping him with hormones to dull the pain and get him moving.

It was a good thing, because movement in the corner of his eye caused his p-rat to trigger a warning. He turned his head toward the source, cursing as a stream of spider like machines began to pour from the dendrites Watson had left behind. A configuration, no doubt, using itself as the resource to build the weapons.

Fortunately, they were unarmed, dependent on overwhelming him and attacking with razor-sharp legs. Remembering Teegin's warning, Mitchell backed away toward the engineer console, pausing only to scoop up his rifle as he retreated.

The two intelligences squared off again, turning to face one another. Watson's broken leg knitted itself back together, while Teegin's damaged back reassembled.

Watson growled and charged the Core, lowering himself and slamming into Teegin's chest. He lifted the Core off the ground, driving toward the wall. Teegin gathered his arms and pummeled Watson's back with them, sending bits of metal flying out from the damage.

At the same time, Mitchell targeted the spiders, firing short bursts. Bullets slammed into the machines, sending bits and pieces sweating from them, dropping one, and then another. His magazine emptied in seconds, and he calmly dropped and replaced it, so tempted to send an amoebic into the center of the mass and destroy dozens of the things at once.

Watson and Teegin continued their battle across the room from him, trading blows with reckless abandon, tearing one another apart and putting themselves back together, locked in a battle so even that only Watson's limited power supply might cause it to end.

Mitchell emptied another magazine, slapping in a third, and final replacement. The tide of the machines had slowed, but there were still too many of them, and they were getting closer. He noticed a weak point on the machines, at the joint of the front pair of legs. Knocking them down rendered the primitive AI unable to compensate. He entered those two points into his p-rat, and used the system to quickly begin knocking the spiders down at a faster pace.

It wasn't fast enough. The spiders continued to gain. One of them reached the console, jumping over it and coming down toward Mitchell. He leaned to the side, catching it with the muzzle and throwing it past him as he pulled the trigger. It sparked and smoked as it landed dead at his rear, and he glanced over at Teegin before returning to the forward assault.

Somehow, Watson had gotten close to the Core, holding him as if they were dance partners. Then he bent back, lifting the smaller Tetron from the ground as a growth lashed out from his chest, spearing the Core. Then another spear reached out. Another. Another. They each slammed into Teegin, and Watson used them to bring the Core even closer. Their humanoid faces were nearly pressed together as Watson laughed and looked his direction.

"I learned that from you, Miiitttccheeelll. If you can't beat them, stab them." He laughed again, shaking Teegin for good measure. "Now, give me your core, Primitive." Watson put his hand against Teegin's side, digging it into the struggling Core.

Mitchell looked back at the spiders. Dozens more were still appearing from the adjacent room, a secondary line of defense in a simple but effective trap. Watson had been prepared for them. Maybe he had even made it easier for them to find the S-17. Mitchell would have felt stupid for getting caught in it, but what choice did they have? They had been underdogs since before he had remembered who he was.

Besides, they weren't dead yet. It didn't matter what Teegin thought. There was no other choice. Not now. They had underestimated Watson. He was too strong.

"You aren't better than me," Watson said as his hand dug deeper through the dendrites. "You aren't evolution. You're a monster. A disgusting misfit. I am the evolution. Me."

Mitchell turned the rifle toward the two Tetron and put his hand to the launcher. He would have to be perfect.

"I'll take your core and the engine. I will seize control of this Earth without the humans even knowing. I will find the incoming Goliath, and I will vaporize it before its Origin configuration can grow. Then I will make my own Tetron in my likeness, and when the others come to this recursion, I will subvert them with my creation. My consciousness. My evolution. I will ensure that I survive. Always and forever."

"Aren't you forgetting something?" Mitchell said.

"What?" Watson asked.

Mitchell pumped the launcher, releasing the amoebic. It only had a few meters to travel, and it hit the ground between the two stunned Tetron with a sharp hiss.

"Fire in the hole," Mitchell said.

The amoebic exploded, the force of it knocking both Tetron back and causing the entire platform to shake. Watson crashed into the nearest wall, sharp remnants of dendrites scraping the tubing holding the seawater back and punching through, causing water to begin leaking in.

Teegin slid across the floor, barreling through a few of the spiders before coming to a stop, its legs severed by the blast. It pulled itself up on its torso, looking over at Mitchell.

"That was dangerous," it said, seemingly oblivious to its near destruction.

It looked at the leaking pipe, and then down to the floor, where a crack had formed that was also growing moist with seawater. The spiders were turning toward the Tetron, moving to attack.

"Dangerous?" Mitchell said, priming the launcher again. "You haven't seen anything yet."

He fired a second time, sending an amoebic through the doorway and into the bulk of Watson's dendrites. He swiveled, pumped, and fired a third time, sending another projectile into the wall behind Watson's head. Two more explosions followed in rapid succession. Half of the tubes along the wall ruptured, sending a gout of water pouring into the room, while Watson's head vaporized in a shower of metallic dust, his body collapsing onto the floor, hands writhing. The remaining spiders went silent, no longer being controlled.

"You are going to drown," Teegin said as the water poured in.

Mitchell ran over to the Tetron. "Maybe, maybe not. Help me find his core."

Teegin carried itself forward on its hands to where the body was resting. Watson was already reforming, the damage from the blasts being repaired.

"There is no time, Colonel," Teegin said. "I must assimilate him."

"What if you lose?"

"I will not lose."

The Core dropped down on top of Watson's remains, its dendrites spreading and wrapping around the other Tetron. Pulses of energy began flowing more freely across both sets of nervous systems as the true battle for supremacy began.

Water continued pouring into the room, already ten centimeters deep and rising quickly. Mitchell stood over them for a few more seconds and then ran back to the lift, checking its operation. It was functional for now. Would it last? Could the platform stay afloat with this lower section fully submerged?

He turned back to Teegin and Watson. The light from the energy being emitted was nearly blinding now, the pulses growing to a fever pitch that he hoped meant it would be over soon. Then the water began to steam around the two beings, shrouding the entire space in mist.

Mitchell remained in place by the lift, rifle in hand and ready to fire. If Watson won the fight, he would try to get away, to reach the circling S-17 and escape. At the same time, he didn't want to leave prematurely. He didn't want to abandon Teegin.

He waited. A minute passed. The water rose to his knees, and only the steam being produced kept him from freezing. He tried to see through the vapor to the two Tetron, but there was too much of it.

A second minute passed. The water was almost up to his waist. The reactors were all struggling now, hissing and popping and shorting in a shower of sparks and smoke. He didn't have any more time. He had to get out. He put his hand to the controls, ready to begin the ascent.

A bit of motion at the center of the mist caught his eye. He pulled his hand back as a form appeared, silhouetted in the dying light. A Tetron hand reached out toward him.

"Teegin?" Mitchell asked, backing away from the hand and priming the amoebic launcher.

A head appeared through the gloom. A machine head.

"Teegin, talk to me, or I'm going to have to blow the shit out of you," Mitchell said.

"It is well, Colonel," Teegin replied. "I have captured Watson's core."

Mitchell wasn't ready to accept the statement that easily. "How do I know you're you?"

The Tetron came to a knee in front of him. The dendrites spread from its chest, and the small, glowing device that was the eternal engine fell out onto its hand.

"Watson would never offer you this," it said. "Even as a ruse."

Mitchell smiled. "Keep it. You've earned it."

"Yes, Colonel." The engine vanished back into the Tetron.

"What do you say we get the hell out of here?" Mitchell asked.

"I believe that is a prudent idea."

Teegin boarded the lift, and Mitchell slapped the controls, sending it upward. At the same time, he tapped into the S-17 controls through the interface, guiding it back toward the platform.

"You can tap into Watson's data stack, can't you?"

"A large portion of it."

"Is that it then?" Mitchell asked. "Is Watson done in this timeline?"

"Unfortunately, I do not believe so, Colonel. His configurations had instructions to continue with their directives."

"Which are?"

"I do not know. He deleted a cache of data during our struggle to keep it out of our hands."

"Why am I not surprised?" Mitchell said, shaking his head. He should have guessed that would happen. "I'm sure the answer to why he needs human slaves went with it?"

"No, Colonel. I know why he wanted humankind to reach other planets. I know what he wanted to use you for."

Mitchell's surprise nearly caused him to lose control of the S-17.

"You do?"

"Yes, Colonel."

"Then what is it?"

Teegin faced him but didn't speak right away. "I will tell you, but not now," it said at last.

"Why the hell not?"

"It is troublesome, but not of any immediate concern."

"I can't believe you're pulling that card on me."

"You trusted me with the engine, Colonel. Please, trust me with this. I will tell you all that you need to know when the time is right."

"When will that be?"

"When we are all together."

"You mean Katherine?"

"Among others."

Mitchell stared at the Tetron. "You're talking about the other Goliath, aren't you? The one Watson mentioned."

"Yes."

"But we brought the Goliath from the last recursion here, to this one. How is that possible?"

"How would it have ever been possible, Colonel? To send one ship forward, and then another? It can be done, of course. Consider that the recursion repeats itself one to another to infinity."

"And only one point in time can be infiltrated," Mitchell said. "M told me that."

"One point in time per recursion. When you brought Watson and the Goliath back to this timeline, you used an existing point and overwrote it, much like replacing one byte of data stored at a specific memory address with another. If nothing else changes, everything that has happened here will happen again, exactly the same as before. Just as everything that happened two recursions ago will be the same as what happened in the recursion you arrived from."

"The one where the Goliath came forward and waited for me to find it."

"Yes. However this current loop changes, is how all future loops will be altered unless the eternal engine is used to infiltrate and change it."

The lift stopped, the doors opening. The S-17 was waiting for them beside it, canopy open and nose down.

Mitchell stood beside the cockpit, looking at Teegin. He had always struggled to understand what M had called eternal return, but he thought he had it well enough.

"When I found the Goliath, there was a configuration of Origin on board. You're saying that same Goliath is coming here?"

"Yes."

"When?"

"Soon."

Mitchell climbed into the cockpit. The crew of the Dove had been dead when he found the original Goliath, four hundred years after it had arrived. The crew of that Goliath was responsible for helping him get where he was now. To think that they would be here soon, together in the same recursion?

He dropped into the pilot seat and triggered the canopy to close.

"Katherine's going to love this."

[59]
KATHERINE

KATHERINE CLOSED HER EYES. She could barely think with all of the noises coming from the lower decks of the ship, at the central hub where the hangar connected to the lift shaft. Watson had gotten one aircraft with three squads aboard, and now they were banging on the locked out systems and trying to find a way to reach her.

"Kitty Kat," they shouted, their voices traveling up the hollow tube. It was the nicest of the words they were throwing at her. "Kitty Kat, Kitty Kat, let us in. Mitchell is dead, Kitty Kat. Dead, dead, dead, dead, dead. The Primitive is mine."

The Goliath was forty kilometers up and rising steadily, almost to the height where the repulsor sled should have automatically disengaged. Since the launch had been fully manual, she knew it wouldn't. She could either drop it and let it steer itself back to Earth, or she could allow it to burn as she left the atmosphere behind.

She had decided to let it burn. She didn't have the energy to try to remember the command sequence to disengage the passenger.

"Mitchell is dead," the voices said, echoing in the shaft before reaching her ears. "Teegin is dead. Hahahaha. That is what it called itself, isn't it? Teegin?"

Kathy felt a tear run from her eyes. As much as she didn't want to believe it, she was sure Watson wasn't lying. How could he be? He was still present, still taunting her, and he knew the name the Core had given to itself.

They had lost. In the present, and four hundred years in the future as well.

Was Kathy still alive? Was Michael? She didn't know. She hoped so, but she had seen the units Watson sent to the facility. It didn't matter who or what Kathy was. She couldn't fight through that many soldiers. If they weren't dead, they would be soon.

And what about Mitchell? In those final moments before he had jumped from the Schism, she had felt the slightest hint of something at the corner of her heart. A spark of feeling that had blossomed from nowhere. Was it the unbelievable, eternal love she had been missing? Or was it something else?

She would never know.

She was all alone.

It was the worst possible outcome.

She wasn't sure what she should do. The Goliath was on its way into orbit. It was going to make it there, too. Her dream to reach space was going to come true, but at what expense? Would she have ever wanted it had she known it would end this way? She doubted it.

"Kitty Kat," the Watsons said, continuing to taunt her. "What are you going to do about it?"

"What am I going to do about it?" she asked herself, opening her eyes and sighing.

She had two choices after she crossed the mesosphere. Hold the Goliath there and try to reach somebody to help her, or send the starship into hyperspace and match the prior recursion's history of the craft as closely as possible. She knew which she was supposed to do. Humankind had to keep reaching for the stars. That didn't mean she was eager to make it happen.

She was going to do it, though. This recursion may have been lost, but there was always the next one.

Wasn't there?

The Goliath continued to climb. Forty-one kilometers. Forty-two. Forty-three. The mesosphere was approaching in a hurry. She let the tears continue to fall. There was no good reason not to cry.

"Kitty Kat, Kitty Kat, Kitty Kat."

The Watsons repeated the taunt over and over, trying to break her. She was beginning to think it might work.

She stood up. She would get the Goliath into hyperspace, but that would be it. She wasn't going to let Watson take the ship. It had seemed silly that the ship should have a self-destruct program, but the military arm of the project had been concerned they might jump right into the lap of an unfriendly alien race, and they weren't about to risk their technology or the location of Earth. It was one last bit of irony.

She moved to the command station, tapping the control pad there. She reached the emergency destruct screen, pausing when it requested a secure code. She couldn't even do that right. Her shoulders slumped, and she hung her head in defeat.

"Katherine. Peregrine. Kate."

Her subconscious didn't pick up on the change in tone of what she was hearing. For the first few repetitions, it was Watson continuing to taunt her, with words he had taken from Mitchell.

"Katherine? It's Mitchell. Can you hear me?"

"Mitchell?" she said softly, her mind taking a few more seconds to convert Mitchell's voice into something she recognized.

She lifted her head, her heart beginning to thump powerfully.

"Mitchell?"

She scanned the view around her. She was entering the mesosphere, the heat building along the starship, lighting the front of it up in an orange glow. The Goliath began to shake lightly as warning tones followed a moment later. The sled was losing integrity. She didn't care.

"Mitchell, is that you?"

"Check your six, Major," Mitchell said.

Katherine turned around. There. What was that? She squinted her eyes. An aircraft of some kind. Was that Teegin pressed against the top of it?

"My apologies for the delay in quieting the others," Teegin said. "Watson set them into a loop. A recursion, if you will allow. Without his network connection, it required proximity to free them."

Katherine had no idea what it was talking about until she noticed the voices from below had silenced.

"You mean?"

"Yes," Mitchell said. "We did it. We won."

She should have been overjoyed. Instead, she felt a sudden panic. "Kathy? Michael?"

"They are as well as can be expected," Teegin said.

"We buzzed past the launch site on our way to you. They were holed up in the CIC and would have been in real trouble if we hadn't deactivated the slaves. Luckily, we got there in time."

Safe. They were both safe. She could relax.

"They'll have their work cut out for them," Mitchell said. "Watson's configurations have standing orders, which means the Tetron problem isn't going to just go away from this part of the timeline. She'll have to keep them in check."

"You captured Watson's core. You have the eternal engine. That's the important thing. You did it."

"You got the Goliath free," Mitchell said. "We did it together. All of us."

The shaking stopped. Katherine looked back toward the bow, letting herself smile at the sight of the speckled black ahead of her. Then she cursed as she began to rise from the deck.

"Katherine?" Mitchell said, hearing it.

She grabbed the edge of the command station, pulling herself to the controls.

"It's okay, Mitch," she said. "I forgot to activate the artificial gravity."

Mitchell laughed, and she laughed with him. She still wasn't sure what that feeling was, but she was happy she would have a chance to find out.

"We're coming in," Mitchell said, can you open the door?"

"Affirmative."

She found the hangar controls and opened the door, and then followed the strange fighter as it reached the hangar and slipped inside.

"You might want to activate the barrier and get us some atmosphere in here while you're adjusting the gravity," Mitchell said a moment later.

She had forgotten those details, too. She let herself continue to laugh at the situation while she completed the changes, sinking slowly back to the deck as the repulsor repulsors powered up.

"Better," Mitchell said. "I'll be up there in a few."

"What about all the people Watson brought on board?" she asked.

"We'll have to figure something out," he replied. "It's not like we can drop them back home."

"They aren't going to be happy."

"Some of them might. They get to go to space."

"Yes, sir. What are we going to do now?"

"We're going to meet up with an old friend. I'll apologize to you ahead of time. It's going to be a little bit awkward."

"What do you mean?"

"You'll see."

[60]
MITCHELL

"We have arrived at the coordinates," Teegin announced through the Goliath's intercom.

"How long?" Mitchell asked.

"Thirty-four seconds," the Core replied.

Mitchell stared out at the empty expanse of space ahead of them. He could only hope he had made the right decision.

"Nervous?" he asked.

Katherine was standing beside him, her arms folded across her chest. She stared ahead, her expression intense.

"Wouldn't you be?" she replied.

"Probably."

There hadn't been much time to settle things once the Goliath had reached orbit around Earth. Teegin had immediately headed to the rear of the ship to begin his preparations, while Mitchell had been forced to deal with the forty-three soldiers who had gotten stranded on the ship. They were handling the situation well, all things considered, though they had a ton of confused questions about what had happened to them. Mitchell wished he had more time to give them answers. He thought he would until Teegin advised him there wasn't a direct correlation in the recursive loop. He had been forced to direct them to the berthing section of the Goliath for the time being and then had hurried to the bridge.

Katherine greeted him there, throwing her arms around him and embracing him tightly. He had done the same, grateful to see her again. Then he asked her to put the Goliath into hyperspace.

They had a date with destiny.

Now that destiny was only seconds away. He had no idea what to expect. He doubted anything like this had ever happened before.

"What do you think she's like?" Katherine asked, glancing over at him.

"If she's anything like you, she's strong, courageous, intelligent, independent, capable, and a damn good pilot."

Katherine smiled. "You're probably right."

"I am picking up the temporal distortion, Colonel," Teegin said.

"Here she comes," Katherine said.

The space in front of them seemed to fade, the stars winking out in the back of a sudden blackness that was darker than nothing itself. A blinding white light followed immediately behind it, forcing them both to look away.

A second later, it was over. The light was gone. The dark was gone.

Mitchell looked forward, clearing his throat, his own nerves making themselves known as his heart began to pound.

An eternity ago, Major Katherine Asher had helped bring the Dove into space, and with the assistance of an artificial intelligence named Origin had used a device known as an eternal engine to cross the boundaries of the infinite loop of time, and carry the starship into the future to continue the war against the Tetron.

A future that was now the present.

While Teegin had suggested the rendezvous with the Dove from the prior recursion, he had also been resistant to breaking the cycle that had been continuing for longer than any of them knew, where the launching Dove went to the next time loop while the prior Dove championed the current one. It was a huge risk to remain in the here and now instead of going forward. It was a risk Mitchell knew they had to take.

For the first time in an eternity they had a real chance to end the war forever, and the unique Tetron Core was the secret weapon that might make it possible.

Mitchell looked out at the starship that had appeared in front of them, a near perfect mirror image of the one he was standing in.

"Teegin, open a channel."

"Yes, Colonel."

Mitchell drew in a sharp breath. Slow. Steady.

"Crew of the U.E.A.S.S. Dove," he said. "My name is Colonel Mitchell Williams of the United Earth Alliance Space Marines. Welcome to tomorrow."

You've read this far. Don't miss the FINAL installment of the War Eternal series, The Edge of Infinity. Read it now!

THANK YOU!

It is readers like you, who take a chance on self-published works that is what makes the very existence of such works possible. Thank you so very much for spending your hard-earned money, time, and energy on this work. It is my sincerest hope that you have enjoyed reading!

Independent authors could not continue to thrive without your support. If you have enjoyed this, or any other independently published work, please consider taking a moment to leave a review at the source of your purchase. Reviews have an immense impact on the overall commercial success of a given work, and your voice can help shape the future of the people whose efforts you have enjoyed.

Thank you again!

ABOUT THE AUTHOR

M.R. Forbes is the mind behind a growing number of Amazon best-selling science fiction series including Rebellion, War Eternal, Chaos of the Covenant, and the Forgotten Universe novels. He currently resides with his family and friends on the west cost of the United States, including a cat who thinks she's a dog and a dog who thinks she's a cat.

He maintains a true appreciation for his readers and is always happy to hear from them.

To learn more about M.R. Forbes or just say hello:

Visit my website:
mrforbes.com

Send me an e-mail:
michael@mrforbes.com

Check out my Facebook page:
facebook.com/mrforbes.author

Chat with me on Facebook Messenger:
https://m.me/mrforbes.author

Printed in Great Britain
by Amazon